For the first time _____ looked to his mother... He seemed confused. Carol Marcus patted him on the shoulder. "Would you excuse us a moment? I have to discuss something with Dr. McCoy."

As the doors shooshed closed behind the boy, she returned the doctor's scrutiny. There was a decidedly no-nonsense cast to her features—something Bones would have called defiance under different circumstances.

"Dr. McCoy," she began, lifting her chin slightly, almost exactly the way the boy had earlier. "A long time ago, I knew Jim Kirk quite well."

He nodded. "The captain has mentioned you once or twice. But—"

"He doesn't know about David," she interrupted. "And I want to keep it that way."

Suddenly all the pieces fell into place. McCoy cursed softly.

"You understand what I'm saying," she observed.

"You're damn right I do," he said. "That boy is Jim's son."

Look for STAR TREK Fiction from Pocket Books

Star Trek: The Original Series

Star Trek: The Next Generation

STAR TREK®

FACES OF FIRE

MICHAEL JAN FRIEDMAN

POCKET BOOKS

New York   London   Toronto   Sydney   Tokyo   Singapore

An *Original* Publication of POCKET BOOKS

POCKET BOOKS, a division of Simon & Schuster Inc.
1230 Avenue of the Americas, New York, NY 10020

Copyright © 1992 by Paramount Pictures. All Rights Reserved.

STAR TREK is a Registered Trademark of
Paramount Pictures.

This book is published by Pocket Books, a division of
Simon & Schuster Inc., under exclusive license from
Paramount Pictures.

ISBN: 0-671-74992-7

First Pocket Books printing March 1992

10 9 8 7 6 5 4 3 2 1

POCKET and colophon are registered trademarks of
Simon & Schuster Inc.

Printed in the U.S.A.

For Gene Roddenberry

with white foam about some dark rocks, and in a third

28

Historian's Note

This story begins on Stardate 3998.6, which would place it about halfway through the starship *Enterprise*'s original five-year mission.

FACES OF FIRE

Prologue

As KIRUC ADVANCED on the ancient, abandoned observation post, he naturally anticipated the possibility of a trap. Certainly, it had all the makings of one.

First, the way he'd been summoned—the secrecy and mystery surrounding it, not to mention the anonymity of the summoner. Then, the location—secluded, unfamiliar to Kiruc, rife with potential hiding places—especially now, in the blackness of night. And finally, the instruction to leave his men behind as he approached.

He glanced back over his shoulder at Zibrat and Torgis. They looked like hunting beasts tethered against their will, prevented from accompanying him, though their duty as his bodyguards was clear. Recalling the vehemence and persistence of their protests, he smiled a thin smile and turned again to face his destination.

The observation post was a dark and craggy thing, looming up out of the colorless hills like a swamp spider. A one-eyed swamp spider, for a single window of the place was illuminated with a faint, orange light.

His every Klingon sense cried out danger. Like anyone of his political stature, Kiruc had no lack of enemies. Any one of them might have arranged this encounter, using his curiosity as bait. And yet, he hadn't dared ignore the invitation.

Because if he was right about who had called him here, so far from the imperial space routes, the greater danger by far would have been *not* to come.

As Kiruc got closer to the post, he could make out the individual buildings that comprised it. They were squat, stark, designed entirely for function and not esthetics. None of them had been used in half a century, since the Klingons subjugated the last of their enemies along this border and incorporated their worlds into the body of the empire.

Fifty meters from the outermost structure, he discerned Klingon silhouettes among the shadows. Instinctively, his hand wandered to his hip, where his empty holster reminded him of that other condition he'd been given: no weapons, not even a dagger.

Not that a single disruptor could have made a difference anyway. If this was truly a snare fashioned by his enemies, he would certainly be vastly outgunned—and he was out here in the open, whereas his adversaries could take advantage of concealment.

Perhaps, then, the silhouettes were a good sign. An indication that he'd been right about whom he was meeting. On the other hand, maybe they were just a decoy, a way of enticing him to come closer so his adversaries could get off a better shot.

He would know the truth before very long. Clenching his teeth, he narrowed the gap. In the distance, a winged predator shrieked, calling out its claim on some earthbound prey. An omen? His father would have said so. But then, his father was a superstitious man.

And I am not, he told himself. I am of the new breed, one who makes use of the superstitions of others. Still, it was difficult to ignore the uncanny timeliness of the flyer's cry.

Kiruc was close enough now to see more than just silhouettes. He could see faces—hard eyes, cruelly shaped mouths. Having had ample experience in judging men at a glance, he could tell these were not the average run of hired warriors. These were specialists.

And that gave even more credence to his theory.

Holding his arms up, he showed them he was unarmed. Once they saw that, they swarmed around him, surrounded him. They themselves were armed to the teeth, some of them even holding disruptor rifles at the ready.

But he was not jostled. He was not treated roughly. In fact, he almost had the feeling he was being protected.

One of the men gestured—a sharp, quick chop with the barrel of his pistol. It seemed he was the leader. As he headed back toward the heart of the installation, the others followed. Kiruc went with them.

They negotiated a path around this building and that, all the time getting nearer to the main edifice, the one that held that baleful eye of a window. A dark figure was visible now in the soft glow, someone who seemed to be standing with his hands locked behind his back, watching.

At the door to the edifice, Kiruc found additional

warriors—even more than he had expected. He had the feeling that there were weapons trained on him that he couldn't see.

Then the door opened and he was ushered through. The place was as stark inside, he noted, as outside. Just a few pieces of severe furniture, the kind an administrator would have had in the days when this post was operational, were caught in the meager light of a single standing fixture.

But his gaze didn't linger on the furnishings. It was drawn to the Klingon who stood by the window—the massive form that turned as he entered and fixed him with his gaze, one eye still hidden in the shadows.

"Leave us," the massive one said. His voice was deep, strident, commanding.

Kiruc expected the warriors to protest. They did not. Without a single word, they filed out; the last one closed the door behind him.

"Sit," the figure commanded. With a casual sweep of his arm, he indicated a chair beside a large, gray desk.

Inclining his head slightly, Kiruc did as he was told. The room smelled musty. There were spiderwebs in the corners where the walls met the ceiling, and patterns of dust on the floor.

The figure moved toward another chair, one closer to the light. As he left the concealment afforded by the shadows, his features were thrown into stark relief.

Even though Kiruc had suspected all along who had summoned him, the sight of the man still came as a shock to him. He swallowed involuntarily.

Careful, he told himself. It was important not to show weakness. And to be caught off-guard was most definitely a weakness.

As his host sat, there was silence. Their eyes met and locked. "You know who I am?"

Kiruc nodded. "You are my emperor."

Kapronek, the most powerful being in the Klingon empire, grunted. "Very good. First, I should tell you this: I have not brought you here to threaten harm to you or your kinsmen."

"I am relieved," Kiruc replied in earnest.

The emperor's eyes bore into him. They were a pale and startling sea green—very unusual for a Klingon. "What have you heard about the 'loyal opposition,' Kiruc, or, to use their proper name, the Gevish'rae?"

Ah. So *that* was what this was about. The rise of the Gevish'rae—the clans of the homeworld's southern continent, thoughtless fools who would plunge the empire into premature war with the Federation. The Gevish'rae—literally, the Thirsting Knives.

Kiruc thought for a moment. "I have heard they are gaining ground in the council," he responded. "Increasing their influence."

Kapronek harrumphed. "That is a polite way of putting it. The Gevish'rae are sending my councillors to early retirements—by whatever means seems most expedient in each case. Some they are buying off; others they simply assassinate, blaming their deaths on one obscure blood feud or another."

The visitor nodded. His intelligence had been accurate, then; his spies were to be commended.

The emperor's lip curled in savage and magnificent disdain. "Noisemakers like Dumeric and Zoth are gaining in stature. And the proud and noble Kamorh'dag—my people and yours, who have ruled the empire for ten generations—are sinking like a herd of puris in a salt-marsh."

5

An apt image, Kiruc mused. In his youth, he had seen a puris sink in a marsh east of his family's hereditary lands. Too bad, too. The beast had been fat and sleek; it would have fetched a hefty price at market.

What's more, puris were indigenous only to the northern continent—like the Kamorh'dag themselves. That lent the image an additional shade of meaning.

"We are losing our grip on the empire," Kiruc's host went on. "We are *dying*. For I assure you, once the Gevish'rae gain the upper hand in council, they will not be as tolerant of us as we have been of them."

All very likely true, Kiruc conceded. Still, what did it have to do with him? What role did the emperor have in mind for Kiruc, son of Kalastra?

Kapronek looked at him with hooded eyes, the eyes of a hunter. Not a puris but a bird of prey. "I will not see my people trampled, Kiruc. I will not see the empire brought down by southern-continent barbarians. And I most definitely will not give up my throne without a fight." A pause. "Emperor Kahless, the most famous Kamorh'dag of all, warned us of times like these, when our rule would be challenged. You are familiar with his teachings?"

The visitor nodded. "I am." In fact, he had been a student of Kahless for years, ever since he gained access to the family library as a youth.

"I thought you would be. Do you recall his advice? In his *Ramen'aa?*"

The words were very much alive in Kiruc's memory. He recited them out loud: "Darkness will fall. Enemies will circle us 'round and 'round, their swords as numerous as the trees of the forest. But we will not yield. We will wear faces of fire."

"And what does this mean to you, this phrase *faces of fire?*"

"According to the commentaries I've read, it has two meanings. One pertains to the quality of determination—in other words, if one's strength of will is great enough, he can surmount any obstacle."

"And the second meaning?" the emperor asked.

"A reference to one's skill at deception. An admonition to remain circumspect in all one's dealings—particularly with one's enemies, or potential enemies."

Kapronek made a sound of approval deep in his throat. "Very good." He leaned forward, his eyes narrowing to slits. "I've chosen well, it seems."

Kiruc shifted his weight in his seat. His heart was beating hard, but he dared not show it. "How may I serve you?" he asked.

The emperor sat back again and smiled grimly. "How indeed."

Chapter One

As Captain James T. Kirk entered sickbay, he saw Leonard McCoy standing in front of one of the new biomonitors that hung over each bed. The doctor was shaking his head in dissatisfaction.

"Bones?" the captain interrupted.

McCoy turned at the sound of his voice. "Damned new-fangled displays," he said. "They *still* don't work right." He sighed. "What's on your mind, Jim?"

Kirk eyed his chief medical officer critically. "You mean besides that paunch you're carrying around?"

"Now don't you get started, too. M'Benga was all over me a couple days ago. Five pounds and it's like the world ended!" McCoy patted his stomach, and smiled sourly. "I've got an exercise regimen all mapped out—as soon as I'm done working out the kinks in all this new hardware."

Kirk chuckled. "Good. I can't have my ship's surgeon setting a bad example for the crew."

"You know," said McCoy, "you're beginning to

sound like me. And the last thing this ship needs is another me." He turned back to the biomonitor. "So? Is my paunch all you came to talk about?"

Knowing the doctor's feelings about the topic he was about to bring up, Kirk wasn't exactly looking forward to this. But a captain had to do what a captain had to do.

"We've got an assignment, Bones. We're picking up an ambassador at Starbase Twelve. And we're taking him to the Alpha Maluria system, which is about six days from here at warp six."

McCoy's smile faded. "An ambassador. Terrific. I hope that wasn't meant to cheer me up."

Kirk sighed. "He comes highly recommended. From what I understand, he worked wonders at Gamma Philuvia Six."

The doctor harrumphed. "Sure. They're all highly recommended. Then they show up, and they get under your skin like Mechlavion mountain ants."

On the other end of sickbay, Nurse Chapel was calibrating the new batch of tricorders. She looked at McCoy disapprovingly.

The doctor returned her look. "Don't give me that, Christine. If you had to deal with the damned diplomatic corps, you'd feel the same way."

"Bones," said the captain, trying to be reasonable, "he's not exactly the Klingon emperor, you know. He's on our side."

"I think I'd rather he were the Klingon emperor," the doctor went on. "That way, we would only have to worry about a frontal assault."

Truthfully, Kirk had no more love for ambassadors than McCoy did. But that didn't mean he was going to let it show.

"Doctor," he pushed on, "you can't judge the man before he sets foot on the ship. He could be the exception to the rule. He could be . . ." He searched for the right word. "Helpful," he said finally.

McCoy snorted. "Right. And mugatu have wings."

"Listen," the captain said, a little more forcefully this time, "he'll be beaming up in about forty-five minutes. I'd like you to be in the briefing room when he arrives."

"I figured as much."

"And I want your word you'll at least be civil. No pokes at the diplomatic corps. No comments about their success rate. And definitely no suggestions that we'd be better off without them."

"Even if it's true?"

"No matter *what,*" Kirk underlined.

The doctor shook his head. "I'm not making any promises, Jim."

Finally, the captain played his trump card. "It isn't a proposal, Bones. It's an order."

McCoy cursed under his breath.

"What was that, Doctor?"

"I said I'll see you in the briefing room," Bones told him. "And I'll be on my best damned behavior."

Kirk smiled. "That's the spirit. Remember—forty-five minutes."

McCoy grunted. "I'll count the moments."

By the time McCoy reached the briefing room, it was already occupied. As he entered, Spock looked up from the table that dominated the place.

"Doctor," the first officer said, inclining his head ever so slightly. His eyes were hooded but darkly piercing, his long, narrow features completely devoid of emotion. Impeccably Vulcan, McCoy noted, as always.

"I see you've been roped in as well," the doctor said.

The first officer cocked an eyebrow. "Roped in?" he echoed.

"Included against your will," Bones translated. But before he'd finished, he realized that Spock might not have dreaded the presence of an ambassador the way the ship's other officers did.

After all, the Vulcan philosophy of IDIC—infinite diversity in infinite combination—taught tolerance for even the most repugnant life forms. And the diplomatic corps, even in McCoy's purview, was no more repugnant than a Tellarite bloodworm.

"I believe you are mistaken," Spock told him. "I have not been included against my will. In fact, it is necessary to the fulfillment of my responsibilities as first officer that I be apprised of—"

The doctor held up a hand for relief. "Never mind, Spock. Just never mind."

The Vulcan regarded McCoy, more like a scientist studying some new form of plant life than someone who'd just been rudely interrupted. "As you wish, Doctor," he replied simply.

"Thank you." Bones pulled out a chair and sat down.

A moment later, of course, the briefing room doors opened and the captain ushered in their guest. The doctor frowned at his sense of timing and got to his feet again. Across the room, Spock did likewise.

"Gentlemen," Kirk said, flashing that pleasant smile he normally reserved for state occasions and ravishing redheads, "this is Ambassador Marlin Farquhar. He has been assigned by the Federation to mediate a civil conflict on Alpha Maluria Six." He indicated the Vulcan, then the doctor. "First Officer Spock and Chief Medical Officer Leonard McCoy."

Farquhar was nearly a head taller than the captain, though he seemed to stoop a little at the shoulders. His age was difficult to ascertain—somewhere between forty and sixty, McCoy judged, though even that was just a guess. The man had thin, sand-colored hair, neatly combed except for a cowlick that stuck up obtrusively, almost comically, at the back of his head. His eyes were a watery blue; they didn't move, they darted. Like frightened fish, McCoy mused. His mouth was a thin, straight line, which dropped at the corners as he surveyed the Vulcan and then the doctor.

A true son of the diplomatic corps. McCoy sighed too softly for anyone to notice. It had gotten to the point where he could smell the type a light-year away. They came in a dozen different shapes and sizes, but the defining attributes were always the same: first, an irritating devotion to literal translations of Federation policy; and second, an inability to recognize the importance of any mission besides their own.

In rare cases, those less than endearing qualities were concealed beneath a veneer of fellowship and backslapping good cheer—a facade that was disingenuous but occasionally amusing. Even more rarely, they were fueled by an almost naive earnestness—something one could understand and even respect, if not quite embrace.

Unfortunately for Farquhar, he seemed to have neither of these attributes going for him. He was the standard model if McCoy had ever seen one.

Spock inclined his head. "Ambassador Farquhar," he repeated, in flat, even tones. His manner was reserved but not unfriendly.

The ambassador's reply was a simple one. "Commander Spock," Farquhar said, in a surprisingly deep and melodious voice that belied his appearance. Was it possible he'd misjudged their guest? McCoy wasn't so hardheaded he couldn't give someone the benefit of the doubt.

Bones held out his hand. "Nice to meet you." He searched for something innocuous to say. "Did you have a good flight out?"

"You could call it that, yes," Farquhar responded. The watery eyes narrowed, making their darting look even more furious. "Why? Has there been a problem with that route?"

Oh Lord, the doctor commented silently. "No, no problem," he assured the ambassador. "Just making conversation."

Farquhar looked at him. "I see." His mouth did that turning-down thing again. Abruptly, he turned to the captain. "I suppose we should get started now."

Kirk nodded. "Absolutely." Gesturing for the ambassador to take an empty chair, he pulled out another one for himself. "I'm sure we all want to hear about Alpha Maluria and what's going on there."

As the captain sat and pushed his seat in, McCoy could have sworn there was a "but" hanging in the air. It turned out he was right.

"But before we go any further," Kirk said, casting a couple of warning glances at his officers, "I should tell you there's been a change of plans."

Farquhar's brow wrinkled. "A change of plans?" he echoed, putting a more ominous spin on the phrase.

"That's right," the captain confirmed. "We received new orders only a few minutes ago—just before you arrived, Ambassador. I hope this doesn't cause you any inconvenience."

The ambassador leaned forward, temples working, cheeks ruddy. "I'm afraid I don't understand." His voice had a distinctly confrontational edge to it.

"We're still going to Alpha Maluria," Kirk stated emphatically. "But we're going to make a stop on the way." Reaching for the monitor in the middle of the table, he pressed a button. The screen displayed a star map.

"Beta Canzandia," the Vulcan announced, recognizing the configuration. "On the fringe of Federation space. Home to a research colony headed by Dr. Yves Boudreau, the Federation's leading expert on terraforming."

"Boudreau," McCoy repeated, picking up the ball and running with it. The longer they could keep away from the subject of Alpha Maluria, the more time Farquhar would have to cool off. "Isn't he the one who developed that G-Seven unit—the one that accelerates plant cell growth?"

"The same," Kirk affirmed. "What's more, Bones, you'll get a chance to meet him. You'll be conducting routine medical checkups for the entire colony." He turned to the Vulcan. "Spock, you'll be busy as well, assimilating data for a report on the terraformers' scientific progress. They're vastly overdue for a checkup in that respect as well."

Spock nodded. "I am quite interested to see how Dr. Boudreau's research is coming along."

The captain turned to Farquhar, whose gaze he'd been studiously avoiding. "All in all," he said, smiling hopefully, "it needn't be a long stopover. We can still be at Alpha Maluria inside of two weeks."

The ambassador's reply was anything but cooled off.

"This is an *outrage*," he fumed. "I can't believe what I'm hearing. Doesn't anyone at Starfleet have even a modicum of intelligence? Don't they see that a political cauldron like the one on Alpha Maluria Six must take precedence over *everything* else—much less a routine visit to yet another research colony?"

So much for the benefit of the doubt, Bones told himself. This joker's the ambassador to end all ambassadors.

"Medical checkups may be performed at any time," Farquhar went on. "But the Malurians need us *now*. Surely you can all see that."

The captain regarded Farquhar with equanimity. "Ambassador," he said, "I am merely following orders. Just as you are."

Farquhar eyed him. "There is a difference. I may not diverge from my orders. As the captain of this ship, you have the discretionary power to rearrange your itinerary if you feel it is necessary."

Kirk's shoulders straightened. McCoy knew what that meant: the captain would remain polite if it killed him, but he would not make a change he didn't believe in. And that was that.

Unfortunately for the ambassador, not to mention the rest of them, he had no such knowledge of Kirk's body language. He pressed his case.

"Starfleet knows nothing of Alpha Maluria Six," Farquhar persisted. "They have no idea what the Malurians are like, or of the lengths to which they will go in their devotion to their religious ideals. To them, it is just another world, another civil dispute." He snorted. "Idiots, that's what they are. Old men, who can no longer tell the difference between a beer barrel and a powder keg."

The captain was chewing the inside of his cheek. McCoy noticed and knew Farquhar was on the verge of being reined in.

"It's up to you, Captain." He pointed to Kirk. "You must turn your ship around and discharge your responsibility to the Malurians. Anything else would be—"

Kirk held up his hand. "I have to interrupt, Ambassador." Leaning forward, he met Farquhar's indignant stare head-on. "You've made your position clear. Now let me do the same." His voice took on a new note of authority. "You may think routine colony visits are a waste of time; they're not. I can't tell you how many lives have been saved because a ship's surgeon found some alien disease spreading through a Federation population."

The ambassador dismissed the idea with a wave of his hand. "That's—"

"Irrelevant?" the captain suggested. "Not to me. Lives are lives, and every one is important. I know that's hard to remember when you're focused on one planet, one set of circumstances, but that's the code I've got to live by." He frowned. "Now, you may say the Malurians are on the verge of civil war—and you may even be right. But I've got to go by the information available to me, including not only your opinions but the documentation the Federation has provided. And I must tell you, I see no reason to diverge from my orders. I'm not discounting the Malurian problem by any means, but those colonists have gone too long already without medical attention."

Farquhar fumed. "I see. And that's your final word?"

Kirk nodded. "My final word," he said without emotion.

McCoy admired the captain's restraint. In Kirk's place, he would have given the ambassador some friendly advice about interpersonal relations. But then, he wasn't the captain, was he?

A moment later, the ambassador got up and walked out. As the doors shooshed closed behind him, the captain looked at his officers.

"Well," he said, "that could have gone better."

McCoy grunted. "You sure you wouldn't have preferred the Klingon emperor?"

Kirk didn't answer. He just sighed.

David shaded his eyes from the frosty glare of Beta Canzandia and considered at the fissure at his feet. It was so deep that the bottom was lost in shadow. He kicked a medium-sized stone over the brink; it didn't hit bottom for a full three seconds.

Deep, all right. He felt its breath—a cold and clammy updraft, even chillier than the wintry air all around him. Protected as he was by his parka, it still made him shiver.

Of course, it wasn't all that unusual to find crevices in these cold, reddish brown highlands. His mother had told him the way they'd been formed; it had something to do with the ice that covered this part of the planet a long time ago.

But this was no small crack. The fissure was as wide

18

as David was tall. No, he decided, even wider than that. It had to be a good six feet from one side to the other.

"What's the matter?" Riordan asked him, grinning crookedly beneath his broad nose and wide-set, pale green eyes. His breath froze on the air, seeming to prolong his words. "Don't think you can handle it?"

That stung. Timmy Riordan was the oldest of them. He'd had more practice in finding a person's soft spots.

David studied the other four children who surrounded them. They looked back with varying levels of concern and anticipation: Pfeffer, with his tight curls of red hair and his red, freckled cheeks; Wan, with her shiny, black ponytail and her delicate features; Medford, with her chocolate brown eyes and complexion to match; and Garcia, whose dark, narrow face looked painfully sharp between his windbitten, jug-handle ears.

"Well?" Riordan prodded. "Are you going to take the dare? Or is it too dangerous for you?"

It *was* too dangerous. David knew that. If his mother had any idea what he was up to, she'd have restricted him to their dome for the rest of his life.

"Nope. Not too dangerous for me," he told the older boy, though the cold made his words seem hollow.

Riordan grunted. "Good."

"I think we ought to go home," Medford announced. "This is stupid. Someone's going to get hurt."

Riordan dismissed her with a roll of his eyes. "You're a girl. What do *you* know?"

Medford seemed to recoil, as if she'd been dealt a

19

physical blow. "I know we're not supposed to be here," she insisted, though she seemed less sure of herself than before the disparaging remark.

"The only way anybody's going to know is if one of us says something," Riordan pressed. "And nobody's going to do that. So what's the big deal?"

Pfeffer and Garcia grunted their assent. They couldn't look like yellowbellies. Not in front of the girls. And definitely not in front of Riordan.

That settled, the older boy turned back to David. "So?

He took another look at the fissure. Maybe Medford was right. Maybe this was stupid.

"I've changed my mind," he said. "I'm not doing it."

Riordan's expression changed from one of challenge to one of derision. "Not doing it? What are you, chicken?"

David could feel his cheeks turning as red as Pfeffer's. He shrugged, bunching the shoulders of his parka up around his ears.

The older boy smiled. "It's all right. I guess it's hard when you don't have a *father.*"

David stiffened at the jibe. He could feel everyone looking at him, reminded of the fact that out of all the colonists' children, he was the only one who didn't have a male parent.

Riordan stood there with his arms folded across his chest, daring David to make the jump. It seemed to the younger boy he no longer had a choice in the matter.

He had to prove he was a man. He had to prove he had become one without a father.

Even if he was only ten.

"All right," David said, screwing up his resolve. "I guess I'll do it after all."

There was no possibility of Riordan going first. That just wasn't the way it worked around here, and it never had been. Riordan had ruled the roost since they'd all arrived on this world nearly two years ago.

Taking a last look into the fissure, David backed away from it a good twenty paces. He knew he'd need a running start; if he was at anything less than top speed, he'd fall short of the far brink. And more than likely, get himself killed.

For a fleeting moment, he had a vision of the eerie, cold darkness flying up at him, and the sound of crunching bones, and the sickening knowledge that the bones being crunched were his. Then the vision passed.

Riordan was silent. He must have sensed there was no longer any need to prod. Taking a deep breath, watching it dissipate on the wind, David crouched. His youthful muscles coiled like springs.

He was suddenly aware of the sounds that haunted these hills—the sighings and hootings of the wind as it explored every tiny niche and hollow. He could hear his heartbeat as well, big and loud in his chest.

Lowering his head, he began to sprint, to gather as much momentum as he could. After a second or two, he raised his head and saw the fissure looming before him, bounding closer and closer like the open jaws of some beast too big to comprehend.

As he passed the other children, he heard someone gasp. Medford, he thought. He didn't let it distract him, though.

Putting a little extra into his last two strides, he leapt high and far. Incredibly, there was an opportunity to think an entire thought between the time he became airborne and the time he saw the other side rushing up at him.

What he thought was this: *I'd better not die or Mom will kill me.*

And then his heels hit the ground and he was past the fissure, skidding and rolling and finally coming to a breathless halt on all fours. He stayed that way for a moment, gathering himself, trying to make his heart stop beating so fast. Then he got up and looked back at his companions.

Riordan was laughing. The others didn't know what to make of it, though Pfeffer looked like he wanted to laugh too. As David brushed himself off with his gloved hands, he barked, "What's so funny?"

The older boy pointed at him. "You are. I can't believe you did it. What a *skeezit*."

David flinched at the word. Riordan had told them it was a Klingon curse, and it meant the lowest, most disgusting thing in the whole galaxy.

"You dared me," the younger boy protested.

Riordan spread his arms wide, palms out, in a gesture of disbelief. "So? You do everything everybody tells you to?"

Riordan laughed again. And finally understanding, Pfeffer joined him. Garcia ventured a chuckle as well.

But David wasn't buying it. The older boy had changed the rules in the middle of the game, and that wasn't fair.

"No way," he called across the fissure. "You dared me and I did it. Now *you* do it. Or are you too scared?"

Riordan reddened. His smile became stiff, and for a second or two, he seemed ready to accept the challenge. Then he shrugged it off—and somehow got away with it.

"First," the older boy decided, "you jump back the other way."

David shook his head. "Why? So you can make fun of me?"

The truth was, he was still trembling a little from his first jump. He had a bad feeling about trying it a second time.

Riordan grunted, as if he'd exposed David's brave leap as a fluke. Pfeffer grunted too, like an echo.

"Suit yourself," Riordan replied. Then, turning to the others, "Let's get back." He flung a backhand gesture at David. "Chicken here can take the long way around."

"Yeah," Pfeffer added. "The long way around."

David wanted to punch his face in. If the crack in the ground hadn't separated them, he might have. Then again, if the fissure weren't there, Pfeffer probably wouldn't have had the courage to say it.

As Riordan started back in the direction of the colony, the other four children fell into line behind him, though Wan hesitated a moment before she departed.

Overcome with anger, David's lower lip started to tremble. He almost threatened to tell their parents about what had happened here—almost. But he stopped himself in time. It wouldn't help him any to become a snitch; it would just make things worse.

Besides, he was the only one who'd jumped the fissure. The others would look innocent by comparison.

Suddenly, maybe half a dozen meters from the

crevice, Medford did an about-face and started back. Riordan stopped for a moment to stare wonderingly at her; like puppets, the others stopped too.

"Forget something?" he asked, just a hint of a taunt in his voice.

She didn't look at him. Maybe she couldn't; maybe she'd reached the limits of her defiance already.

"Nope," she said, a determined expression on her face. "I'm just going to wait for Marcus."

"He might be awhile," Riordan warned her, his tone decidedly more mocking now. More threatening, though David wasn't sure exactly what the threat was.

"That's okay," she said, wrapping her arms about herself as if she were cold, despite her parka. "I'm not in a hurry."

The older boy seemed about to say something more. He must have thought better of it, though, because he simply turned his back on David and Medford and left—with the others in tow, of course.

After a minute or so, when Riordan and his companions had dropped out of sight down an incline, Medford looked at David. To his surprise, she smirked. To his greater surprise, he smirked back.

"You know," she said, "he wasn't wrong. Riordan, I mean. You should never have jumped this crack, no matter who dared you."

David nodded freely. "I know. It was stupid." But somehow, he didn't feel so bad about it anymore. "You don't really have to wait for me, Medford."

"I know," she answered. She jerked a thumb over her shoulder. "But I sure as heck don't want to go back with them."

He laughed, then scanned east along the fissure— easier than scanning west, which would mean looking right into the yellow-white sun. The crack ran as far as the eye could see, though it seemed to get narrower as it went. In another hundred meters or so, it wouldn't take much of a jump to get across it.

David pointed and told Medford of his intention. "It shouldn't be any problem," he assured her.

She shook her head. "Nothing doing. We'll walk—you on that side and me on this side—and we'll *keep* walking till we find the end of this thing."

He started to protest but stifled it. "Whatever you say," he agreed. After all, he owed her something. Putting the sun at their backs, they began walking.

Chapter Two

KARRADH'S ESTATE was situated in the fog-shrouded foothills outside the imperial city. It was a typical Kamorh'dag residence, a combination of cunning angles and long, elegant curves, constructed of dark, polished woods that reflected the dying light. It managed in its pride and stolidity to look even more ancient than the hills surrounding it.

As Kiruc walked up to the front door, Zibrat and Torgis followed closely behind. They were greeted at the door by Karradh's housemistress, an elderly woman named Wistor with a narrow face and deeply set eyes. Once Karradh's wet nurse, Wistor had been elevated to her present position of authority after the previous housemistress's death—or so the story went.

"You are expected," the woman said. Her voice was stronger than Kiruc would have guessed. "I greet you on my lord's behalf." She indicated the interior of the house with a movement of her withered hand. "Would you like to come in?"

"I would indeed," Kiruc told her.

Wistor turned and led them into the reception hall. Like the exterior of the house, it was very much in keeping with tradition. The smooth, wooden walls were covered with weaponry, most of it antiquated and well worn. Freeform metal sculptures filled the corners of the room, at once fitting in with the weaponry and providing a contrast.

Torches blazed in blackened braziers, throwing up streams of oily, ebony smoke that commingled in the exposed wooden rafters. Each torch threw its own set of shadows, so that Kiruc felt as if he were moving amidst an army of ghosts with each step he took.

Wistor stopped in the center of the hall and turned to Kiruc. "You will wait here. Karradh will be with you presently."

She did not wait for him to acknowledge the information. She simply resumed her progress across the reception hall. At the far end, there was a semicircular doorway that led out into the water garden. She vanished through it.

After a moment or two, Karradh filled the doorway with his bulk. Except for the advanced graying of his whiskers, he seemed no older than when Kiruc saw him last, though that must have been a good five or six years ago—when Kiruc's father had been alive, and Karradh had been master of security for the Second Fleet. That meeting had been quite productive. Kiruc hoped *this* encounter would prove likewise.

"Welcome," Karradh said in his booming voice, approaching his visitors with a bit of a limp. The hall reverberated with his enthusiasm. "It has been a long time, Kiruc."

Kiruc grasped the older man's hand. Karradh's grip was as firm as ever. "Too long, friend of my father."

The former security master looked to Zibrat and Torgis. "Kiruc's friends are my friends," he announced. He gestured to an alcove off the main hall, where a wrought-iron table and chairs awaited in the soft light of a standing brazier. "Make yourselves comfortable while I entertain my guest."

There was nothing impolite about the suggestion; bodyguards did not take part in private conferences. Nor did anyone anticipate trouble here. Karradh had been a friend of Kiruc's family for some years. Nonetheless, both Zibrat and Torgis shot glances at their master.

With a curt, almost imperceptible nod, Kiruc gave them leave to do as Karradh said. Satisfied, they headed for the alcove and the table.

The older man looked at Kiruc. "Do you permit them to drink while on duty?"

The younger man shook his head. "I used to, but not anymore. Times have changed, friend of my father."

Karradh grunted. "So they have." He took Kiruc by the arm and led him in the direction of the semicircular doorway. "Fortunately," he went on, "you and I are under no such restriction. I think you will enjoy the ale. The keg was opened only yesterday."

As they emerged from the doorway, Kiruc nodded approvingly. The water garden was laid out in the lap of the mist-laden hills, according to classic design precepts, with every form and texture of movement represented. Here, two channels clashed and eddied, azure with reflected firelight; there, another gurgled with white foam about some dark rocks; and in a third place, there was the hissing glamour of a waterfall, made ruddy by the rays of the setting sun. There were levels and levels, as far as the eye could see through the gathering haze. Squat, spiky shrubs, gray boulders, and graceful, overhanging dwarf willows worked in harmony with the water courses, hiding the least interesting portions from view. And of course, there were the torches held forth by dark, cunning shapes—metal abstractions of demons from Klingon mythology, half hidden in the intricate shadows—which did the additional duty of keeping away biting insects.

All in all, quite pleasing. Kiruc said so.

"I am glad you like it," the older man responded. "For better or worse, I have had a great deal of time to cultivate it, now that I have retired from the fleet." He showed Kiruc to a table made of flat stones, that sat on a peninsula extending into a miniature lake. As they took their seats, Kiruc noticed the tiny whirlpools that came and went along their shore. Marvelous, he mused. He wondered if Karradh would tell him the secret of creating them some day.

Karradh poured the ale from a crude wooden pitcher into ceramic goblets. They drank. The former security master was right, Kiruc mused. The ale was sharp, enjoyable; it attacked the taste buds like a warrior.

"Ahh," Karradh said, replacing his goblet on the table. "Impeccable."

Kiruc nodded. "And even more delicious, I'll wager, for your having snatched it from the hold of a Romulan ship."

The older man's eyes narrowed. "You know that story, eh? Good. It *should* be known. It was a glorious victory. A model for future encounters with the

Romulans." Wiping his bearded lips with the back of his hand, he drummed his fingers against the tabletop. "Speak, Kiruc. You didn't come here to chew the fat off the bones of old war stories."

The younger man smiled. "True." He paused. "At one time, Karradh, you were privy to a great deal of information. Some say even more than the emperor himself."

Karradh shrugged slyly. "It was my job, my duty, to be well informed. Though I would not say I was more knowledgeable than the emperor, at least not to his face." He measured his visitor with his black, stony eyes. "What sort of information were you looking for?"

Kiruc told him, in the vaguest terms possible. He was particularly careful to avoid any further mention of Kapronek. Nor did his host ask for additional information. He seemed quite comfortable with the vagueness.

"The Gevish'rae," Karradh repeated. "I, too, have been concerned about them. I am glad to see I am not alone."

"Yes," Kiruc replied. "Now all we need is a way to penetrate their defenses. To disrupt their movement."

The older man looked at him. "It seems to me," he said, "there is a young Gevish'rae named Grael, of the Nik'nash clan. A little more than a year ago, he committed an indiscretion—an act of violence directed against his own kinsmen. A play for power, you understand, if a rash one. The act never bore fruit, but neither was it discovered." Karradh leaned forward. "One armed with knowledge of this indiscretion might find Grael willing to do his bidding. After all, if others in the Nik'nash clan got wind of his treachery . . ." His voice faded meaningfully.

"Grael," Kiruc echoed. "I will remember the name." He smiled. "And what about you, friend of my father? Is there nothing I can offer you in return for your assistance?"

Karradh shrugged. "I am Kamorh'dag. In working against the Gevish'rae, you work on my behalf." His eyes narrowed ever so slightly. "However, if you are bent on showing your gratitude, there *is* one small favor you might render me."

"Ask," the younger man advised him, "and if it is in my power, it will be done."

The former master of security poured them more ale. The mists were rolling down the hillside as darkness fell, mingling with the trees and shrubs of the water garden, deepening the mystery in them.

Having finished pouring, Karradh looked up. His eyes reflected the firelight. "I have a son, Kell. He serves as second officer on the battlecruiser *Fragh'ka*, and does a damned good job of it. The first officer is a man by the name of Kernod, by all accounts a capable individual as well. However, for Kell to move up in the ranks . . ." As before, he let his voice trail off.

"Kernod must meet with an accident."

"Precisely." A pause, in which the older man showed some discomfort. "The normal way of the world would be for my son to perform the task himself. However, Kell is not always as ambitious as he should be, and he has a great respect for Kernod. Left to his own devices, I fear, Kell would remain a second officer the rest of his days."

"You need say no more," Kiruc assured him.

"Kernod will be eliminated at the earliest opportunity. And there will be no connection between your clan and the assassination."

Karradh nodded. "I am grateful," he said.

Kiruc waved away the suggestion. "It's nothing. As the expression goes, it is easier to defend oneself with two hands than one."

The older man grunted. "You're a student of Kahless."

"I am," Kiruc confirmed. He picked up his goblet. "To Kell."

Karradh followed suit. "Yes. To Kell. And to the Kamorh'dag."

They drank.

As Kirk stopped before the door to McCoy's quarters, he announced himself: "It's me, Bones."

There was no reply.

Strange, he thought. Had the doctor forgotten the invitation he'd extended only this morning? It wasn't like McCoy to let something like this slip his mind. Starfleet regulations, maybe. On occasion, the name of a planet or two. But never a date to shoot the bull.

Maybe he's fallen asleep, the captain decided. He was about to announce himself again, this time a little louder, when out of the corner of his eye he noticed someone approaching.

Turning, he saw his chief medical officer dressed in sweat-soaked gym togs. The man didn't look any too happy; he was walking with a decided limp and he had a dark bruise just above his left eye.

"What happened to *you?*" Kirk asked him.

McCoy swept away the question with a swipe of his hand. "Don't ask."

Suddenly, the captain remembered their discussion of a few days ago, before Farquhar came on board and started turning things upside down. "Bones, this doesn't have anything to do with that remark I made about your being out of shape, does it?"

The doctor stopped in front of his door and glared at his friend. "I *said* don't ask. And don't expect me to get within fifty meters of that gymnasium, either. A man could get killed there."

The door slid aside with a soft whoosh and Kirk followed McCoy inside. "If you want," he suggested, "we could make it another time . . ."

"No," the doctor told him firmly, wincing as he started to strip off his top. "I'll just be a few minutes. Relax. Make yourself at home."

Then he turned the corner and vanished from sight. A moment later, the captain heard the hard hiss of the shower.

It didn't take long, however, before he followed Bones's instructions and relaxed. Sometimes, Kirk mused, he felt more at ease in McCoy's quarters than in his own. After all, in his own quarters, there was always the temptation to work—to finish up odds and ends he hadn't gotten to while on the bridge, or to get a head start on the next day's agenda.

But here, in the chief medical officer's suite, there was no such temptation. Not that he couldn't have signed on to the computer system from McCoy's terminal as easily as from his own; it was just that it didn't seem appropriate, any more than catching a nap in Sulu's botanical garden or having dinner in engineering. This was a place for old war stories, for shared meditations, for exchanges of clever witticisms. And let's face it, Kirk told himself—for escape.

These days, he needed one. Even if he wasn't about to say so out loud, he'd had about all he could take from Ambassador Farquhar. The man had been harassing him and his officers at every opportunity, plying and replying his case for skipping over the colony on Beta Canzandia Three and heading straight for Alpha Maluria Six.

Fortunately, the one officer Farquhar hadn't approached was Bones—perhaps because, at some level, he sensed the doctor's dislike of him. And that made McCoy's quarters more of a haven than ever; for the duration of the captain's visit here, he was safe from the ambassador.

Smiling at the thought, he lowered himself into McCoy's easy chair and considered the furnishings: the matched set of intricate *phornicia* shells, which symbolized the healing arts on Magistor Seven as the caduceus did on Earth; the large and ostentatious oil painting of a graceful antebellum mansion, reputed to be somewhere on the outskirts of Atlanta; the miniature black knight Yeoman Barrows had sculpted for him—rearing charger and all—just before her transfer to the *Potemkin*.

Barrows. Kirk grunted. Now there had been a—

His observations were interrupted by a familiar grumbling from the next room. A moment later, McCoy appeared in a Starfleet-issue black jumpsuit. Looking at least a bit more sociable than before, he rumpled his hair, which was still damp from the shower.

"Bones—"

The doctor peered at him through narrowed eyes, one of which had swollen up. "Let's pick another topic, shall we?"

The captain held his hands up in surrender. "Fine. Whatever you say."

McCoy headed for his bar, which was amply stocked, as usual. He selected two glasses from a hidden compartment and plunked them down on the counter in front of him. "Name your poison," he said.

"Brandy," Kirk replied, getting up again—no easy task, considering the amount of stuffing in McCoy's chair—and crossing the cabin.

"Saurian?"

"What else?"

"Saurian it is." The doctor selected the appropriate container—a rather elegant one the captain hadn't seen before.

"Nice decanter," he remarked.

"Just got it," McCoy explained. "It was a gift. From Cal Forrest, an old med school buddy." Taking the top off, he poured ample quantities into both glasses. Then he replaced the lid on the decanter.

Kirk picked up one of the glasses and swirled its contents around, watching the patterns the brandy made as it slid down the inside of the glass. "Cal Forrest, eh? I don't believe I've ever heard you mention him."

The doctor chuckled. "Cal's one of those people you don't see for a long time, but when you do it's as if you saw him just yesterday. You know what I mean?"

The captain said that he did.

McCoy lifted his glass. "To old friends," he said, and sampled the brandy.

Kirk did likewise. After taking a moment to savor the bittersweet flavor of the liqueur, he set his drink down on the bar.

"Good?" the doctor asked.

"Very good," he answered. Bones seemed to have forgotten his ornery mood. But then, Kirk's company often had that effect on him. Even as he watched, the doctor's eyes seemed to light up.

"And while we're on the subject of old friends . . . ," he said.

The captain looked at him. "What about them?"

"I came across an interesting name on the Beta Canzandia colony roster that was sent out to us. Meant to mention it earlier, in fact, except Farquhar has been keeping you so busy with his infernal litany about Alpha Maluria Six, I didn't have a chance." He muttered a curse. "Lord save me from little minds . . ." His voice trailed off as he became lost in thought.

Kirk tried to remain patient. "Bones?"

"Mm?"

"The *name*. An old friend, you said."

McCoy met his gaze. "Right. Sorry. It's Carol Marcus."

It caught the captain by surprise. "Carol Marcus?" he repeated.

Actually, she was a lot more than an old friend. Carol had been someone special—someone with whom he'd come damned close to initiating a permanent relationship, until their careers got in the way.

And she was on Beta Canzandia Three. Small galaxy, wasn't it?

McCoy tilted his head to one side. "What's that grin about? Thinking of picking up where you left off?"

Before Kirk could answer, a beeping sound invaded McCoy's quarters. The two men looked at one another.

McCoy said: "You know what that's about, don't you?"

The captain nodded ruefully. Apparently, he wasn't so safe here after all. Heading for the doctor's intercom unit, he laid his hand over the metal strip.

"Kirk here."

"Sir, I dinnae like to interrupt yer personal time, but—"

"It's all right, Scotty. What's up?"

As if he didn't know.

"Captain, it's Ambassador Farquhar."

Kirk sighed. "What about him, Scotty?"

Abruptly, the ambassador's voice replaced the chief engineer's. "I'm perturbed, Captain. I thought you understood the urgency of my mission."

McCoy rolled his eyes.

"I understand it quite well," Kirk replied. "What leads you to believe otherwise?"

"Lieutenant Commander Scott does," Farquhar told him.

"Now wait just a bleedin'—"

The captain cut him short. "Not to worry, Scotty. Ambassador, just what is it Mr. Scott told you?"

He could picture Farquhar drawing himself up to his full height. And Scotty's expression of frustration as he looked on, unable to defend himself.

"That the *Enterprise* is traveling at warp six."

Kirk saw the problem. "And you'd like our speed to be greater, I suppose?"

"Certainly. The faster we reach Beta Canzandia, the faster we leave Beta Canzandia. That is, unless you've changed your mind about going there first."

The captain smiled grimly. "No, I haven't changed

my mind. What's more, I have no intention of increasing our speed."

An uncomfortable pause. "And why is that, if I may ask?"

Kirk could feel a dull ache starting over the bridge of his nose. "Because I wish to conserve some power for tactical reasons. As I'm sure Mr. Scott would have told you, if you'd given him a chance, Beta Canzandia is situated in fairly close proximity to the Klingon Empire. And while there hasn't been any trouble in that star system historically, I'm not ruling out the possibility of it."

The ambassador made a derisive sound. It was loud enough to be heard clearly over the intercom system.

The captain ignored it. "I trust that explains the situation to your satisfaction?"

"It explains it," Farquhar answered, "but by no means to my satisfaction."

Kirk was formulating a response to the remark when the intercom suddenly went dead. Obviously, the ambassador saw no purpose in continuing the conversation.

Just as well, the captain told himself. He might not have liked what he was about to hear.

Turning back to McCoy, he shrugged. "Sorry about that, Bones. Now, where were we?"

"Carol Marcus," the doctor reminded him. "I was asking if you had any intention of fanning the embers."

Kirk smiled at the metaphor. Leaning against the bulkhead, he thought about it. And thought some more.

After all, it had been a long time—for both of them. People could change a great deal in all that time.

Or they could not change at all.

"Well?" McCoy probed.

The captain looked at him. He didn't know what to say.

The doctor chuckled. "Knowing you, I'll take that as a yes."

David tried not to show how tired he was as he tramped into the warm, domed quarters he shared with his mother. She was sitting in the section reserved for their personal computer, no doubt going over some calculations that had eluded her during the workday.

Hearing him come in, she turned and smiled. *"There* you are."

The tone of her voice sent a bolt of fear up his spine. Had she found out where he'd been? Had someone squealed?

"What do you mean?" he got out.

She pointed to the chronometer that hung from one of the gently curving walls. "It's nearly dinnertime. You're cutting it pretty close these days, young man."

David breathed a sigh of relief—though actually, he mused, he might have been more relieved if she had found out. Then he wouldn't have to keep it secret from her.

For as long as he could remember, his mother had been his best friend. Sometimes, when they'd lived in colonies without other children, she'd been his *only* friend. He hated not being able to tell her about the crevice.

But there was no way he was going to tattle. He liked the company of the other children here at Beta Canzandia, despite their not always being real nice to him. Even Riordan wasn't so bad to have around, compared to having no one to play with at all.

"So what did you do after school today?" his mother asked. "Anything interesting?"

David shrugged. "You know. Hung out with the other kids."

Her eyes lost some of their good humor. "How's that Timmy Riordan treating you?"

"Fine, Mom, just fine." Pulling down on the zipper of his parka, he took it off and hung it up. "Really."

His mother looked at him. She seemed to see something there. "Are you sure? I'm not shy, you know. I could talk to his parents ag—"

David held up his hands. "No!" he said a little too loudly. And then, "It's all right. We get along just great now."

She didn't look convinced. "You're sure, Lamb?"

Inwardly, he shivered. "I'm sure, Mom. And you said you wouldn't call me that anymore."

His mother chuckled. "That's right, I forgot. You're too big to be called Lamb. Too much of a man, now that you've turned ten."

"Come on, Mom. Give a guy a break."

For a moment, she looked wistful. He'd seen her look that way before, but never when she knew he was looking back.

"All right," she agreed. "I'll give a guy a break. But first the guy's got to go wash up for dinner."

David started to do that, grateful that she'd hadn't pressed him any harder about the day's activities. Or for that matter, about Timmy Riordan.

Then something weird happened. He stopped halfway to the washroom, as if he couldn't make himself move any farther. "Hey, Mom?"

Shut up, he told himself. *What are you doing? You had it made in the shade!*

His mother turned to face him again. "Yes?"

The boy swallowed. "Mom, do I need a father? You know, to become a man?"

Her face seemed to lose some of its color. "A father," she repeated, trying without success to sound as cheerful as she had before. "Where did that come from?"

He frowned. Why couldn't he have kept his mouth shut? "I heard somebody talking about it today, saying that fathers were important things to have and all." He licked his lips. "And I wondered if maybe I should have one, like the other kids."

His mother sighed. "I knew something was wrong. The kids were giving you a hard time, weren't they?"

David nodded. "Sort of."

She got up from her work station, came over to him, and put her arms around him. "I know it's not easy being different, but you've got to make the best of it. You've got to remember that you're as good as *you* think you are—not as good as *they* think you are."

He nodded some more, but it didn't help as much as his mother intended. He didn't want to be different. He wanted a father—if not his real one, the one that had died a long time ago, then someone else.

His mother held him away and looked at him. "You understand what I'm saying, right? Father or no father, you're still the best kid around."

"I understand," he got out. But more than he'd ever wanted anything in his life, David Marcus yearned for a man he could look up to.

Chapter Three

DARK AND UNPOPULATED, the bridge of the *Kadn'ra* seemed more spartan than ever, more passionately Klingon, as Vheled entered it and took his place in the captain's chair. On the forward viewscreen, there was an image of Alalpech'ch, the vassal world where he and his crew had laid over while their ship was being equipped with an improved grade of photon torpedo launchers.

Not that any improvement mattered a damn, in the long run. Battles were waged by captains and crews, not machines.

Stretching his long arms and legs, he could still feel the dull pain of his half-healed wounds, acquired in the course of a bloody brawl in one of Alalpech'ch's public drinking houses. Even if his crew had not emerged victorious against the scraggly Kamorh'dag cowards they'd encountered there—victory being measured by the relative number of men still standing at the end—the brawl would have been the highlight of his down time.

Vheled, captain of the *Kad'nra,* loved to shed Kamorh'dag blood. It was his greatest pleasure in life to show those high-and-mighty northerners—scheming puris like Kiruc of the Faz'rahn clan—how a *real* Klingon carried himself. He smiled at the memory of the stocky, broad-shouldered Kamorh'dag who'd pulled out his dagger, hoping to skewer Vheled on it, only to be skewered himself on a broken chair leg.

But enough of such pleasantries, he told himself. Now it was time to pursue more weighty matters, to continue on the path of glory he'd been blazing since he entered the imperial fleet. Bringing his fist down with a thud on one of the metal studs in his armrest, he altered the picture on the viewscreen.

Instead of the curving, cloud-strewn horizon of Alalpech'ch, it showed the familiar countenance of Dumeric, his maternal uncle—and the newest member of the high council. Dumeric was an older version of Vheled—dark, swaggering, and powerful, especially for one who had so many threads of gray in his hair. His smile was thin-lipped, his gaze intense; a nearby torch cast a red glow over one side of his craggy face.

"Ah. Right on time, nephew. Your punctuality is to be commended."

Vheled inclined his head. "I am your servant," he said, reeling off the proper response.

"Good." A beat. "You are certain this channel is secure?"

"It is secure," Vheled assured him. "I have checked it myself; I would stake my life on it."

His uncle grunted. "You already have. If the Kamorh'dag intercept this communication, not only the *Kad'nra* but our entire movement will be at risk."

"I understand," Vheled confirmed. "And I maintain, there is nothing to fear."

Dumeric leaned back in his seat. He was ensconced in the shadowy, stone-walled library of his estate on Tiv'ranisch Island, off the coast of the southern continent.

Vheled had been there on a number of occasions, the most recent of them less than a year before. He recognized the crossed red-metal blades on the wall behind his uncle, presented to him for bravery during the Ia'kriich campaigns. Of course, that was a long time ago, before the Gevish'rae were organized enough to be perceived as a threat to the emperor.

"You have heard of the world called Pheranna?"

Vheled thought for a moment. "In the nineteenth ring, yes? The sector *disputed* by the Federation?" Of course, the Klingons had no real claim on the place, and privately they recognized the fact. Vheled had placed an ironic emphasis on the word.

"That is the one. The humans and their allies call it Beta Canzandia Three." He licked his lips. "According to our spies, they have established an important research colony there."

Vheled looked at him. "In what way important?"

"They are developing a technology to remake barren planets in the mold of the human homeworld—as incredible as it may sound. Their goal on Pheranna, it seems, is to carry this out in bits and pieces. But once they have learned all they need to learn there, they intend to alter entire worlds."

The captain of the *Kad'nra* shook his head. "Alter

them—to resemble their homeworld. How is such a thing possible?"

"I told you it sounded incredible." Dumeric's brows knit. "Of course, it is entirely possible the project will end in failure. Nonetheless, the emperor is curious about this sort of technology. He wants it seized while it is still within easy reach of the empire."

Vheled shrugged, as if to say *the emperor's whims are his own.* No technology really mattered unless it could be used as a weapon against one's enemies.

"What has this to do with me?" he asked his uncle.

Dumeric smiled savagely. "Regardless of what you or I may think, the emperor attaches great importance to this objective. He has said so in council." The older man tilted his head to one side. "Originally, Kapronek wished to assign the mission to one of his kinsmen. I argued, however, that no one is better suited to such a task than my nephew."

Vheled touched a soreness at his temple, where he'd been bludgeoned with something in the course of the brawl. It was certainly true—not only was he a better captain than the emperor's kin, he was somewhat more familiar with the sector in question.

And should his mission be a successful one, it could only enhance the standing of the Gevish'rae in the Great Hall. On the other hand . . .

"I know what you're thinking," Dumeric said. "The Kamorh'dag will not exactly cheer you on. Quite likely, they will try to thwart you—even humiliate you, if at all possible—all the while making sure not to give away their hand in it. After all, as much as your triumph will strengthen our position in the empire, a failure would knock us down twice as far. People will say the Gevish'rae can't be trusted with anything important. The Kamorh'dag were right, they'll say, to keep the reins of government all to themselves." His lip curled. "That is why we dare not falter. It is why I have chosen *you*—because I know you will prevail, no matter what the Federation and the Kamorh'dag throw against you."

Vheled acknowledged the praise with a quick nod of his shaggy head. He didn't like being a pawn in Dumeric's council games. All this plotting, it seemed to him, had little to do with the way of the warrior.

However, these were political times; one had to accept the lot one was given. And besides, it was a chance to rub Kapronek's Kamorh'dag nose in the dirt.

Pounding his chest with his closed fist, Vheled responded: "It is my duty to serve my emperor's pleasure."

Dumeric chuckled dryly. "See to it," he advised, "that you don't please him *too* much."

As Kirk came out onto the bridge, he half expected to see Farquhar waiting for him there. He was pleasantly surprised to be in error.

Spock was sitting in the captain's seat. Noticing Kirk's arrival, he stood and moved to one side.

"Thank you, Spock. I trust nothing unusual took place while I was gone."

The Vulcan turned to face the forward viewscreen, where the stars were streaming by at nearly four hundred times the speed of light. "Actually," he said, without the slightest hint of annoyance in his voice, "there *was* one event worth noting."

As he took his seat, the captain had a sneaking suspicion what it might be. "Don't tell me. Ambassador Farquhar filed an official protest, claiming that our travel at warp six reflects an inappropriately casual attitude toward the problem on Alpha Maluria Six. Or something to that effect."

"The word he used was *cavalier*," the first officer remarked.

Spock's nostrils flared. Not many people would have noticed, but Kirk did.

The captain tapped his fingertips on his armrest. "I see."

"Will that be all, sir?"

Kirk gave the Vulcan a look of empathy. The ambassador was trying all their souls, even the nonhuman ones. "Yes. That'll be all, Spock."

Without another word—as if he didn't trust himself to utter one without giving away his feelings of vexation—the first officer turned and left the bridge.

The captain shook his head. He almost wished he'd never been given the Beta Canzandia mission. Then they'd be heading directly for Alpha Maluria, and the ambassador wouldn't have anything to complain about.

But then, if they hadn't been assigned Beta Canzandia, he wouldn't have had a chance to see Carol Marcus again. And that, at least, was something he was looking forward to.

"Carol?"

She looked up at the sound of her name and saw Dr. Boudreau standing at the open entrance to the roofless enclosure. He was smiling genially, but as soon as he saw the look of concern on her face, his smile faded.

"Everything all right?" he asked, his breath freezing.

She frowned. "It's the fireblossoms."

Actually, she had something else on her mind as well. She'd been thinking of David and what he'd said to her before dinner the night before. But that wasn't something she wanted to discuss with the colony administrator.

Boudreau's eyes narrowed as he stooped to come inside. His gray thermal jumpsuit bent stiffly; the material was still new. "The Klingon specimens? I thought they were doing so well."

Carol grunted. "They're doing fine. The problem is, they're turning out to be lousy neighbors. Everything around them is dying."

The colony administrator grunted as he approached. "Lousy neighbors—like the Klingons themselves, from what I understand." Kneeling beside her, he touched one of the long, deep blue petals of the nearest fireblossom, accidentally brushing against the plant's prickly-looking stamen as well. A gray-blue dust came off on his gloved fingertips. "Too bad. Are you going to take them out of the mix?"

She shook her head. "No. They're still outdistancing all our hybrids in terms of growth and oxygen production. Which is a bit strange, considering they come from such a humid place, and there's so little water here. Tenuda and Harcum were right in their assessments of the fireblossom. It's turning out to be incredibly hardy—incredibly tenacious."

"Furthering the comparison with the Klingons themselves," Boudreau commented. "So what will you do? Transplant its neighbors instead, and try others?"

She nodded. "That's what I was thinking. You disagree?"

"Not in the least," he said. "But keep in mind adaptability and oxygen production are of no use if the damned things won't coexist with Terran plants when the time comes. Our ultimate goal, remember, is to terraform; the fireblossom, or whatever else we come up with, is just a natural means of speeding up the process."

Carol didn't really have to be reminded of their objective. Nor, she was sure, did the colony administrator believe otherwise. But like many scientists she had known, Boudreau had the habit of repeating his aims out loud. Maybe he thought that made them more tangible somehow.

Boudreau tried to blow the fireblossom dust off his fingers, but some of it remained. With a look of resignation, he wiped it off on the front of his jumpsuit, where it was barely visible. "Even its pollen is stubborn," he commented dryly.

Carol chuckled. "Apparently." She got up and brushed the red-orange dirt off her own thermal garment; it left a bit of a stain. "So, what brings you out here so early in the day? I thought you hated the cold."

"I do," he confirmed. "But I just had some news, and I wanted to tell you before someone else did. We're expecting visitors."

She looked at him; a moment later, understanding dawned. "Medical exams, right? Is it time for those already? I feel like we just got here."

Boudreau shook his head. "It's time. In fact, it's past time. And our health isn't going to be the only subject under examination. They'll also be checking on our scientific progress."

Carol crossed her arms over her chest, realizing a

moment later that she'd executed the classic defensive posture. In recognition of the fact, she let her hands drop to her hips.

But it was too late. The colony administrator had seen the gesture and read it for what it was. "You're not exactly looking forward to the scrutiny, are you?" he asked.

She sighed. "Maybe not. I've always got it in the back of my mind that the Federation's agenda might be different from our own. I mean, look how long and hard we had to campaign to get our funding, and all of a sudden we got twice what we asked for. What made them decide suddenly that terraforming should be a priority? Just a bureaucratic coincidence? Or some purpose we haven't been told about?" A pause. "I know how paranoid that must sound, but . . ." She shrugged. "What can I say? I can't help but think that way."

Boudreau regarded her sympathetically. "I have never been able to figure out Federation research policy myself. It's best, I've found, not to even try. It just taxes the brain, which is better used for other endeavors."

She smiled ruefully. "I guess you're right. Which ship is it, anyway?"

She was sure Boudreau knew the reason for her question. It was said that the relative importance of the ship visiting a colony was an indication of the esteem in which the Federation held that colony—and therefore its chances of continuing its research.

"The omens are good," he told her. "It's the *Enterprise.*"

Carol felt a shiver run through her. "Oh?" she responded.

Boudreau tilted his head to one side. "You mean it's not a good omen? Isn't the *Enterprise* a Constellation-class vessel?"

She waved away any suggestion to the contrary. "Yes, it is. And it's most certainly a good sign."

"But?"

"There is no but. It's just that I know the ship's captain. A man named Jim Kirk."

"Really? I've never heard you mention him."

She turned back to the fireblossom. "I knew him a long time ago," she said. And then: "A *very* long time ago."

51

Chapter Four

THE ROOM WAS CIRCULAR, made of dark, red-veined stone, with columns that only half emerged from the walls to support a great sandglass dome of a ceiling. The dome was ablaze with the ruddy fury of the setting sun, though it offered little in the way of illumination.

As Kiruc entered, he saw a dancer. She was only half concealed by the scarlet veils that swirled around her.

On the divans that lined the walls, scores of Klingons glared at her with lust in their faces. There were shouts of approval, lewd comments, hoots of laughter at some joke that was making the rounds.

So supple were the dancer's movements, so suggestive, that at first Kiruc thought she might have been an Orion. Then she wove herself into a cluster of divans where the yellow brazier light was stronger, and he saw that her skin was more blue than green. And at second glance, her features were wrong as well—her eyes too far apart, her lips too full, her hairline half a handsbreadth too low.

A Laurudite, he decided. She must have been second generation, too. It had been years and years since they'd seized any ships full of Laurudites.

Nonetheless, she executed a good *imitation* of an Orion, undulating to the rhythm of a hidden drummer—or more likely, a recording of one. Reaching into the pouch beneath his tunic, which hung by a leather thong from his neck, Kiruc withdrew an imperial and flung it at the Laurudite's feet. She glanced at him briefly, her eyes flashing gold fire in the flickering luminescence, and bowed to sweep up the tribute as if it were only another part of her dance. With infinite allure, she tucked it into a gossamer harness she wore beneath her breasts. Until he saw the coin disappear, he hadn't even noticed the harness— that's how cleverly it was concealed by the flutter of her veils.

Kiruc smiled to himself. It had been some time since he'd visited the pleasure compound at Tisur. For the most part, it was one of those frequented by the young, those who had not yet acquired a subtlety of tastes when it came to female companionship. Hence the Laurudite, while in a more refined compound there would have been an Orion.

Not that the intimacies offered in this place were repulsive to Kiruc; far from it. In fact, if he hadn't had a specific reason for coming here, and a serious one at that, he might have been tempted to relive some of the coarser pleasures of his youth. Maybe even purchase the services of the dancer for an evening—he *had* liked the way her eyes glittered when she beheld him.

A husky voice: "My lord?"

He turned to the pale, almost white Mitachrosian who stood before him, her slender figure draped in long, blue robes, her hair a purplish silver. Apparently, she was in charge here—the agent of the owner, who was reputed to be a member of the council, though these things were never common knowledge. Like all of her kind, the Mitachrosian was tall; her eyes, as blue as her garment, were almost on a level with Kiruc's own. Two tendrils protruded from beneath her jawline on either side of her face; they wriggled as she spoke.

Not particularly attractive, he noted. But then, in her position, she didn't have to be. She just had to have a good head on her shoulders and a little bit of charm.

"Would you like a divan brought out for you, lord? Those out already are all occupied. Or may I offer you a private booth?"

There were other options as well, but she would not offer them. It was considered impolite, and some people came here only for the music and the dancing and the strong drink. Klingons took enough orders in the course of their lives; they didn't come to a pleasure compound to be told what to do, or even to have it suggested to them.

"A private booth," he told her. He leaned closer, to be heard over the din. "I am meeting someone. He may already be here."

The Mitachrosian nodded. She smelled faintly of fireblossoms. "Yes. A young man. He arrived just a few moments ago and told me you would be coming soon after. Follow me and I'll take you to him."

She led Kiruc out of the round main chamber and

down one of the corridors that projected from the room, like a spoke from the hub of a wheel. There were booths on either side of the corridor. The Mitachrosian stopped at the fourth one on the right and knocked on one of the wooden uprights.

A moment later, the opaque, blood-red curtain that concealed the booth was drawn aside. A pair of eyes took them in; a head nodded, shaking a mane of hair worn long and braided at the ends. The braids marked the man as a Gevish'rae; he hàd a goblet in front of him.

"Bring me whatever *he's* drinking," Kiruc told the Mitachrosian.

Nodding, she vanished discreetly. Drawing the curtain aside even more, Kiruc slid into the booth opposite its occupant. Yellow eyes glowered at him in the light of a squat candle on a dull silver tray.

"You are Kiruc," the younger man said.

It wasn't a question, but Kiruc answered it anyway. "Yes. And you are Grael." For a second or two, he let it stay at that.

"You called me here for a reason," Grael prodded. "Or was it just to trade pleasantries?" He grunted as if at a private jest, but his bravado wasn't heartfelt. Kiruc had ended his message with but two words: *I know.* But it had been enough to put Grael on notice.

"No," the older man replied at last. "It was not to trade pleasantries. I have work for you to do. And make no mistake, you will do it. Or I will place you in a position a wise man fears above all others: to be hunted by his own clan."

Grael's eyes narrowed. "What could possibly make them want to do that?"

Kiruc smiled. "You already know, or you wouldn't have risked your reputation responding to a Kamorh'dag's invitation. But I understand. You wish to test the weight of my threat." He sat back comfortably on his bench. "Somewhat more than a year ago, I believe, you arranged the assassination of your older cousin, a man named Teshrin. If he died, you would have succeeded him as head of your clan, young as you are."

"You lie!" Grael spat.

Kiruc leaned forward again. He showed his teeth, though he kept his voice down. "Don't interrupt me again, Gevish'rae, or you'll regret it."

Grael's eyes smoldered, but he remained silent.

"As I was saying," the older man went on, "you arranged your cousin's murder. He was traveling to Szlar'it for a secret meeting of clan elders. You hired a handful of men to kill him and his mate, instructing them to make it look as if they'd been accosted by robbers. However, the men you hired never made it that far; they got drunk and became embroiled in a fight along the way—one that proved fatal to all but one of them. So Teshrin was never accosted at all. And of course, he never knew about your plan to replace him."

The muscles in Grael's jaw worked. "How did you discover this?" he hissed.

Kiruc shrugged. "The assassin who survived, of course. Some months later, he found himself in the dungeon of a fairly prominent Kamorh'dag, for reasons I will not go into. To earn the Kamorh'dag's mercy, he offered information. As it turned out, it was enough to get him his freedom."

The younger man nodded. "How much do you want?"

Kiruc looked at him. "How much? As in money?"

"If not money," he growled, "then what did you come here for?"

The older man smiled with half his mouth. "Why, your cooperation, of course. Only a small thing compared to what you dared before."

"What I dared has no meaning," Grael said. "Nothing happened."

"And by this time, no doubt," Kiruc commented, "you're glad of it. You've seen that the leadership of the clan is not a thing to be taken lightly. It's a responsibility, a great weight—one that would deprive you of pleasure compounds like this one, which is what men your age *really* want. And having come to this realization, you would go to great lengths to make sure your cousin survives." Kiruc paused for effect. "But what was done was done; the attempt was made. And Teshrin won't care that it never succeeded. All he'll care about is that his cousin plotted to murder him."

The younger man had turned a shade paler as Kiruc spoke. He licked his lips. "If I do as you say," he asked, "how will I know that my secret will remain a secret?"

Kiruc nodded. He had expected that question. "A fortnight after you've carried out your task, you'll find the head of the man who survived under the im'pac tree on your estate."

Grael shook his head. "And what proof do I have that the matter will end there? If he opened his mouth to the Kamorh'dag who imprisoned him, and to you, then who else might he have spoken to? And how do I know *you* won't betray me—or that the other Kamorh'dag might not someday see fit to do so?"

The older man snorted. "You don't. But at least you'll be one head closer to burying the matter. That's something, isn't it?" He leaned back again. "And besides, what choice do you have? If you don't cooperate, I will most certainly betray you."

The Gevish'rae nodded reluctantly. "I see." His eyes found the candle flame. "I will settle for the head of the assassin, then. Tell me what I have to do."

Kiruc told him. The whole time, Grael continued to stare at the candle, as if he could not contemplate treachery and look into a man's eyes at the same time.

Kiruc didn't blame him. He didn't think he could have done it either.

When he was finished, the younger man nodded. "It will be done."

"Make certain that it is." Kiruc rose. "Incidentally, Grael, I would not count too much on the men you have posted outside—the ones you hired to kill me. You see, I am older than you, and wealthier. I was able to hire better men, and more of them."

To his credit, the Gevish'rae didn't say anything. He even managed a small smile.

"Remember," the older man told him. "And make no mistakes. Your life depends on it."

Then he pushed the curtain aside, left the booth, and walked away down the corridor. As he passed other booths, each with its mystery, its own secrets, Kiruc pondered the seeds he had planted.

Would Grael do as he'd been instructed? Kiruc believed he would. He would do anything to save his life, even if it meant compounding his earlier treachery with another one.

In Grael's place, Kiruc would simply have poisoned himself. It would have been the only honorable thing to do.

But then, Kiruc mused, I am a Kamorh'dag, and better acquainted with matters of honor.

When Kirk materialized in the colony's main dome, alongside Spock, McCoy, and Christine Chapel, there were two people waiting to greet them.

One was Yves Boudreau, whose gray goatee and deep-set eyes he recognized from holographic representations in the *Enterprise*'s computer files. The man was even taller and more distinguished-looking in person than he'd appeared in the holograms.

The other was Carol Marcus.

It was all the captain could do to focus on the colony administrator first, as protocol demanded. Extending his hand, he said: "I'm Captain James T. Kirk. Pleased to meet you, Doctor."

Boudreau took the hand and nodded. "And I you, Captain. I'll tell you right from the start, I'm not one of those administrators who thinks periodic medical checkups are a pain in the proverbial ass. Our work isn't so urgent we can't spare a moment or two to protect our health."

Not one to mince words, was he? Kirk liked the man instantly.

Boudreau indicated his colleague. "I understand you and Doctor Marcus have met before?"

Uncertain of how much Carol had told her fellow colonist, the captain simply nodded. "That's true."

She smiled. "Good to see you again, Jim."

Kirk smiled back. "Likewise."

It seemed to him Carol hadn't aged a day. She was wearing her hair a bit shorter, and there was a hairline scar just below her mouth that hadn't been there before. But outside of that, she was just as he remembered her.

And what did she think of him? He looked into her eyes, but he couldn't tell. They were impenetrable, as if she'd put up a shield there.

He must have been engrossed too long in his observations, because before he knew it, Bones was shaking hands with the colony administrator. "Leonard McCoy. I'll be conducting the medical exams with the help of my nurse here, Christine Chapel."

Chapel looked a little surprised when Boudreau took her hand as well. "It will be a pleasure to have you with us, Nurse. I believe one can never surround oneself with too many beautiful women—as Dr. Marcus can attest."

Expressed by someone else, it might have sounded like an attempt at an entrée to a more intimate encounter. However, Kirk didn't read it that way. It seemed to him Boudreau just had a habit of speaking his mind.

Nor was Christine the least bit uncomfortable with the praise. "Thank you, Doctor. It's nice to be . . . er, appreciated."

As she spoke, she cast a glance at Spock, who had remained a paragon of patience while the humans around him exchanged pleasantries. Kirk winced at the oversight.

"And this," he said, "is my second in command,

60

Mr. Spock. He's also the *Enterprise*'s science officer, so he'll be the one to report on your progress here."

Boudreau evidently knew enough not to try to shake the Vulcan's hand. "Mr. Spock," he said, inclining his head slightly.

The Vulcan responded in kind. "I am looking forward to our working together, Doctor. I have followed your work closely over the years."

Boudreau smiled. "Have you now?" He looked approving. "In that case, I'm certain we'll get along quite well, Mr. Spock. Quite well indeed."

"It pleases me to hear that," the first officer returned. And then, changing tacks: "I would like to get started as soon as possible."

"Of course," the terraformer assured him. "I will accompany you myself." He turned back to McCoy. "We have cleared out an unused storage dome for your use. I trust it will be suitable as an examination area."

Bones shrugged. "As long as it's clean."

"It is that," Boudreau said. "Carol, why don't you show the doctor and Nurse Chapel to their accommodations? And then, after they're taken care of, perhaps Captain Kirk would like to explore the Bois de Boulogne."

"Bois de Boulogne?" the captain repeated. "As in the park at the outskirts of Paris, back on Earth?"

"One and the same," the administrator confirmed. "I miss the city of my birth. Of course, our Bois de Boulogne is somewhat humble compared to the original. But on this world, it is the grandest forest of all."

Kirk nodded. "In that case, I look forward to it."

"Then it's settled," Boudreau told him. "And after

Michael Jan Friedman

all your endeavors are under way, we'll meet again for dinner. Agreed?"

McCoy looked at the captain, as if to say: the less time we have to spend back up on the ship, the better.

"We'd be honored," Kirk replied.

As if on cue, his communicator beeped. With a glance at McCoy, he reluctantly flipped it open.

"Go ahead, Scotty."

There was no mistaking the tone of exasperation in the engineer's voice. "Sir, I hate t' bother ye, but . . ." A pause. "It's the ambassador again."

The captain sighed. "What is it now, Mr. Scott?"

"He's insistin' that I leave you down there and take the ship to Starbase Seven."

"Starbase Seven?" Kirk was at a loss.

"Aye, Captain. He's figured out that he can make better time with the *Hood*—and she's currently at Starbase Seven on shore leave."

Kirk frowned. It sounded like the kind of thing he'd have to deal with in person, unless he wanted his ship spirited out from under him.

"Have Kyle beam me up," he said. "And tell the ambassador I'll meet him in the briefing room in five minutes."

"Aye, sir." Scotty sounded more than a little relieved.

The captain turned to Boudreau and Carol. "Sorry. It looks like we've got a bit of a bureaucratic problem."

"Quite all right," the colony administrator told him. "I've encountered my share of those."

Kirk smiled wistfully at Carol. "I'm afraid I'll have to take a rain check on the tour, Dr. Marcus. But with any luck, I'll be down again in time for dinner."

She nodded. "I understand."

It wasn't the first time he'd heard her say that, not by a long shot. But then, understanding was one of the things she used to do best.

Boudreau's laboratory was housed in the colony's central and largest dome. As Spock followed the doctor inside, he took in the facility at a glance.

Along the curve of the wall, there was a continuous rank of some thirty work stations, about two-thirds of which were currently occupied. Some of the colonists looked up for only a second or two and went back to their computations. Others stared a little longer.

"My staff," the doctor told Spock. "All experts in their fields. You say you've followed my work, Commander. You weren't just being polite, were you?"

"Not at all," the Vulcan replied. "In fact, I have read every monograph you ever published."

Boudreau made a face. "Even the early ones? Where I postulated that radiation could be used to encourage amino acid formation?"

Spock nodded. "Yes, even the early ones. Nor is there any need to be embarrassed, Doctor. While your findings were erroneous, as you have apparently come to concede, they were nonetheless fascinating."

The doctor affected a shudder. "You're too kind, Mr. Spock. Fascinating was hardly the word for them."

"It is a word that seems appropriate to me," the Vulcan said. He directed his attention toward a smooth, shiny cylinder suspended halfway between floor and ceiling by a lattice of long, narrow tubes. "After all, your early efforts laid the groundwork for the G-Seven unit."

Boudreau turned toward the unit as well, and smiled. "Yes. I suppose it did at that."

Together, they approached the G-7 cylinder and inspected it more closely. About a meter long, with a diameter about half its length, the G-7 reflected their visages in its flawless surface.

"You have been pleased with the results?" Spock asked.

"I have, yes. But then, I am principally concerned with the reproduction rates of the specimens under study—rates that have well exceeded our expectations. In the Bois de Boulogne, which is our oldest experiment, we've gone through six annual cycles in a little more than a year. And in Sherwood Forest, named by our head mathematician, Dr. Riordan, the specimens have multiplied at an average annual rate of seven times."

"Impressive," said Spock.

"I agree. However, if you ask Dr. Marcus about our results, she'll tell you that the specimens' oxygen production is not what it might be. And I must concede her point, though I believe it is limited. If our specimens are reproducing like mad, what difference does it make if each produces a little less oxygen than it should? In the end, we will still get what we want—an atmosphere breathable by most species in the Federation."

Spock reserved comment on that count. "What about the beam itself? I understood you were working on increasing its effective range."

"Quite correct. In fact, we've made great strides in that regard. When we began, we were only able to effect specimens within a tenth of a kilometer radius.

Now, we have a grouping as distant as three kilometers."

"And the actual affected area? Has that remained the same? Or have you been forced to narrow the beam?"

"The affected area has remained the same," Boudreau replied. "We've just found ways to step up the input-to-output ratio. I'll show you how we did it, if you like."

"I would like that very much," Spock told him.

"This way, then. I'm sure Dr. Wan would be glad to run through his calculations with you. After all, he was the brains behind the input-to-output enhancements."

Kirk confronted Farquhar across the briefing table. "I understand you have another objection to the way we're handling things," he said.

"To say the least," the ambassador replied.

He leaned forward, planting his elbows on the table and clamping his hands together, unconsciously making them into a club. The captain had no illusions as to whom the ambassador would like to beat over the head with it.

"I've been doing some thinking, with the help of the computer," Farquhar said. "And I've come to the conclusion that I'd be better off on another ship. Starbase Seven is only a day's journey from here—"

"And the *Hood* is there for shore leave. Mr. Scott filled me in on that part."

"Good. Then you know there's no reason for not complying with my wishes. You could drop me off and be back before Dr. McCoy can finish his work here.

And since the *Hood* is presently uncommitted, it can take me directly to Alpha Maluria Seven."

Kirk shrugged. "That wouldn't be a bad idea, providing it was only shore leave the *Hood* was in for. The fact of the matter is, there was a virus running rampant among the crew—a rather serious virus, though I understand the medical authorities have a handle on it now. But so as to avoid panicking the population of the starbase, the *Hood*'s visit was officially listed as 'shore leave,' and not something closer to the truth."

The ambassador looked at him. "You have proof of this?"

"Of course not. It was communicated to me on a confidential basis. And if you'd come to me even a couple of days ago, during the crisis, I couldn't have said anything about it."

"Then the crisis is over?"

"Yes." The captain knew what Farquhar's next question would be. "But don't expect the *Hood* to just take off as if nothing happened. Its people are going to need some time to recuperate." He smiled. "Ambassador, if Starfleet had an uncommitted ship available, don't you think you would have been on it? The reason you're on the *Enterprise* is that every ship in the fleet has been deployed for one reason or another."

Farquhar smiled back, but in a sour-grapes sort of way. "You'd better be telling the truth about the *Hood*, my friend. I don't like to be misled."

Easy, Jim. Better men than he have tried to provoke you and failed.

"I have no reason to tell you anything but the truth," Kirk returned, his voice so calm and even it surprised him. He stood. "And now, if there's nothing else I can help you with, I'm headed back to the colony."

The ambassador scowled. But he had nothing else in his arsenal except a parting shot. "Take your time," he sniped.

Seeing no need to dignify the remark with an answer, the captain walked past Farquhar and exited the briefing room.

Chapter Five

"MORE CHONDRIKOS, DAVID?"

Dr. Medford extended a plate of the stuff in his direction. It smelled terrible—not at all like the fragrant, alien fir trees from which it had been harvested.

The boy looked down at his plate, where the only evidence of the baked chondrikos casserole was an oily film and a few yellowish fibers, and regarded Dr. Medford anew. "No thank you, sir. I think I've had about all I can handle."

The big man's eyes narrowed beneath his large brows and his even larger mustache. The overhead lighting was reflected in his bald spot.

He looked from David to his daughter and back to David again. "Does that mean you liked it and you can't eat any more? Or that you hated it and you don't *want* to eat any more?"

David shifted in his seat, not sure how to respond.

His mother had always told him to tell the truth, but these circumstances seemed to call for something else. He pretended that a piece of chondrikos had caught in his throat and coughed into his cupped hand to clear it.

Finally, Medford responded for him. "He hated it, Daddy. I *told* you he would hate it." She smiled and leaned closer to David. "Don't worry. My mom can't stand the stuff either. That's why Daddy only makes it when she's working late."

Dr. Medford grunted. "Let the boy speak for himself, Keena." He rested his elbows on the table and regarded their guest. "Now tell me, David. Did you like it or didn't you?"

"It's all right," Medford told him, putting her hand on his arm. "You can tell him; he won't get mad."

David swallowed. "Actually," he began, meeting Dr. Medford's gaze, "I, uh . . . I didn't like it."

For a long moment, Medford's father just sat there, staring. David wondered if his friend had miscalculated and he was about to get kicked out of their dome for insulting the cook.

Then, ever so gradually, the man's expression changed. His brows lifted and the lower half of his face stretched out into a rueful grin.

"Well," Dr. Medford said, "at least you're honest." He sighed. "It was that bad, huh?"

David nodded, encouraged by the man's smile. "The worst."

Medford whooped, clapped a hand over her mouth, and laughed so hard she was almost in pain. Her father, after a second or two of indecision, began laughing too.

David chuckled, caught up in the spirit of it. "To tell you the truth, it was worse than the worst. It was—"

Dr. Medford held up a meaty hand. "Enough," he said, still grinning. "There's only so much criticism a man can take." He straightened. "That is, before he cancels dessert."

Suddenly, his daughter found the self-control to stop laughing. Her lips pressed together, she shot her friend a look of mock warning.

Taking the cue, the boy went deadpan. He looked at Dr. Medford, awaiting his verdict.

"That's better," the big man said. He got to his feet. "Now you two wait here, while I get the homemade ice cream." He looked at his daughter. "He won't hate that, will he?"

She shook her head. "No way."

Dr. Medford nodded approvingly. "Good. I'd hate to have him tell his mom we poisoned him or something." He winked at David. "Right?"

The boy nodded. "Right."

As her father crossed the dining area, Medford leaned toward David again. "I think he likes you. That's good, you know. Daddy doesn't like everybody."

David watched the man open the refrigeration unit and remove a container. "I like him, too. He's the kind of . . ."

. . . *man I could look up to* . . . The phrase flashed in and out of his mind.

". . . he's kind of neat," he finished, ignoring his thought.

Medford nodded. "Yeah. I think so, too."

The boy looked at her. "It's nice of you to have me over," he said.

His friend shrugged. "When my mom was invited to the big dinner they're having for the starship people, and she found out your mom was invited too . . ." She shrugged again. "She didn't want you to have to eat alone."

Actually, the Pfeffers had asked David over to dinner as well, and so had the Chiltons. But he was glad his mom had accepted the Medfords' offer first. The Chiltons didn't have any children. And he much preferred Keena Medford's company to Will Pfeffer's.

Of course, David thought, if I had a father like everybody else, I could've had dinner with him. There wouldn't have been any need to find a place for me with someone else's family.

But it wasn't that way. And there was no use wishing otherwise.

"Your mom was very thoughtful," David said.

"I had something to do with it, too," Medford told him. "I mean, you're my friend, right? Friends have to stick together."

The boy smiled. "That's right. We do, don't we?"

She lowered her voice a notch. "So have you seen any of them yet? The starship people, I mean?"

He shook his head. "Mom asked me to stay out of their hair, so that's what I'm doing."

"Aren't you curious about them? At least a little?"

David thought about it. "Not really. Mom says they're people like anybody else."

"Well, I'm curious. And I heard they're not just here for medical checkups."

He looked at her. "What else would they come for?"

Medford glanced in her father's direction. Satisfied he wasn't listening in, she said: "I heard they're going to be grading us. You know, like Mr. Fredericks does in school. And if we don't get a good grade . . ."

She made a cutting movement with her hand across her throat.

"We're dead meat?" he asked.

"The colony's dead meat," she told him. "They'll cut off our funding faster than you can say Jack Robinson. At least, that's what my mom told my dad."

David pondered the information. Cut off their funding? After his mother had worked so hard to get it in the first place?

"That doesn't seem fair," he said.

The words were barely out of his mouth when Dr. Medford started back to the table with three bowls of frosty, yellow ice cream in his big hands. The spoons were inserted between his fingers.

"Here it is," he announced. "Just like I promised."

Bending over the table, he set David's ice cream down first, then his daughter's, and finally his own. It looked good—real good. So good, in fact, that the sight of it pushed David's concerns about the future of the colony to the back of his mind.

As Dr. Medford sat down, he said: "Dig in, everybody." And then, to David: "I hope you have a hankering for chondrikos. We were all out of chocolate."

The boy paused in mid-dig. Medford slapped her father on the forearm. "Daddy! Will you cut it out?"

The big man grinned at David. "Actually, it was the

chondrikos we were out of. That's vanilla." He paused. "You do like vanilla, don't you?"

David chuckled. "I like vanilla fine, sir."

Dinner, which was held in the rec dome on a series of stripped-down Ping Pong tables, was modest but tasty. Kirk sat between Spock and McCoy, opposite Boudreau, Carol, and a colleague of theirs named Medford.

"I take it you were able to clear up your bureaucratic problem?" Doctor Medford asked.

The captain shrugged. "For the time being, yes. But you know how it is with bureaucratic problems. They have a way of coming back."

"In this case," McCoy explained, "we've got a crazy ambassador on our hands, who can't wait to get to Alpha Maluria Seven."

Kirk shot him a remonstrating glance, like a warning shot across his bow. No matter what the ship's officers thought of Farquhar, it wasn't good form to rail at the man behind his back.

Bones frowned at the suggestion of self-censorship but complied with his captain's wishes. "I guess I shouldn't tell tales out of school," he said.

"Alpha Maluria, eh?" The colony administrator shook his head. "Can't say I'm familiar with it. But then, I can barely tell you where Beta Canzandia is."

"If you wish," the Vulcan said, "I can show you its location on a starmap."

Boudreau smiled. "That won't be necessary, Mr. Spock. Even if I knew, the information would be meaningless to me. I'm afraid astronomy is not my strong point."

McCoy grunted. "It's all right, I'm the same way. If

the captain relied on me to navigate, the *Enterprise* would be circling the Klingon homeworld right about now." He stood. "On the other hand, I know my way around a buffet table just fine. Anyone care to join me?"

Carol shook her head. "Not I, Doctor. I've got enough here to last me for a while."

"Looks like you're on your own, Bones."

"Fair enough," said McCoy. "If I'm gone too long, send out the dogs."

Chuckling, Medford watched the medical officer go. "A very amusing man, your Dr. McCoy." She turned to Spock. "He must keep you entertained all the time."

The Vulcan was as deadpan as ever. "That is one way of putting it," he remarked. "The doctor has a unique point of view."

The captain decided it might be a good idea to change the subject. Turning to Boudreau, he said: "Mr. Spock tells me your research is going quite well."

The colony administrator turned to Carol. "What do you think, Dr. Marcus?"

Medford smiled. "Actually, that's a constant bone of contention between them."

"A friendly bone of contention," Boudreau amended.

"But a bone of contention nonetheless," Carol amended further. She turned to Kirk. "It has to do with oxygen production. Our specimens simply don't perform in the field as well as they should."

Spock nodded. "Dr. Boudreau mentioned your dissatisfaction. I am curious to know more about it."

Carol shrugged. "It's pretty simple, really. Before we send our specimens out in the field, we observe them under controlled conditions in a little garden I've set up. And in the garden, their oxygen production is terrific. Then we plant them outside the colony and their production falls off." She frowned. "My current theory is that the G-Seven beam is altering the plant's DNA somehow, but I'm nowhere near proving it. So far, I haven't found any differences at all in the genetic material—not in the first generation or any other."

The Vulcan looked more than casually interested. "Fascinating," he commented. "May I see your notes?"

"Of course," Carol replied. There was a slight flaring of her nostrils, though, that told the captain that she was at least a little put off by the bluntness of Spock's request. Why? Because it implied that he could find the answer when she couldn't?

Kirk wondered if he was the only one who noticed her pique. After all, it had taken him a long time to be able to read Carol's little quirks, and they'd had something a lot more intimate than a professional relationship.

"Miss me?"

The captain and everyone else at the table looked up at McCoy as he rejoined them. His plate was once again heaped with selections from the simple buffet.

"You know," said Kirk, "these people are going to think we don't feed you on the ship, Doctor."

"Pshaw," McCoy replied. "Only a fool turns down home cooking." He leaned closer to the center of the group as he took his seat. "Though I have to admit, there was one dish there that must have gone bad a couple of weeks ago. Or at least, it smelled that way."

Medford looked at him. "Was it kind of yellow and oily looking?"

"That's the one," Bones confirmed. Suddenly he blanched. "Don't tell me you cooked it. I'll want to crawl under a rock."

The black woman shook her head. "No, I didn't cook it."

"That's a relief," said McCoy.

"My husband did."

The doctor's jaw dropped.

And Medford began laughing out loud. When she finally got control of herself, she added: "It's all right. *Everybody* thinks it smells terrible. But he did the cooking tonight for—"

She exchanged a quick glance with Carol, which the captain missed the significance of.

"—for my daughter, and he insisted I bring some of the stuff along to the buffet. He thinks people *like* it."

Kirk smiled. So did Boudreau and Carol. Finally, Bones smiled too. Only Spock remained expressionless, as usual.

"Well then," said McCoy, "I'm glad I didn't offend anyone."

"Just my husband," Medford replied. "But believe me, no one's going to tell him. No one dares."

The whole table chuckled—again, with the exception of Spock. Kirk looked at Carol; he'd always loved her smile, and now he remembered why.

He wished she smiled more often these days. But then, maybe she did, when she didn't have to contend with the presence of an old lover.

Suddenly she turned and saw him staring at her. If she was surprised, she didn't show it. She simply returned the look.

And then surprised *him.* "If you want to cash in on that rain check, Captain, you'd better do it soon. It gets pretty cold here after dark."

Kirk nodded. "In that case, we can go as soon as you're finished eating."

She shrugged. "I'm finished now."

Vheled was in his quarters, sharpening his favorite knife with a honing stone, when he heard the rap on his door. Rising, he replaced the dark, abraded stone on the low shelf where he usually kept it.

Next, he tucked the knife into the space between his belt and the small of his back. Finally, feeling prepared for anything out of the ordinary, he barked, "Enter."

At his command, the heavy door to his quarters slid aside, revealing the lean, proud form of his gunnery officer. Inclining his head by way of a greeting, the young man took two steps into the cabin; the door closed behind him.

No threat here, Vheled mused. Removing the knife from its hiding place, he flipped it point first into the throwing board on his wall. It hit with a soft thud and remained fixed among the board's many scars.

The young officer smiled approvingly. "You are skilled with the dagger," he noted. "I trust that is not your only weapon, however."

It was. If a warrior could not rely on his own senses, of what use were weapons?

"Of course not," Vheled lied. He indicated a seat across the room, near the tapestry that had been in his family for twelve generations. The man made his way there and sat down, but not before the captain did. For a moment, they sat in silence.

77

"Why have you come?" the captain asked finally.

"There is to be an assassination," the younger man told him.

Vheled's eyes narrowed. He was interested, but he wouldn't let on *how* interested. It was never a good idea to let a warrior think he had an advantage over his captain. "Are you my security officer," he asked, "that you should warn me of such things?"

"No, excellency. But I have some experience in these matters."

Vheled knew that, of course. "I see. And who is to be assassinated?"

With just the slightest amount of hesitation, the gunnery sergeant replied: "Gidris."

The captain grunted. Gidris was his first officer, an efficient and dedicated man. Not one who was widely liked, but that was of no importance to the captain; popularity wasn't necessarily a virtue on a bird of prey.

"And the assassin?"

The man's narrow features hardened into a scowl. "Your second officer seeks advancement. I believe he intends to create an opportunity for himself sometime in the next couple of days."

Vheled looked at him askance. "You have evidence? Or has the second officer confided in you?"

The other man shrugged, ignoring the taunt—and impressing the captain with his self-control. "No evidence. But it is obvious, nonetheless."

Vheled digested that. He had served with this officer long enough to know his capabilities.

Besides, the report came as no great surprise. Vheled's second officer was an ambitious sort, Gevish'rae through and through.

Under normal circumstances, the captain would have allowed the assassination to proceed. After all, it was part of the process by which Klingons remained strong, ensuring themselves that the most capable and aggressive personalities were always at the forefront.

However, these were not normal circumstances. Vheled wished his crew to be as stable as possible when they arrived at Pheranna. He would brook no distractions, nothing that might upset the quick and efficient fulfillment of their task. There was too much riding on this mission to let any one man's desires get in the way.

The captain nodded to the younger man. "You've made your report. You may leave."

"As you wish, excellency."

He turned and exited the cabin. Vheled watched him go, not without a certain amount of satisfaction. Haastra, his current security officer, was getting old. He believed he had just found his replacement.

After all, Grael was Gevish'rae, too.

Boudreau was right, the captain mused. This world's Bois de Boulogne was somewhat humble compared to the original.

Actually, it was a cluster of perhaps fifty golden-needled conifers, none of which was more than a dozen feet tall. As Kirk walked among them with Carol at his side, the foliage was barely thick enough to block out his view of the white colony domes.

"You say these are hybrids?" he asked.

Carol's cheeks were already beginning to turn ruddy with cold. He remembered that about her—how red her face used to get, and how beautiful it made her eyes look by contrast.

"Half Aldebaran eristoi, half Marraquite casslana," she answered. She was all business; he could have been a complete stranger. "We planted four of them to start out; none were more than a foot high. Obviously, they thrive in this kind of environment. And they responded very well to the G-seven beam. What's more, we think they'd get along fine with Terran flora. But as I mentioned at dinner, they don't produce as much oxygen as we'd like—not as much as I'd like, anyway, and I set the standards for them. In that respect, they're a disappointment. And oxygen production is, after all, the most important trait of all."

"So you'd call this group a failure?"

She shook her head. "I wouldn't go quite that far. On the other hand, I obviously wouldn't call it a success, either. I guess it's somewhere in between."

"A step in the right direction?"

"Yes. A step in the right direction. And when we get over this oxygen production bugaboo, we'll have taken even a bigger step."

"You're optimistic, then?"

Carol nodded. "Very optimistic. We've had other obstacles, and we've always gotten past them. There's no reason for me to believe we won't get past this one as well. And someday, we'll reach our goal—"

"A plant that can reproduce like crazy and spew out oxygen even faster . . . a plant that can help turn a freezing ball of dirt into a class-M world."

Carol hesitated, then looked at him. "My words?"

"Your words, after you got that job working on Schwimmer's terraforming project. I only heard them on subspace radio, but I'll never forget how excited you were."

80

For a moment, a silence hung in the frosty air. In a way, it was more personal than any of the talk that had passed between them, more lush with feeling. Then the moment subsided.

"Anyway," she said, "for the time being, we've pretty much turned our attention away from Bois de Boulogne and Sherwood Forest and all the other little woodlands we've created down here in the valley. We've set our sights on a couple of projects up in the hills—so we could test the range of G-seven technology."

Kirk nodded. "And a new batch of hybrids?"

"Uh huh. Though the next batch I'd like to test isn't a hybrid at all. Ever see a Klingon fireblossom?"

He half smiled. "No, I can't say I have." And then: "Where did you get hold of a Klingon plant?"

"Not just one—a number of them. Remember the Klingon ship found a few months ago by the *Potemkin?* Or should I say the *wreckage* of a ship?"

"Sure. The one whose impulse engines blew. It had every admiral in the fleet buzzing for weeks. But—"

"A couple of compartments survived intact. One was the captain's quarters. And his hobby, it seems, was cultivating fireblossoms."

The captain chuckled. "I see. How convenient."

"The funny thing," Carol said, "is that the fireblossom is outperforming everything else in the garden. And I didn't have to splice any genes to make it; it occurs as naturally as you or I. Of course, it has its share of drawbacks: specifically, it can't seem to get along with its neighbors. But I'm hoping we can find neighbors it'll like a little better."

Kirk looked around at the tops of the golden

81

conifers, emblazoned against the crisp, blue sky. "All right. Let's say you find a way to tame your fireblossom, or you come up with a hybrid that does what you want, or you isolate the glitch in the G-seven beam and correct it. Then what?"

"You mean where do we go from here?"

"Yes. What's the next step?"

Carol shrugged. "Provided we can continue to make the Federation believe in us, we find another planet. Not like this one—where it's already got a bona fide oxygen atmosphere, and just hasn't produced any organisms yet—but one of those marginal places where there's barely enough warmth and oh-two to support life. And we terraform it. We make it into a garden." She grinned, her mind focused on that distant paradise.

He grinned, too. Beyond the branches, the sun was sinking, turning the colony domes pink with its dying light. "You sound happy," he observed.

She fixed him with her eyes, and for the first time since his arrival, it was truly Carol looking out at him. "The happiest I've been in a long time. I mean, I complain about oxygen production and such, but we're making real strides here, Jim, real progress. For the first time, I can see the day when we'll be able to terraform any planet at all."

"It's hard to imagine," he said sincerely.

"Nonetheless, it's going to happen. I don't know when, but it's going to happen." She regarded him, the sunset light in her eyes. "And I've got at least a small chance to be a part of it. That's about the most exciting thing I can think of. It's what I've worked all my life for."

The captain looked back at her. "Good. Lord knows, you deserve it. No one's lobbied harder than you have to make terraforming a priority for the Federation."

Carol shrugged. "I don't know about *that*. Dr. Boudreau's the one who got this colony off the ground. Without him, I'd still be conducting research in a lab back on Earth." She paused. "And what about you, Jim? Are *you* happy?"

He thought about it. "I guess I am, most of the time. I mean, being a starship captain isn't all glory and adventure. People die—people who depended on you to keep them safe and secure. And too often, you have to compromise your ideals—your sense of justice— for the sake of policy." He took a deep draught of the cold air, which was getting colder by the minute. "But it's got its up side, too, of course. You get an opportunity to travel the stars. You get a chance to see something new every day, maybe something no one has ever seen before. And every now and then, you strike a blow for something you believe in."

She nodded, then turned away, as if some nuance of movement in the tree branches had caught her eye. When she spoke again, there was a distinct note of emotion in her voice.

"Would you trade it for something else?"

The captain hesitated, understanding completely the significance of the question. After all, he'd heard it before, in a slightly different form. But there was still only one answer.

He shook his head. "No. I wouldn't. Or rather, I couldn't."

It might not have been what he wanted to tell her. It

might not have been what she wanted to hear. But it was the truth—no less today than eleven years ago.

Carol nodded again, still not looking at him. "I had a feeling you'd say that."

Instantly, Kirk regretted making the conversation personal. He regretted asking her if she was happy, and the line about the freezing ball of dirt.

He could have left things as they were. He could have let the past be the past, and nothing more.

But now, the memories of their loss were bubbling to the surface. The old emotions were coming back unbidden.

He felt awkward, off-balance. And a little sad— maybe more than a little. He could only imagine how she was feeling, the things that were going through her mind.

It had been a mistake to recall what they'd had together. If he could have taken the words back, he would have. But it was too late. Hell, it was too late for a lot of things.

"I'm sorry," he told her. "I didn't mean for this to happen."

Carol turned to him. "It's all right," she said. "If you hadn't brought it up, I probably would've done it myself." She sighed. "I guess neither of us has changed very much. We're still two people going in different directions, though we may wish it were otherwise." Smiling ruefully, she added: "Funny how life gives you just what you really want, isn't it?"

He didn't know what to say to that. Fortunately, Carol didn't leave him twisting in the wind too long.

"Care to take a look at Sherwood Forest?" she asked him. "Before it gets too dark?"

It didn't require much thinking on his part. Anything was preferable to standing here like this. "Sherwood Forest it is," he replied.

They started walking. Before long, they emerged from Bois de Boulogne and felt the wind on their faces again. It seemed to clear the air a bit—not completely, but enough for them to feel comfortable with one another.

As they skirted the colony, headed for a somewhat smaller cluster of trees, the captain's attention was drawn to something moving up in the hills. When he turned to look, he saw that it was only a white plastic playground set, with some swings moving in the wind.

The playground was the standard model, of course. He'd seen it a dozen times before on colony worlds. Nor were the swings themselves anything remarkable.

But for some reason, he found them fascinating. As if there were something to be learned from watching them, as if they held the key to some sort of ancient and obscure wisdom.

Then the fascination faded, and it was just a playground again. He turned back to Carol.

And noticed she was watching him—not circumspectly, as before, but with plain and terrible intensity. Then she saw the look in his eyes, and she became interested in something else, or pretended to.

But there was a rouge in her cheeks much deeper than that imparted by the weather, and a tightness around her mouth that he recognized from days gone by, when she'd been angry with him about things neither of them could control.

"Is something wrong?" he asked her.

She shook her head. "No, nothing at all." When she

regarded him again, she was smiling, though he sensed it was only for his benefit. "Really."

Kirk didn't probe into it any further. He'd done enough of that already.

Without another word, he let Carol guide him into the shade of Sherwood Forest.

Chapter Six

IT HAD BEEN a lonely night. And a restless one.

Sighing, Kirk sat up in his bed and surveyed his quarters. They had that uncertain, not-quite-real look, the predictable result of not enough sleep.

"Damn," he said out loud.

It was his own fault. If he hadn't resurrected the past the night before, if he hadn't stirred it up . . . Although the way Carol had looked in the failing light might have been enough to do that all by itself. That, or the sound of her voice, or the almost tangible nearness of her . . .

Kirk's musings were interrupted by beeping from the personal monitor on his desk. Swiveling into a sitting position, he got up and crossed the room on bare feet. Then he tapped the stud that activated the device.

A familiar image came up on the screen—that of Lieutenant Uhura. "Sorry to bother you so early, sir, but it's Mr. Spock. He's calling from the colony's communications center."

"Spock?" Immediately, the captain's mind snapped into command mode, anticipating a dozen different reasons for the call. "Something wrong down there?" he asked.

"I don't think so, sir."

"Put him through, Lieutenant."

In the next instant, Uhura's sultry beauty was replaced by the Vulcan's poker-faced calm. "Good morning," he suggested.

"Is it? It's difficult to tell at this point, Spock. I mean, the damned thing's hardly gotten started."

Kirk's surliness surprised even himself. The Vulcan merely arched an eyebrow; to him, sleep was something one could occasionally do without, and he sometimes overlooked the fact that humans were different in that respect.

"I apologize," he said, recognizing his error. "Perhaps we should speak a bit later in the day."

"No," the captain insisted. "I'm the one who should apologize. I just didn't get a whole lot of sleep last night is all. What's on your mind?"

"I wish to make a request," said Spock.

A request? "Certainly, Commander. Ask away."

The Vulcan paused, as if ordering his thoughts. "I believe, as Dr. Marcus does, that there is a flaw in the G-seven unit's operation that is leading to decreased oxygen production. I would like an opportunity to find the flaw, and perhaps to correct it."

Kirk frowned. "You want to stay with the colony?"

"Yes. At least until the ambassador's mission to Alpha Maluria Six is completed. You can pick me up on the ship's return trip through the sector."

The captain thought about it. He hated to lose an officer like Spock, even for a short time.

On the other hand, diplomacy wasn't one of the Vulcan's strong points. Kirk had planned on making him a member of the negotiating team, but his presence at Alpha Maluria Six was far from necessary.

"You think you can make a difference?" he asked Spock.

The first officer nodded. "I think it is possible."

"All right, then," the captain said. "You've got my blessings."

"Thank you," said Spock.

"No need," Kirk told him. "Just find that flaw."

"I will endeavor to do so," the Vulcan assured him. "Spock out."

An instant later, the screen went blank, and the captain was alone again with his thoughts.

McCoy was washing his hands at the sink as the doors to his makeshift examination room whispered open and his next patient walked into the room. Glancing over his shoulder to acknowledge the colonist's presence, he was surprised to find a boy looking back at him.

"Howdy," the doctor said.

"Howdy," the boy echoed, trying out what was plainly a new word for him. He had curly blond hair and soft brown eyes. "Are you the doctor?"

McCoy shrugged. "I'm one of them. My name's Leonard. What's yours?"

The boy raised his chin a little. "David."

Though the boy couldn't have been more than nine or ten, he didn't exhibit any of the childish qualities the Pfeffer and Garcia kids had. There was no wariness in him, no hanging back. Just a lot of healthy curiosity.

"David. That's a good name," McCoy commented. "Are you here all alone, David? Usually, kids come to see me with their parents."

"I was supposed to meet my mom here," he said without hesitation. "But I was a little early, so . . ." His voice trailed off.

The doctor turned a kindly eye on the boy. "So you decided to come see what this medical exam business is all about."

David nodded. "I guess so."

"Well," McCoy told him, "there's not much to see." He picked up the only instrument he'd brought down with him, the only one he needed. "Just this, really. It's called a tricorder, and I use it to—"

Abruptly, the doors hissed open again. This time, a woman came in—and a rather striking one at that.

Bones nodded once by way of a greeting. "Dr. Marcus. Can I help you?"

The woman was a little out of breath, as if she'd been rushing. Frowning a little, she glanced at the boy.

David turned to greet her. "Hi, Mom."

Hi, Mom?

McCoy cursed himself for a fool. Now that he saw them together, there was no mistaking their relationship. They had the same coloring, the same proud cheekbones and graceful bearing.

Not that the boy was a clone of his mother, or anything even close. Where his eyes were warm and dark, hers were an almost alarming shade of blue. And where David's hair was a mass of tight curls, hers was long and almost perfectly straight.

But the resemblance was still striking. He should have seen it when David walked in.

Carol Marcus stroked her son's hair. "Hi," she said. Then she turned to McCoy. "I see David beat me here. I hope he hasn't been any trouble."

Bones shook his head. "None at all." He looked at the boy again, this time in a new light. Apparently, Dr. Marcus hadn't let any grass grow under her feet. But then, why should she have? It wasn't as if Kirk hadn't pursued a number of romantic relationships in the years since he'd known her. What was good for the goose was good for the gander, right?

He grunted softly, remembering how he'd felt when he found out one of *his* old girlfriends had gone off and gotten married. As Nancy's face flashed before his eyes, he felt a twinge of pain. Of course, that was another story entirely.

McCoy dragged his thoughts back to the situation at hand. Clearly, he mused, the captain had a surprise in store. Or had he already met Marcus's son and put the surprise behind him? Bones had no idea. He'd been so busy with these medical checkups, he hadn't seen Jim Kirk in a day or so.

"Well, then," he said, turning to the personal computer Dr. Boudreau had been kind enough to provide, "why don't we get started?" He called up the colony's roster, figuring that he could identify the boy by his first name alone. Unfortunately, when he keyed on it, the machine came up with *two* Davids.

Of course, neither of them were David Marcus, but McCoy had known that in advance. If there'd been a second person by the name Marcus, he would have taken note of it back on the ship.

Apparently, the boy had been given his father's surname. But not knowing who David's father was, Bones had no choice but to ask.

"What's your *last* name, son?"

For the first time since they'd come in, David looked to his mother. He seemed confused. McCoy wondered about that. Surely, it wasn't a difficult question for a child that age, especially one with such obvious intelligence in his eyes.

"Tell the man," his mother advised him.

David turned to McCoy again. "Marcus," he answered. "Like my mom."

Bones absorbed the information. "I see," he said.

"Is something wrong?" David asked. He was perceptive, McCoy remarked inwardly. Definitely that.

"I wouldn't call it *wrong,* exactly. It's just that you're not listed on the colony personnel roster." He regarded the boy's mother. She didn't seem all that surprised, he thought. "Could David have been listed under some other surname for official purposes?"

She frowned slightly. And a moment later, she turned to her son. "Would you excuse us a moment? I have to discuss something with Dr. McCoy."

David shot her the kind of withering look children give their parents when they're excluded from conversations. But he didn't question her; he just left.

As the doors shooshed closed behind him, Carol Marcus returned the doctor's scrutiny. There was a decidedly no-nonsense cast to her features, something Bones would have called defiance under different circumstances.

"Dr. McCoy," she began, "David is on the colony personnel roster. He's just not on the one you have.

And the reason he doesn't appear there is that Dr. Boudreau was doing me a favor."

Bones didn't understand. He said so. "What were you trying to do? Keep me from examining him?"

She shook her head. "No. I'm not that foolish." She lifted her chin slightly, almost exactly the way the boy had earlier. "A long time ago, I knew Jim Kirk quite well."

He nodded. "The captain's mentioned you once or twice. He spoke well of you. But that doesn't explain—"

"He doesn't know I have a son," she interrupted. "And I want to keep it that way."

McCoy began to ask why. But before he could get the words out, all the pieces fell into place.

Kirk's relationship with Carol Marcus had ended about ten years ago. And there was something about the boy's eyes that seemed rather familiar, now that he thought about it. He cursed softly.

"You understand what I'm saying," she observed.

"I think so, yes. The boy is Jim's son."

"Yes, but only biologically. As I'm sure you know, your captain has no inkling David exists." She sighed. "I wish they'd sent some other ship—some other doctor, who wouldn't have noticed at a glance that David's genes matched up with Jim's. Someone who wasn't aware of our relationship and wouldn't have been able to put two and two together. But they didn't. They sent *you.*"

He looked at her. "They sent me, all right. And once you knew I was coming, you convinced Dr. Boudreau to give me a personal computer, separate from the colony's main processor. And to delete David's name from my roster so Jim wouldn't suspect." He shook his head. "But why go to all this trouble? Why don't you want him to know?"

She looked away from him. "That's none of your business, Doctor."

He glared at her without meaning to. "Doctor—it's his *son!* He has a right."

Dr. Marcus shook her head. "No," she said softly. "He doesn't. It's up to me what he knows and what he doesn't."

"That's not fair," McCoy protested. "I don't know what took place to make you bitter—"

"I'm not bitter," she told him, her eyes turning hard—though she still looked away.

"Maybe not. But you've made this choice, and it's the wrong one. Blazes, Doctor, put yourself in Jim's place. Imagine someone keeping that kind of thing from *you.*"

She met his gaze. "I don't have to justify my actions, Dr. McCoy, not to anybody."

Bones snorted. "Of all the stubborn—" With a major effort, he managed to rein in his galloping emotions. "For godsakes," he rasped, "give this a little more thought. In a couple of days, the *Enterprise*'ll be gone, no matter what you decide. It'd be a damn shame if the captain left without getting to know David—even a little."

Her nostrils quivered. "You don't have to agree with me, Dr. McCoy. You just have to respect my wishes. I believe that's called patient privilege."

Bones bit his lip. She had him there.

The muscles in his temples working, he glared at her. "I *know* my responsibilities, Doctor." At least one of us does, he added silently.

She nodded. "Good. I'll go get David."

As she turned away from him, he called after her: "At least give it some thought," he said. "At least that."

She didn't answer. Then the doors opened in front of her, and the conversation was at an end.

"So McCoy wanted you to reconsider," said Boudreau.

Carol nodded. "That's right."

"And did you?"

"Uh-huh. But my decision was the same as before. David is my business. Jim's not to know about him."

"I see."

They were in the lab dome, working at adjacent terminals, speaking in low tones, so no one else could hear unless they were really trying. And in a colony as small as this one, people respected one another's privacy.

She turned to look at him. "You don't approve?"

Boudreau shrugged. "It's not my place to approve or disapprove. You ask me to keep David's name off the roster that goes up to the *Enterprise*, I do it. You ask me not to mention the boy in front of Captain Kirk, I do that too."

"But you don't approve, do you?"

The colony administrator sighed. "Now that I've met the man, I can't help but feel for him a little. He's not a bad sort. In fact, he strikes me as the kind I wouldn't mind having for a friend."

Carol frowned, remembering. "You wouldn't be disappointed, either. He's a very good friend."

Boudreau smiled sympathetically. "That's part of the problem, isn't it? If he was a real bastard, the choice would be easy. If you hated him, you wouldn't feel so guilty. But you don't hate him."

He didn't say the rest; there were others in the room, and even respect for privacy had its limits. But she knew the rest.

You don't hate him. You love him. Still.

It was part of the problem, all right. The night before, when they were walking in the woods, she'd almost weakened. She'd almost said she wanted him back, no matter what.

But it wouldn't have worked, not any better than it worked a decade before. And now there was more than just the two of them to consider—there was David as well. So she pulled in the reins and kept herself from following where her heart wanted to lead.

"No," she agreed. "I don't hate him. But that doesn't change anything. I've still got to look after my son's best interests. And that means sticking to my guns."

"Did I hear something about guns?"

In a long, dizzy moment, Carol whirled and saw Jim standing behind her. She felt her cheeks grow hot.

Had he heard her mention David? She searched his eyes for the answer.

"Something wrong?" the captain asked. He was smiling.

No. He hadn't heard. Her secret was still a secret.

"Nothing," Carol answered. "Nothing at all. You just startled me, that's all."

"Sorry. I just came to say good-bye."

"Good-bye?" she echoed numbly. *So soon?* she thought. It seemed as if he'd just gotten here.

Jim nodded. "Dr. McCoy tells me he's finished his checkups, and everyone's got a clean bill of health.

And as you know, Spock's staying on a while. So there's no excuse for us to linger."

She managed a smile, but it was nowhere near a match for his. "Well then," she said, "I guess we'll see you on your way back."

For just a fraction of a second, his smile faltered. And she knew by that sign that she wouldn't see him on the way back. The *Enterprise* would come back for Spock, but the captain wouldn't beam down.

He didn't comment on the possibility directly—which was tantamount to telling her that her suspicion was correct. All he said was, "It was good seeing you again, Carol."

She met his gaze. "Likewise."

He turned to Boudreau and held his hand out. "Doctor."

The colony administrator clasped it. "Thank you for your help, Captain."

And then he was leaving, and Carol felt an ache in her throat. Suddenly, before she knew what she was doing, she called after him.

"Jim! Wait!"

He stopped, turned around, and looked at her expectantly.

Why had she called out? What had she meant to tell him? She didn't know.

And then, something came to her. Something that seemed fitting, somehow—and more important, something that would postpone his leaving by a moment or two.

Carol came up to him and took his arm. "Come on," she said.

His eyes narrowed with mock trepidation. "Where are we going?"

"You'll see," she told him.

As they headed for the exit, the doors swooshed open before them. Then they were outside, in the bright, brittle sunshine.

"You shouldn't be out here without a jacket," he said.

"It'll only be for a minute."

Once they crossed the open space and entered the garden enclosure, it wasn't quite so cold. Still holding on to his arm, she guided him to their destination.

It took him a moment to realize what they were looking at. He smiled. "These are the Klingon flowers, aren't they? The ones you were telling me about?"

"Yes," she confirmed. "The fireblossoms."

Letting go of him, she got down on her knees and dug into the red soil with her bare hands. It wasn't easy to free up the fireblossom's roots; they went deeper than they had a right to. But after a while, he saw what she was doing and bent to help.

Together, they managed to wrest the alien plant from the ground. Smiling as much as she dared, brushing aside a strand of hair that had gotten in her eyes, Carol handed it to him.

"Water it occasionally," she advised him. "At least once a month. Outside of that, you don't have to worry. They're tough to kill."

"A parting gift?"

"Something like that."

"In that case, thank you."

"In that case, you're welcome."

He regarded her. "It always was hard to say goodbye to you."

"You always managed," she reminded him, without rancor.

Jim nodded. Managing it one more time, he took out his communicator. "One to beam up," he said.

In the next couple of instants, he began to shimmer, and then to fade. Finally, he was gone altogether.

Carol took a deep breath, let it out. Her breath froze on the air. Turning to the opening, she exited the enclosure and headed back for the lab dome.

That was the easy part, she told herself. The hard part was still ahead of her.

After all, Spock would be with them for some time. It would take some work to keep him from finding out about David.

Chapter Seven

VHELED TURNED to see his second officer enter the starboard weapons room, responding promptly to his summons. Big-shouldered and strapping, taller than most of the crew by half a head, his large, protuberant eyes sought the captain's. It was easy to read the question in them.

They were still a good day's journey away from Pheranna, and Vheled had inspected the weapons room just a couple of days ago, to see how the new torpedo launchers worked. What could have drawn him back here so soon?

The second officer halted in front of the captain and pounded his chest with his fist. "Is something amiss, sir?" He spoke slowly—a product of the S'zlach hinterlands that had spawned him, and not any lack of intelligence.

Instead of providing an answer, Vheled made a sweeping gesture with his left hand. A moment later, the room was empty of all personnel except the two of them: himself and Second Officer Kruge.

Kruge's dark, wispy brows came together over the bridge of his nose. He seemed on the verge of repeating his question, then appeared to stop himself. Perhaps he'd seen someone repeat a question to a captain on the last ship he was attached to.

Vheled stroked the starboard disruptor console, allowing Kruge to squirm a little. It was good to remind one's officers who was in charge, particularly when one was about to give so unusual a command.

At last, the captain looked up and met Kruge's gaze. "No," he said, "nothing is amiss. At least, nothing that can't be fixed with a minimum amount of effort."

The crease between the second officer's brows only deepened. "I don't understand," he replied frankly.

Vheled decided he'd played captain long enough. "I have discovered you intend to assassinate First Officer Gidris."

Kruge didn't flinch, but something in him stiffened. To his credit, he didn't ask how Vheled knew; he just accepted the fact and went on from there. "That is correct," he confirmed.

The captain shrugged. "Normally, I do not interfere in such matters. I leave it to the parties involved." A pause for effect. "However, this time is an exception. This time, I will stand in your way."

Kruge absorbed the information with stony equanimity. "Is it permitted to ask why that should be?"

Vheled nodded. "You've served me well since you arrived on the *Kad'nra*. You've shown great promise. Great skill, and great determination. You deserve an explanation."

And the captain gave him one. He left out precious little, so that by the time he was done, Kruge knew almost as much about their mission as he did.

"So you see, Second Officer, there is no room for personal ambition on this ship—at least until we complete our mission. For a while, you will have to put the Gevish'rae before your own ends."

Kruge nodded. "I will do that gladly. Like you, I have no love for the Kamorh'dag. However, I have one request."

"And that is?"

The second officer's mouth turned up slightly at the corners. "That you refrain from informing Gidris of my intention to kill him. It would, after all, make my job that much more difficult when the time comes."

Vheled thought about it for a long time, while Kruge patiently awaited his answer. "All right," he said finally. "I will keep your intention a secret. But that's as far as I'll go. I won't stand in the way of his finding out from others."

Kruge grunted. "Fair enough. And when I am first officer, I will make you wonder how you ever tolerated a puris like Gidris."

The captain chuckled, finding new respect for his second officer. "See that you do, Kruge. See that you do."

"Beautiful, isn't it?" asked Sulu, arranging the soil around the fireblossom with loving care, admiring the place's newest acquisition. Nor would he have been any less attentive if someone other than the captain had placed it in his hands for safekeeping.

Uhura sniffed it. "No scent?" she asked.

"None that *we* can smell," the helmsman told her. "But if you were of a slightly different humanoid species . . ." He let his voice trail off meaningfully.

Chekov gazed at the Klingon plant, with its flower the color of a twilight sky over Petrograd. The overhead illumination in the botanical garden gave the long, full petals an almost iridescent quality. "It is wery beautiful," he agreed, then paused. "But there is something about it . . ."

Uhura looked at him. "Yes?"

The ensign shrugged. "Something . . . predatory. As if it vere about to leap up and take your head off."

Sulu chuckled. "No chance of that. It's not even carnivorous."

Chekov grunted. "As far as ve know."

Uhura shook her head. "As far as we know," she echoed. She put her arm around the ensign. "You know, Pavel, for someone who aspires to be the captain of a starship one day, you're a little too eager to ignore the facts."

The helmsman nodded as he finished his ministrations. "And a little too cautious of the unknown." Giving the soil one last pat, he brushed his hands off. "If you're afraid of a Klingon plant, what are you going to do when you come up against the Klingons themselves? Run the other way?"

"For your information," Chekov replied, straightening, "I have come up against the Klingons. And I sairtainly did not run."

"You were sitting on the bridge," Sulu reminded him, "right next to me. I'm talking about meeting the Klingons face to face—mano a mano."

The Russian harrumphed. "It vould make no differ-

Michael Jan Friedman

ence. I am not afr—" Suddenly his eyes fixed on the
fireblossom and went wide. "Vatch out!" he cried.

Reacting instinctively, Sulu snapped his hand back
and clutched it to his chest. It was only after
he'd reacted that he realized how badly he'd been
duped.

"Vat are you afraid of?" Chekov asked, smiling
innocently, his own hands clasped behind his back.
He tilted his head. "Not a little plant, I hope?"

Uhura put her hand over her mouth to conceal her
grin. She looked at Sulu.

Gradually, the helmsman smiled too. "I guess you
got me that time, Pavel."

Chekov patted the plant in an almost paternal way.
"I guess I did at that."

McCoy was on his way to the gym when Kirk caught
up with him.

"Didn't you hear me calling you, Bones?"

The doctor had heard all right. "Calling me?" He
shrugged. "I didn't hear a thing," he lied.

The captain looked at him penetratingly. "I've got
to tell you," he remarked, "if I didn't know better, I'd
say you were avoiding me."

McCoy returned the look as if that were the furthest
thing from his mind. "Listen, Jim, this whole fitness
thing was your idea. I'd have thought you'd be glad
that I'm finally getting into shape."

As they reached the door to the gym, the doctor
turned in to enter the place. Kirk followed.

Lord help me, Bones told himself. If he doesn't
leave, I'm actually going to have to do something in
there.

The captain grunted. "I don't get it. Not so long

104

ago, you had no interest in coming back here. Now you're at it every free moment."

McCoy shrugged. "What can I say? When you've got the bug, you've got the bug."

Truth to tell, he hated the idea of physical training more than ever. But his sudden yearning for exercise had been a handy excuse for avoiding heart-to-heart conversations with his friend.

Normally, he enjoyed those conversations, even looked forward to them. But there was nothing normal about the position in which he'd found himself lately—caught between his friendship for Jim and his professional integrity.

Bones was deathly afraid that he'd have a little too much to drink and in an unguarded moment spill the beans about David Marcus. And thereby violate the doctor-patient privilege David's mother had been so quick to cite.

Unable to depend for certain on his willpower, he'd decided to sidestep the possibility altogether. Even if it meant putting his well-being on the line every now and then.

After all, he didn't want word to get back to Jim that he was just hanging around in the gym and doing nothing. That would only rouse the man's suspicion.

"I suppose I shouldn't be so incredulous," Kirk commented. "But . . ." He searched for words. "I can't help it. This just isn't like you."

"I guess you've got to face it," the doctor replied, walking up to the wrestling mat with a courage he didn't even begin to feel. "You've created a monster."

There were three crewmen standing around the mat. All bruisers. Gallagher, a young, brawny security officer, was the smallest of them, though not by much.

Gallagher winced when he saw McCoy coming. The opposite was true as well, though for a completely different reason.

The security officer was wincing because he'd have to toss the doctor around again like a leaf in a windstorm. Bones was wincing because he didn't look forward to being the leaf.

"All right," he told Gallagher, "let's give it another shot."

The younger man actually looked as if he were the one anticipating pain. "You sure, Doctor?"

"Of course I'm sure." It was no picnic tussling with Gallagher. But the other crewmen might hurt him even worse.

The captain shook his head. "I never thought I'd see the day," he muttered.

"What's that?" asked McCoy.

"Nothing," Kirk answered quickly. "Nothing at all. Listen, I think I'll head for the rec cabin and see if I can drum up a game of chess. In the meantime, good luck with your, uh, fitness program."

Bones harrumphed. "It's Gallagher you ought to be wishing good luck. I'm getting pretty good at this."

The captain took one last, long look at him. Obviously, he knew there was something fishy about this—he just didn't know what.

"Right. Well then, I'll see you later, Doctor."

As McCoy watched him go, he wanted desperately to end the charade. He wanted to tell his friend he had a son, a son he'd never met, and see his eyes pop out with surprise and jubilation.

But he couldn't, damn it. He couldn't.

A moment later, the doors to the gym closed behind

Kirk. Screwing up his resolve, Bones turned to Gallagher.

"All right," he said tautly. "Let's get this over with."

Something was going on, Kirk told himself. Something was *definitely* going on.

He couldn't ever recall McCoy acting so strange, so standoffish. And he didn't believe it was simply a sudden obsession with staying fit.

Had something happened down on the colony planet? Something that had made Bones want to keep to himself for a while?

In any case, he mused, as he headed for the rec cabin, it was the doctor's business and no one else's. If McCoy wanted to talk, the captain had made it plain enough that he was available. And if he didn't . . . well, he didn't.

Funny, he thought. Spock's back at Beta Canzandia Three and Bones is acting like someone else. And I feel like a rowboat without its oars.

I guess you never realize how much you depend on your friends until you're deprived of them. Frowning, Kirk watched the doors part for him as he entered the rec area.

Taking the place in with a glance, he saw Scotty sitting at a table by himself, finishing a plate of shepherd's pie. The engineer looked up as the captain approached.

"Mr. Scott," said Kirk.

"Sir?" came the response.

The captain sat down. "Scotty, I'm in the mood for a game of chess. How about you?"

He had a premonition that the man would say he was too busy with a project down in engineering. Or that he had a date to look at the stars with some young woman. Or that he had a new recruit to whip into shape.

But all he said was, "I'd be delighted."

Kirk sat back, relieved. At least he wasn't completely on his own.

"Shall I get th' pieces?" Scotty asked.

"No," the captain told him. "Allow me."

Chapter Eight

ONCE AGAIN, McCoy noted, there were four of them in the briefing room. However, with Spock absent, Scotty had been brought in to round out the diplomatic team.

Clearing his throat, the captain addressed the group. "As you know, we'll be arriving shortly at Alpha Maluria Six, a Federation member planet and the site of a certain amount of civil unrest."

Farquhar's frown, which seemed like a perpetual thing now, deepened. McCoy was pleasantly surprised when the ambassador reserved comment.

"As you also know," Kirk went on, "Ambassador Farquhar has been assigned the task of settling this unrest." He regarded Farquhar. "Ambassador, would you like to describe the situation?"

Farquhar grunted softly but derisively. "The *situation*," he insisted, "is not simply one of unrest, Captain; it borders on civil war."

Straightening in his seat, he seemed to warm to the

topic despite himself. "The planet has two main religious groups, the Manteil and the Obirrhat. Historically, the two populations have coexisted quite peacefully. It is only in recent months that they've come into conflict, over a herd of docile beasts in the region.

"The dominant group, the Manteil, believes that the animals carry the souls of long-deceased holy men. As a result, it insists on allowing the beasts access to anywhere and everywhere as they go about their seasonal migrations—including an ancient city historically important to both religions, which happens to contain the holy places of the other religious group, the Obirrhat."

"And th' Obirrhat," said Scotty, "take offense at th' idea of beasts in th' vicinity o' their sacred places." He paused, his eyes alight with curiosity. "But why's this only now become a bone o' contention? Presumably, both th' beasts and th' holy places have existed for some time."

The ambassador nodded. "Very astute, Mr. Scott. As it happens, the Manteil's sacred beasts were dying off some years ago, until the Federation provided them with a medicine to cure them of their plague. Thanks to us, the beasts are now more plentiful than ever, which is why they've begun to broaden the path of their migrations to include the city's thoroughfares and the Obirrhat's sacred precinct." He shot the Starfleet officers an ominous look. "When the first beasts passed through, some days ago, there were heated protests. But the main part of the herd is still on its way. When *it* passes through . . ."

He let his words hang in the air. They had the

desired effect, eliciting visions of religion-inspired chaos and carnage.

McCoy held up a hand. "Let me get this straight," he said. "These people are ready to go to war over whether or not some *animals* have the right to walk in the streets?"

"To put it succinctly," Farquhar told him, "yes. But remember—to the Manteil, these are more than just animals. These are the souls of their ancestors. And to the Obirrhat, these aren't streets, they're parcels of sacred ground."

The doctor snorted. "And we're supposed to keep them from each other's throats?"

"Precisely," the ambassador returned. "As a member planet, the Malurians have the right to ask the Federation for assistance. And we are providing that assistance—though by the time it arrives, it may be too late to prevent a good deal of bloodshed." With that last thought, he glanced meaningfully at Kirk.

The captain ignored the implication. "Any other questions?" he asked.

McCoy shook his head. So did Scotty.

"In that case," said Kirk, "this meeting's adjourned. I'll have Lieutenant Uhura let you know when we establish communications with the planet."

Without bothering even to acknowledge the captain's last remark, Farquhar got up and left the briefing room. As the doors whispered closed behind him, McCoy turned to his exasperated captain.

"He's got the dramatic exit part down pat," the doctor noted. "Now if only he'd polish up on those soliloquies a bit . . ."

* * *

"Approaching Alpha Maluria Six," Chekov announced, as soon as the captain emerged from the turbolift.

"Slow to half-impulse," Kirk instructed.

"Slowing to half-impulse," Sulu echoed, making the necessary adjustments.

On the forward viewscreen, Alpha Maluria Six was a gradually expanding ball of green and blue, swaddled in sweeps of white cloud. Class-M all the way. Beyond the planet, and partially eclipsed by it, loomed the mysterious purple sphere of its single moon.

At warp six, they'd been able to complete the trip from Beta Canzandia in less than five days—though with Farquhar's constant complaining, it had seemed like that many weeks.

Kirk turned in his chair to face Uhura. "Hail the first minister, Lieutenant. Let him know we're here."

"Aye-aye, sir," his communications officer responded.

Before the captain could face front again, the turbolift doors opened and Ambassador Farquhar stepped out. He looked stiffer than ever.

For a moment, his eyes flicked in Kirk's direction. Then he focused his attention on the viewscreen.

"I see you got my message," the captain told him, resuming his original position. "We should be ready to beam down in a matter of minutes."

Kirk anticipated a blistering response. He wasn't disappointed.

"I've been ready to beam down for days now, Captain. Believe me, there will be no delays on my account."

The captain refused to take the bait, though it was

getting harder and harder to refrain. "I'm happy to hear that, Ambassador."

"There's a response to our hail, sir," Uhura reported.

"Thank you, Lieutenant." Kirk pointed to the screen. "On visual, please."

A moment later, the image of the planet was replaced by that of its highest official, First Minister Traphid. Kirk recognized his image from the holos he'd been studying. Like all Malurians, his skin was as black as ebony, with weblike patterns around the mouth and chin area. Silvery-pale eyes looked out at the captain from cavernous sockets that made them appear even smaller than they were.

Kirk spoke up. "Greetings. I'm James T. Kirk, captain of the *Enterprise*. I believe you were expecting us, First Minister."

Traphid returned his greeting: "Blessed be your every incarnation, Captain. We have indeed been expecting you."

It was the response Kirk had been told to look for. But there was something about the first minister's tone of voice that seemed wrong, out of kilter.

What's more, the textured skin around Traphid's mouth seemed to be twitching. Kirk was certainly no expert on Malurian facial expressions, but he couldn't escape the feeling that something was amiss.

"Oh, no," Farquhar whispered.

There, the captain thought. That confirms it.

Out of the corner of his eye, Kirk observed the ambassador's approach. "You see?" he rasped, too low to be heard by the first minister. "We took too long. We're too late."

Ignoring Farquhar, though that was no easy task

113

under the circumstances, the captain concentrated on Traphid. "You seem discomfited, First Minister. Am I to understand that the discord has intensified?"

Traphid made a strange, gulping sound deep in his throat. "One might say so, yes. Please, beam down to our government hall. I will elaborate."

Kirk inclined his head. "As you wish."

As soon as the first minister's image faded, replaced again by that of Alpha Maluria Six, the captain rose from his chair and headed for the lift. He didn't have to ask Farquhar to accompany him; the man was on his heels like a predator running down its prey.

"Mr. Sulu," Kirk said, "you've got the conn. Ask Dr. McCoy and Mr. Scott to meet me in the transporter room."

"Aye-aye, Captain," Sulu acknowledged.

The lift doors opened and Kirk entered, with the ambassador right behind him. Turning, the captain could see the quick shuffle of personnel on the bridge —Sulu taking the command chair while a female ensign moved smartly to replace him at the helm.

Then the doors closed. Before Kirk could even tap the button representing the transporter deck, Farquhar had launched into his diatribe.

"I told you there was no time to waste, Captain. I told you time and time again." The ambassador locked his arms across his chest, as if he couldn't trust his hands not to damage something otherwise. He glared at Kirk, his jaw muscles working. "Now the conflict has escalated, and who knows to what extent."

The captain regarded him as calmly as he could. After all, as annoying as the man's manner was, he wasn't entirely wrong. The conflict *had* escalated, and a good deal more quickly than Starfleet had anticipated.

"Ambassador," he said, "I suggest we wait to see exactly what has transpired among the Malurians before we formulate any opinions."

Farquhar snorted, looked at the ceiling and shook his head. "Sure, let's wait. Why not? As if waiting wasn't what got us into this mess."

Kirk sighed, silently urging the turbolift to move a little faster. It was going to be a long trip to the transporter room.

The Malurian Hall of Government was a hexagonal space with six long windows alternately tinted green and violet. The walls were made out of some dark variety of stone, with tiny threads of something like silver running throughout. A gray polished-metal ring with six spires hung suspended from the ceiling, its form echoed by a round table with six chairs directly below it.

Kirk and his party materialized in a shaft of bluish light that filtered in through one of the windows. Traphid and three other robed figures were waiting for them.

As the two groups came together, Farquhar took the initiative. "First Minister," he said, touching his index and middle fingers to his temples.

Traphid returned the gesture. "You must be Ambassador Farquhar."

"I am." With a sweep of his arm, Farquhar indicated the captain, McCoy, and Scotty, pausing briefly as he identified each one in turn. "These are my colleagues from Starfleet—Captain Kirk, whom you've met; Dr. McCoy, and Lieutenant Commander

Scott. They have been dispatched to assist me in my mission."

Bones leaned close to Kirk and muttered: "We're his *assistants?*"

Gradually, over the last couple of days, McCoy had come to seem like his old self again. There was none of the standoffishness the captain had sensed just after their departure from the research colony. Whatever it was that had been bothering him, he seemed to have come to grips with it.

"In a nutshell, yes," Kirk muttered back.

Traphid looked to his own colleagues. "Allow me to introduce my fellow ministers, Entrath, Ilimon, and Dasur."

Farquhar looked at the first minister soberly. "And the others?"

The skin in the lower part of Traphid's face did that twitching thing again. "Regrettably, Menikki and Omalas have absented themselves from these premises indefinitely. They have resigned their positions as ministers."

The ambassador nodded. Without a hint of the criticism he'd dished out back on the ship, he expanded on Traphid's explanation. "Menikki and Omalas were Obirrhat; they represented that portion of the population on the council."

"I see," Kirk replied. He engaged the first minister. "And the reason for their departure?"

Farquhar didn't like the idea of the captain speaking directly to the Malurians; that much was certain. But he kept his objections restricted to the sullen look in his eyes.

Traphid regarded the captain. "Earlier, you asked me if our discord has intensified. The fact is, it has intensified to the point of bloodshed. Finding no satisfaction in this chamber, the Obirrhat have taken their arguments to the streets. There have been riots; the rioters have been arrested. But those who instigated the violence—Menikki, Omalas, and others like them—have gone into hiding."

The ambassador's brow creased. "You have no idea where they are?"

The first minister shrugged. "We suspect they are still here in the mother city. But it is only a suspicion; there is no evidence of it."

"That is unfortunate," Farquhar said. "It will complicate matters considerably. However, we can still work toward a solution, even without the Obirrhat in attendance."

Traphid and the other ministers didn't look overly encouraged by Farquhar's suggestion.

"As you say," the first minister replied, "we can work toward a solution."

"You know," Kirk suggested, "it might not be a bad idea for us to visit the Obirrhats' holy places, just to see what they're like. And I'd like to get a look at your sacred animals t—"

"There's no need for that," Farquhar interjected, smiling pleasantly—or at least, the captain thought, that must have been the man's intention. "I'd like to see the holy places as well, but I don't think the first minister would look kindly on our disturbing the beasts."

"On the contrary," Traphid remarked. "If you are to help us, you must get a feeling for the things we hold dear. I will make arrangements for you to see both—the holy places of the Obirrhat and the sacred herd."

Only a slight ruddiness in his cheeks betrayed the ambassador's pique. He touched his fingers to his temples again.

"As you wish, First Minister."

Carol Marcus would have sworn she was alone in her garden, planting new neighbors for the remaining fireblossoms, until some sixth sense prompted her to look up—and see Mr. Spock standing at the entrance to the enclosure.

Gathering her composure, she asked, "Have you been there long?"

The Vulcan shrugged, though it was a more subtle gesture than a human would have made. "Just a few moments," he responded. And without offering anything more, he slowly scanned the garden.

His eyes were darkly inquisitive. And it wasn't only by sight that he explored the place; every so often, his nostrils flared as if he were breathing in the commingled scents.

But had he really come to sample the botanical variety, or was he on to her? Had he stumbled across the truth about David, despite her efforts to prevent it? She couldn't be sure, not just by looking at him. Vulcans didn't exactly wear their hearts on their sleeves. Nor could she very well *ask*.

But she wasn't comfortable with the silence, either. So she said: "I understand you're making good progress with G-seven."

Spock nodded. "Some—though not as much, or as quickly, as I had hoped." He indicated the Klingon specimens with a tilt of his head. "And you?"

She smiled as pleasantly as she could. "Plugging

away. Trying to see if we've got anything tough enough to keep up with the fireblossoms."

For a moment, he scrutinized the Klingon plants, and his eyes seemed to lose their focus for just an instant. The first officer straightened, his lips flattening in a frown, as if he felt guilty about abandoning his work even for a minute, then he returned his attention to her.

"Thank you," said the Vulcan formally, "for allowing me to enjoy your garden."

This time, it was Carol's turn to shrug. "My pleasure," she told him, though she couldn't mean it under the circumstances.

As Spock walked back to the lab dome, she sighed like a balloon with a slow leak. Apparently, her secret was still safe.

From the playground, the domed colony buildings in the distance looked like pearls half buried in the ocher-colored ground. And the lab dome, David noted, looked like the biggest pearl of all.

That's where his mother was, probably. Unless, of course, she was in her garden.

The lab dome was also where Mr. Spock was bound to be, talking with Dr. Boudreau about the G-7 unit, which was about all he'd done since he got here nearly a week ago. Mr. Spock was supposed to fix something the unit was doing wrong—though Dr. Boudreau didn't seem to think it was doing *anything* wrong.

It was all kind of confusing. But it was also important, especially to David's mother, so he tried to understand it. Sometimes he even joined his mom in the lab for a while, listening as she explained what kind of problem she was facing that afternoon and how she was trying to solve it.

Unfortunately, he couldn't visit the lab today, even if his mother was in it. He was supposed to avoid Mr. Spock as best he could—just as he'd had to avoid all the other people from the starship, when they were still here.

The only exception had been Dr. McCoy. Everyone else was off-limits.

His mother hadn't made it very clear why any of that should be. In fact, she hadn't seemed entirely sure herself. But she'd emphasized it over and over again, so David knew it was a big thing to her. Even if he didn't have any other reason, he guessed that one was good enough.

"Hey, Marcus!"

He turned. Riordan was sitting on one of the top rungs of the playground's white plastic monkey bars. Pfeffer and Wan were twisting themselves around a couple of the lower rungs, while Medford and Garcia tossed a football back and forth.

"Daydreaming again?" Riordan jeered. "How come you're always a million miles away?"

David didn't answer. He just walked over to the white plastic swingset and sat down on one of the swings.

"My dad says daydreamers never get anywhere," Pfeffer added, looking to Riordan for approval. "He says they dream their whole lives away."

"Sounds right to me," the older boy decided. Then he whispered something down to Pfeffer and they both laughed, their breath making white puffs on the air.

Since the fissure-jumping incident, their jabs at him

had become more frequent. He imagined he could hear what they were whispering.

... father ... got no father ...

Planting his feet and launching himself backward, he began to swing. Immediately, the air felt even colder against his face. And as he kicked higher and higher and lost himself in the hard, blue sky, he found it easier and easier to forget Riordan and Pfeffer and their little cruelties.

In fact, if he closed his eyes, he could almost imagine himself somewhere else. He could almost make himself think he was back on Earth.

That's where he was born, where the whole human race started, before it expanded out into space in a thousand different directions. And it was green there, lush and full of life—full of grass and trees and birds and animals.

Not like the planets his mother had taken him to over the last several years, places that had no growing things, or so few there might as well have been none at all. Some were cold like this one and some were hot, but none of them was even the least bit like Earth.

"Hey, Marcus!"

It was Riordan's voice, of course. No doubt he'd seen another opportunity to call David a daydreamer and was pouncing on it.

This time, though, David would keep his dream intact. He would stay inside it, happy and safe. And Riordan could shout himself purple—he wasn't going to get the satisfaction of a response.

"Hey, Marcus! *Marcus!*" That was Pfeffer, joining in on the fun.

Ignore it, David told himself. Don't give in. Don't let them take your green place away from you.

121

Michael Jan Friedman

"Marcus!"

The last yelp hadn't come from either Riordan or Pfeffer. It was a girl's voice—Medford's.

David opened his eyes. The other children were clustered around the swingset, their eyes drawn to the colony buildings. He looked that way also and saw a bunch of dark figures making its way from dome to dome. From a distance, they looked as tiny and harmless as any of the colonists.

But they weren't colonists. And they weren't the Starfleet officers, either. As David leaped from the swing and landed on the sandy ground, he saw a flash of light among the domes and heard someone down there cry out.

That's a cry for *help,* he realized. And that flash came from some kind of weapon. But why? Why would anyone want to hurt the colonists?

And then, while he was still trying to put the pieces together, he heard Pfeffer moan a single word that explained everything.

"Klingons."

122

Chapter Nine

DAVID TOOK A second look at the dark figures scurrying all around and knew that Pfeffer was right. They *were* Klingons—the worst killers in the galaxy.

It didn't seem real. Those were their homes down there, the places where they lived. How could there be strangers there with ugly bumps on their heads and eyes full of hate?

He swallowed. Their parents—his *mother*—they were all in terrible danger.

"They need us," Garcia said in a surprisingly husky voice. "We've got to help them."

As he started down the hill toward the colony, Medford grabbed his arm. "No way," she said. "Are you nuts? You think you can stop the Klingons all by yourself?"

Garcia struggled, but Medford wouldn't let go. He began to drag her after him down the hill. Before David knew it, he had a hold on the boy's other arm.

Together, he and Medford kept Garcia from running off.

"Let me loose!" the dark-skinned boy wailed. "Let me go!"

But after a while, his white-hot burst of courage seemed to fizzle out, to turn cold. And finally, they were able to let go of him.

After that, no one moved. No one knew what to do.

For what seemed like a long time, they stood there, watching the dark figures swarm over the domes. Every so often, there was a flash, but there were no more yells for help. Wan began to cry, silently at first, and then a little louder.

Her sobbing, soft as it was, roused something in David. It got his brain working again. It brought him back to reality.

"They're going to come for us next," he said out loud. "Pretty soon, they're going to check the colony roster on the computer and realize we're missing. And then they'll come after us."

Pfeffer looked at him. "But we're just *kids.*"

David shook his head. "No. We're humans. I don't know what they're doing here, but you can be sure they don't want witnesses, even if we are just kids."

Medford darted a glance at him. "Does that mean they're going to . . ." She couldn't quite finish the thought.

But David finished it in his head: *kill our parents.* "I don't know," he replied. "Maybe they're just going to lock them up, so they can't see anything."

Medford nodded. Wan, too. That's what they all wanted to believe. But David knew there were no guarantees, even if he wasn't saying so.

He regarded the others. "I say we go back into the hills. We'll be safe there, at least for a while."

They looked at one another, but in the end all eyes fell on Riordan, just as they always did. Expressionless, he shook his head. "No. It's stupid to run. It'll only get them mad at us."

David was shocked. "What are you saying?" he asked. "That we should give ourselves up?"

It came out more like a challenge than he had intended. The older boy's eyes grew wide suddenly.

And in that moment, David saw the fear in them— not the simple fear for family and self that resided in the rest of them, but something that ran much deeper. A wild and unreasoning fear—of what? Of losing control of the other kids? Of being thought of as a chicken?

Whatever the reason for it, David saw it. And Riordan knew that he saw it and hated him for it.

"All I know is," the older boy said, "if we run and they catch us, it'll make it ten times worse. Who do you want to have to face—a Klingon or an angry Klingon?"

With startling clarity, David understood what Riordan was doing. He was scared to take to the hills, no matter how much sense it made. As calm as he appeared, he wasn't thinking rationally. And he was trying to make the rest of them scared in the same way he was, so he wouldn't look like a coward.

But David wasn't about to let that happen. He wasn't going to let Riordan get them all killed so he could salvage his self-respect.

They had to survive. They had to live long enough to help their parents—not Garcia's way, not by rushing in, but by finding an opening and taking advantage of it.

And if the opportunity never came, at least there would be survivors to tell Starfleet what happened. At least there would be someone to point a finger at the Klingons and say: "It was them. They did it."

"They don't have to catch us," he replied. "We know those hills better than they do. We can hide in a million different places."

"That's true," Garcia chimed in. "We can hide where they'll never find us."

"Remember those caves?" asked Wan in her delicate voice. "The ones we found the first time we went out there?"

"She's right," Medford affirmed. "We could stay in the caves."

Riordan licked his lips. He looked like a cornered animal. And cornered animals were dangerous.

"You're out of your minds," the older boy said. "These are Klingons. They have sensors and stuff like that."

That was true. David hadn't considered the point.

"It doesn't matter," he responded. "Sooner or later, Starfleet's going to find out what happened and come help us. All we have to do is hold out until then."

Riordan shook his head again. "You're talking like a little kid." His voice had gotten louder, more confident. "Dr. Boudreau hardly ever talks to Starfleet. It could be weeks before they figure out something's wrong and send a ship."

"Maybe months, even," Pfeffer piped up.

"No," David countered, remembering the Vulcan. "Mr. Spock is here. They have to come back and get him, right?"

126

The older boy's eyes narrowed. He'd forgotten about Spock, obviously. "Still," he said, "it's going to be a while before they come back for him. And by then, we could all be tortured to death."

"Tortured? To death?" Wan echoed.

Even Medford seemed to flinch.

David bit his lip. It was just like back at the fissure. Riordan was too good at making the others think what he wanted them to think. He could make courage seem like stupidity and common sense seem like cowardice.

The older boy couldn't be beaten at that game. At least, not by any of the other kids.

And the longer they argued, the greater the chance that one of the Klingons would spot them. Then they'd be caught for sure.

David looked at Pfeffer and Medford and Wan and Garcia. He saw that they were still on the fence—that they still might fall on either side of it. But only if he made them decide *now*. Only if Riordan didn't have a chance to sway them any further.

He took a deep breath. "Look," he told them, "I'm not going to just stand here and wait for them to find us. I'm going. Who's with me?"

Nobody moved, not even Medford, who had appeared to be on his side only a few moments ago. She seemed like she wanted to follow him, but she just wasn't a hundred percent sure David's way was the right way, and this was too big a decision to make lightly. There was too much riding on it.

"Well?" he prodded.

No one responded.

Riordan sneered at him. "Nobody's going with you,

Marcus. Can't you see that? They're staying here with me."

David didn't want to go up into the hills alone. He didn't want to leave his friends at the mercy of the Klingons. But he couldn't force them to do what they didn't want to do. Sighing, he turned his back on the other children and started up from the playground.

He'd failed. Maybe the others hadn't been as undecided as he thought. Maybe Riordan had won the game before it ever began.

He wasn't going to think about that now. He was going to concentrate on getting away from here and finding the best place to hide himself. Before he'd gone half a dozen steps, however, he heard a thin, high-pitched wail from down among the colony buildings. Glancing back over his shoulder, he saw yet another flash. The scream ended.

David shivered. That could have been his mother. Part of him wanted to rush down the hill as Garcia had, but he held himself in check. Suddenly, Medford started after him. He could see she had tears in her eyes, but she was coming along. And then, even more unexpectedly, Wan followed. And Garcia as well.

That left Riordan and Pfeffer standing in the playground, in the shadow of the monkey bars. The older boy glared at David and his companions.

"You're crazy," he barked. "You're just going to make it worse for everybody."

But his words seemed strangely flat and lifeless. Riordan had lost his hold on them, David realized. He wasn't sure how, but Riordan's control over them had been broken.

Pfeffer looked at the older boy as if he was seeing him for the first time. Riordan looked back.

"Don't tell me you're going to go, too," he snickered.

Pfeffer swallowed. He couldn't answer. But a moment later, he left Riordan to join the others.

The older boy laughed. "Lamebrains. *Skeezits.* You're making a big mistake."

Still a little amazed at the way things had turned out, David turned his back on Riordan and resumed his trek up the hillside. The others fell in behind him. He could hear the shuffle of their feet on the sandy incline.

Maybe the older boy would come running after them, too, he mused. Maybe his fear of the Klingons would override his fear of being thought a coward and he would come marching up the hill with some clever remark calculated to distract them from his defeat.

But Riordan didn't join them. He just shouted at their backs, his voice cracking like a whip in the chill air.

"You'll see," he called after them. "You'll see I was right."

Riordan was still standing in the playground, glowering at them, when they topped the rise and lost sight of him.

Carol saw it first out of the corner of her eye: a flash of blue-white light outside her garden enclosure. But when she turned toward the source of the flash, there was nothing there.

She was about to chalk it up to her imagination when she saw a whole series of flashes, one right after the other. And then, as she sat back on her haunches and tried to figure out what they might be, a scream for help pierced the stillness.

Her blood froze.

Dropping the Vegan fern she held in her hands, she scrambled for the entrance and would have gone tearing out of the place altogether, were it not for the sight that stopped her like a duranium wall:

Klingons.

A lot of them, too—maybe as many as twenty—swaggering about in their heavy, dark body armor. And they were herding her colleagues out of Boudreau's laboratory dome, waving their weapons around as if they were only too eager to use them.

Carol knew now what the flashes had been. *Disruptor fire.* Had they actually killed anyone? Her stomach clenched painfully at the thought.

As she watched from the enclosure, one of the invaders shoved Irma Garcia, apparently to expedite her exit from the lab dome. But he pushed too hard, and the woman fell to the ground.

The Klingon growled something Carol couldn't make out and brought his booted foot back as if to kick Garcia. But Boudreau came between them, his hands up in a gesture of peace. Unfortunately, peace wasn't what the Klingons had in mind. A second marauder dealt Boudreau a blow to the face that bloodied the scientist's mouth.

Carol almost gave in to her reflexes and came to her friend's aid. But she stopped herself.

Or rather, he stopped her. Because as the Klingons picked up their victims and got them moving again, Boudreau happened to turn toward the enclosure and catch sight of her. Their eyes met, and his were full of fear. But he had the presence of mind to look away again—and quickly.

That's when she realized that she hadn't been

spotted yet and that if she played her cards right, she could be the colonists' ace in the hole. She pulled her head back inside the enclosure.

But she couldn't stay here, Carol told herself. It was only a matter of time before the Klingons got around to searching the enclosure. And when they did, she would share whatever—

Suddenly, she remembered: *David.* Where was he?

In the hills, she thought, not without a pang of relief. Along with the other children. Safe—at least for the moment.

Of course, they wouldn't remain that way for long. All the invaders would have to do is access the computer's personnel files, and they'd know that the children were missing. They were all on the colony roster—not the one that had gone up to the *Enterprise,* with her son's name purposely left off it, but the master list, the one that was on the central computer, in the lab building the Klingons had just evacuated.

Strangely, it was only then that her heart began to race. Because she knew that the children had a chance to stay out of this—and that if she did nothing else, she had to purge their identities from the files.

Maybe then, she could think about sending a call for help, though the communications center was way on the other side of the installation. And though the *Enterprise,* the nearest Federation ship, would take days to respond.

But first, the lab. She had to get to the lab.

Even as she was screwing up her resolve, she saw more flashes, followed by a terrible, plaintive wailing, a sound like mourning. It was cut off abruptly, before it could run its natural course.

She bit her lip to keep it from trembling. Bastards, she thought. Bloody *bastards*.

After that, however, there were neither flashes nor cries. She counted the seconds, not only to measure the time but to calm herself. If she was going to do anyone any good, she had to have her wits about her.

Carol had counted to two hundred before she dared to poke her head out of the enclosure again. There was no one around—neither Klingons nor colonists. Now was the time. Praying no one spotted her, staying low, she made her way across the flat, open space between the garden and the lab-dome entrance.

It couldn't have taken more than a few heartbeats, but it seemed like forever. Then she was at the door, waiting for it to admit her. Come on, she urged it silently. Let me in, damn it!

An eternity later, the door slid aside, revealing the interior of the lab. Carol only got a vague impression of the carnage the Klingons had caused before she slipped inside and pressed her back against the interior wall.

Letting out a breath, she took a moment to gather herself again, then headed for the nearest work station. En route, she couldn't help but notice that many of the monitors had been smashed. Stupid and unnecessary, she mused, as she reached her destination. The marauders had jeopardized all the colony's hard work by giving vent to their destructive natures.

Fortunately, some of the work stations had escaped unscathed. With any luck at all, the central processing unit had remained undamaged as well.

Then she noticed something else. Or more accurately, the *lack* of something.

The G-7 unit was gone. The latticework of energy-transfer tubes that dominated the center of the lab had a gap in it a meter long. Carol swore beneath her breath. No doubt the Klingons were dismantling it at this very moment, to see what was so special about it. And in the process, undoing all that Dr. Boudreau had accomplished.

After all, there was only one G-7 unit in the entire galaxy. If it were accidentally destroyed, it would take years to build another.

Bastards. Turning her attention to the terminal in front of her, she went through the routine of activating it. Her fingers danced over the keyboard; it was second nature by now. A moment later, the screen lit up. The central processor was fine—at least for the time being. Now all she had to do was call up the colony personnel directory. And hope that she could complete the task before a Klingon decided to walk in on her. Moving with feverish speed, she entered the required command.

As soon as the directory appeared on the screen, she began deleting the names of the children in alphabetical order. First Roberto Garcia, then David Marcus, Keena Medford, Will Pfeffer, Timmy Riordan, and finally, Li Wan.

She'd done it. David and the others were safe—at least, as safe as she could make them. Wiping her brow of the perspiration that had accumulated there, Carol stored the directory and signed off. The terminal hummed slightly as it powered down.

Briefly, for just a fleeting moment, it occurred to her to try to join the children in the hills. She'd gone unnoticed so far; maybe she could slip past the invaders and make good her escape.

She grunted softly. *That would be the coward's way,*

Carol. And as scared as you are, you're no coward. She had an obligation to the other colonists, the children included, to stay with her original plan and send for help.

But as she moved toward the exit, the door to the lab dome slid open unexpectedly. Stopping dead in her tracks, heart smashing against her ribs, she saw the grinning Klingon who filled the aperture with his bulk. She clenched her teeth as he aimed his disruptor at her.

For a long moment, Carol stared at the Klingon, certain that her next breath would be her last. The muzzle of his disruptor loomed in front of her, made gargantuan by her imagination.

But her luck held. He didn't press the trigger. He just gestured for her to come outside.

Thank God, she thought. Suddenly, sharing the fate of her colleagues didn't seem so terrible—compared to the alternative.

What's more, the Klingon didn't seem to have guessed that she'd been up to anything. He hadn't even glanced in the direction of any of the work stations.

Buoyed by the knowledge that she'd bought the children some time, Carol moved out of the lab dome. A fraction of a second later, her captor followed.

Chapter Ten

"ARE YOU CERTAIN?" Vheled asked.

Gidris nodded. "Quite certain. Of course, Mallot has only had a day to examine all the research data—hardly sufficient time. But it is fairly obvious, even to a neophyte, that the facility's central unit— the device that makes possible accelerated plant growth—is missing."

Vheled grunted. "Then one of the colonists must be missing as well."

His first officer looked perturbed. "There is no one missing," he reported. "In fact, we have rounded up one individual too *many*."

The captain of the *Kad'nra* leaned forward, planting his elbows on the desk before him, the desk that had so recently belonged to one of the colonists, until Vheled had commandeered that person's dome and made it his headquarters. "Too many?" he echoed. "How is that possible?"

Gidris scowled. "I cannot say for sure. But I suspect his age was a factor. He is twelve years old."

"Too young, perhaps, to be listed as an official member of the colony?"

"That is my guess," Gidris agreed. "Particularly because he is the only nonadult in the colony."

Vheled thought about it. "The Federation maintains lists of all its equipment components . . . why not an individual, no matter *how* young he is?" He shook his head. "There must be another explanation."

His first officer searched for an answer. "Computer-input error?" he ventured.

The captain made a sound of disgust. "Speculation is a waste of time, Gidris. Bring me the boy. Maybe he can tell us himself."

"Damn," Kirk muttered.

"Ye can say that again," Scotty joined in. "I've never seen such a herd."

"The cubaya here are most numerous," their Manteil guide agreed, not without a note of pride in his voice.

"No," said McCoy. "The *stars* are numerous. These critters are *legion.*"

A huge, blue-green valley spread out before them, one of a series of valleys that seemed to stretch to the horizon. In the valley was a broad river, sparkling in the bronze light of Alpha Maluria. And in the river, crowding it from bank to bank, both upstream and down as far as the eye could see, were the cubaya, the beasts at the center of this world's religious conflict.

There were five of them there on the ridge: the three *Enterprise* officers, Ambassador Farquhar, and their guide. All of them were mounted on fleiar—tall, spindle-legged creatures with long, droopy ears and doglike snouts. The fleiar were well-trained; they stood almost completely still, despite the stiff, swirling winds that drove the ground cover in gentle waves.

The cubaya, by contrast, seemed fat and clumsy as they breasted the river current, their migrational imperative aiming them straight for the mother city. From Kirk's vantage point, they looked like small walruses with short, muscular legs instead of flippers. Their coats ranged from a russet color to a very dark brown.

Not a very attractive animal, at least not to the captain's eye. But then, it wasn't the beasts' beauty that commended them to the Manteil. It was their spiritual significance.

"Would you care for a closer look?" asked the guide.

"Absolutely," the ambassador replied. "Please, lead the way."

The Manteil, whose name was Ebahn, urged his mount down the slope. Farquhar made sure he was the next to fall in line, though he looked stiff and more than a little awkward trying to maintain his balance.

As Kirk and his officers prepared to follow, McCoy cast the captain a look. "Who does he think he's impressing?" the doctor muttered.

Kirk grunted. Fortunately, the ambassador's one-upmanship games bothered him somewhat less than they did McCoy. With a flick of the reins that the Malurians employed to guide their mounts, not unlike those used on horses back on Earth, he encouraged his animal to follow Farquhar's.

As they descended the slope, the wind shifted and

they were surrounded by a less than pleasant odor—
something like a chicken egg left too long in the sun.
Nor was it difficult to track down the source.

The cubaya, the captain guessed. It had to be. They
not only looked ugly, they smelled ugly. Some of the
nearest cubaya looked up at them, as if they'd heard
Kirk's mental assessment and taken offense. However,
they didn't seem the least bit daunted by the intrusion.

Ebahn called back over his shoulder: "Do not worry
about getting too close. They are used to seeing riders
around." He pointed upstream, where the captain
could barely make out a pair of Malurians mounted
as they were. "We have men and women patrolling for
predators along various stretches of the river."

"I see," the ambassador replied. "That's very interesting."

McCoy groaned—too softly for Farquhar to notice,
though Kirk was close enough to hear it distinctly.
What's more, Bones had a point—the ambassador
was laying it on a little thick. But then, Farquhar
wasn't the first diplomat who'd been polishing apples
so long he found it hard to know when to stop.

"Actually," their guide went on, "the predators
themselves are not the biggest danger. At least, not in
the way you may think." He pointed to the grassy
ground cover, bent flat now under a sudden gust. "It is
the wind, which carries the predators' scent. The
cubaya may look lethargic now. But if they should
catch the smell of a gettrex, you will find them most
active." He made a fluttering sound with his tongue—
the equivalent of a sigh, the captain guessed. "If we
did not provide protection for the herd, as our fathers

did before us, more cubaya would die in stampedes than in the jaws of the gettrexin."

Scotty, who'd been quiet for the most part, shot the captain a glance. "Begging your pardon, sir, but doesn't that give us a solution to the problem?"

Kirk started to ask the engineer what he meant. But before he could get a whole word out, he stopped himself.

Scotty smiled. "Ye see what I mean, Captain?"

Kirk nodded. "Indeed I do."

Farquhar wheeled his fleiar around and approached them. "Is this something I ought to know about?" he asked.

"Absolutely," the captain told him. "Mr. Scott here may have come up with an answer—a way to satisfy both the Manteil and the Obirrhat."

"And that is?" the ambassador prodded.

Scotty told him.

Farquhar frowned.

"Well?" McCoy said.

The ambassador nodded sagely. "It might work. I'll send word to the Council to expect us."

"Your name?"

The human child swallowed. Vheled recognized it as a sign of fear.

"Timothy Riordan," he said.

The captain of the *Kad'nra* looked to his first officer.

"There are two Riordans listed in the colony personnel file," said Gidris. "One is Martin, the other Dana."

Vheled fixed his gaze on the boy. The swallowing became more pronounced.

"How is it," he asked, "that you are not listed with the others?"

Timothy Riordan—if that was truly his name—shook his head. "I don't know," he said.

Vheled exchanged glances with his second-in-command. Gidris, it seemed, was of the opinion the boy was lying. The captain wasn't so sure.

"The truth," Gidris urged, placing his hand on Timothy Riordan's shoulder. "Or I will see to it that you *suffer*."

The boy's eyes grew red and wet as they looked up at the Klingon. His nose started to run.

It was amazing how easily human children could be broken. Vheled had heard it in the accounts of other captains who'd had dealings with Federation colonies, but he hadn't believed it. And now that he saw it with his own eyes, he felt his gorge rise. Suddenly he wanted to get this over with as quickly as possible.

"Come," he told the boy. "You are hiding something. What is it?"

Timothy Riordan sobbed. "I told them to come back," he said.

Vheled leaned forward until his elbows rested on his knees and his face was mere inches from the human's. "Who? You told *who* to come back?"

The boy caught a ragged breath. "David. And the others." He looked up, eyes wide with fright. "I told them, but they wouldn't listen."

Gidris tightened his grip on Timothy Riordan's shoulder. "The one you call David—and these others. Who are they?"

"They're kids. Like me."

"And they took the G-Seven unit?"

Suddenly the boy looked confused. "G-Seven?" he

140

repeated. He shook his head. "No. The G-Seven unit is in the laboratory dome."

Vheled's first officer snarled. "Do you mean to tell me you don't know what happened to the unit? Before you answer, remember—your *life* depends on what you say to us."

Timothy Riordan looked from one to the other of them, sobbing again. "I don't know anything about the G-Seven—I swear it." And then: "Pl-please don't hurt me. *Please.*"

The captain was caught between anger and revulsion. "Enough, Gidris. *More* than enough." He dismissed the human child with a backhanded gesture. "I cannot watch this display of cowardice any longer."

Timothy Riordan turned a bright shade of red. *Stung by my words?* the Klingon wondered. *Maybe now he will show some courage.*

But nothing happened. The boy just looked away.

That, Vheled thought, was why the Federation would ultimately have to yield to the empire. The humans and their allies were weak. They didn't have the stomachs for confrontation, while Klingons thrived on it.

"Take him away, I said."

Obediently, Gidris dragged the boy out of his chair and flung him in the direction of the door. Timothy Riordan stumbled, recovering only long enough to shoot Vheled a miserable and frightened glance. Then Gidris shoved him out of the dome altogether, leaving the captain alone with his thoughts.

The Klingon shook his head. If one of his sons had turned out like the human child, he would have died long ago—at his father's hands.

Pushing his revulsion to one side, he asked himself

what his next step should be. There was only one answer.

Despite Timothy Riordan's protestations, the other human children—who had also failed to show up in the computer files, apparently—must have taken the G-7 device. And if that were so, they had to be found.

As before, Traphid and his colleagues were waiting for them. This time, however, Kirk and his party didn't transport into the hexagonal hall. They simply walked in, albeit past a squad of security personnel.

Again, there was the exchange of gestures, carried on symbolically for both groups by Traphid and Farquhar. The first minister seemed a bit more impatient than the last time the captain had seen him; so did the other Malurians.

"Matters have taken a turn for the worse," Kirk guessed.

Traphid looked at him. "You are perceptive, Captain. As the cubaya approach the mother city, the rioting is spreading to other cities across our world. We restore order in one place only to find the Obirrhat have created chaos in two others." His face twitched; if anything, it was even more pronounced than before. "The casualties are mounting. The Obirrhat are very stubborn."

And they're not the only ones, Kirk thought. But he kept his opinions to himself.

"I'm sorry to hear that," the ambassador remarked, reminding his companions of who was in charge here. "But we may have found a way to resolve your dispute."

"So I understand," the first minister replied. "Please, present your solution."

For a moment, the captain thought Farquhar might turn the conversation over to Scotty, or at least credit the man for having had the idea in the first place. As it turned out, he had no intention of doing either.

"It seems," the ambassador began, "that we must dissuade the cubaya from treading on the sacred ground of the Obirrhat—and by some means other than physical force. You agree?"

Traphid thought for a moment. "In principle, yes. As long as you understand that it is not only force per se that we object to, but in general anything that may displace the cubaya against its wishes."

"Understood," Farquhar told him. "Now, we understand the cubaya have a strong negative reaction to predator scents," the ambassador began. "In short, they *run* from them."

"True," Traphid confirmed.

"If this is the case, why not domesticate one or two of these predators and leave them in the vicinity of the sacred monuments?" Farquhar smiled ingratiatingly. "This way, the cubaya will not be harmed, but they will be encouraged to stay away—in keeping with the Obirrhat's needs."

McCoy and Scotty stood on either side of Kirk. He darted a glance at each of them in turn. As long as he was in charge here, no one was going to be grimacing at Farquhar's approach, no matter how sickly sweet it was.

The ministers looked at one another. For a moment or two, they conferred in subdued tones. Then they regarded the ambassador again.

"It is unacceptable," Traphid told him.

Farquhar's smile faded. "Unacceptable?" he echoed. "Please explain."

The first minister shrugged. "The Obirrhat will reject the intrusion of the gettrexin in their sacred areas as strongly as they reject the presence of the cubaya. One form of beast is like another to them, in that regard."

The ambassador's mouth was open. He closed it, then darted a sidelong glance at Scotty, as if to say: *I did my best, but it wasn't a very good idea to begin with really.*

The engineer's eyes narrowed, but he didn't say anything. Kirk admired the man's restraint. In Scotty's position, he might not have been so tight-lipped.

Of course, McCoy wasn't as willing as Farquhar to throw in the towel. "Wait a minute," he said, "let's think about this a little. If we can't use real animals, then how about just their scents? We can extract them without causing the gettrexin any pain and—"

Traphid held up his hand. "That would be just as unacceptable to the Obirrhat. Any evidence of a gettrex, even just its scent, constitutes a desecration of their sacred ground."

But the doctor still had some fight left in him. "All right," he said. "Neither beasts nor their scents. Then how about a chemical compound—one that smells like the gettrexin but is created in a laboratory? It would have the same effect on the cubaya as the real thing, but being artificial, it shouldn't put the Obirrhat's noses out of joint."

"Real or artificial," the first minister responded, "it would smell like a gettrex. And the Obirrhat would reject the idea."

McCoy scowled. He was really digging now, Kirk thought. "What if the compound emulates a beast this world has never heard of? Say, a Terran wolverine? Or an Aldebaran kirgis? They'd probably have the same effect on the cubaya."

Traphid shook his head. "I am afraid not. You must understand, Doctor, the Obirrhat are simply not a reasonable people." A pause. "I do not envy you your task."

McCoy cursed under his breath. "Seems to me there's an answer there somewhere, if we can only dig it out."

Scotty patted him on the back. "Whether that's so or not, Doctor, ye gave it a good try."

"But not good enough," Farquhar reminded them. He turned to the Malurians. "I apologize, on behalf of all of us. Next time, we won't waste your time with such a flimsy suggestion."

"Flimsy?" Scotty muttered. "Of all the—"

A look from the captain stopped him in midinvective.

"Ambassador," Traphid said, "you need not worry about making demands on our time. We do not expect you to solve this problem on your own, after all. We anticipated all along that it would require our cooperation."

Farquhar placed his index and middle fingers in the vicinity of his temples. "As you wish, First Minister."

This time, when McCoy looked at him, Kirk looked back. It was one thing to show respect, even deference. But to grovel? Especially when the Malurians seemed less than receptive to it?

He wasn't one to tell someone else how to do his job. But if he were in the ambassador's place, he'd be handling things a bit differently.

* * *

145

"You see, Captain?" said Kruge, who was standing in the humans' garden enclosure. Vheled, who was kneeling, didn't immediately look up at his second officer. He was too busy stroking the long, dark petals of one of the fireblossoms Kruge had pointed out to him.

"And where did the humans say these came from?" the captain asked.

Fortunately, Kruge had asked that question and made sure he got an answer. "The wreck of the *Ul'lud.*"

Absorbing the information, Vheled nodded. "The *Ul'lud*—under Captain Amagh. An effete, Kamorh'dag cultivator of flowers." He grunted. "Yes. That has the ring of truth to it."

He remained there for a moment, kneeling. Kruge wondered what was going through his superior's mind.

Then Vheled spoke again. "Do you understand what they were doing, Kruge, when we interrupted them? Removing the dying specimens from around the fireblossoms so they could plant these others in their place. These lesser organisms"—he held up one sorry example so Kruge could see—"could not stand up to the presence of a Klingon life form. Just as the colonists cannot stand up to us." He shook his head. "The Federation is so weak as to make even the Kamorh'dag seem strong by comparison."

Kruge nodded. The captain was a wise man. If he himself was to be a captain someday, he would do well to listen carefully to Vheled.

Suddenly, he turned and saw Gidris standing in the entranceway. There were two others with him, Loutek and Aoras. A moment later, the captain turned, too.

"You have something for me, Gidris?"

The second-in-command didn't seem pleased to see Vheled and Kruge together, but he managed to submerge his apprehension. "Indeed, Captain. Terrik has completed his sensor scan."

"And?"

"It seems Timothy Riordan was not the only human the computer failed to mention. The sensors have detected five others, huddled together in the hills north of this place. And, sir, all of them are children."

Vheled mulled it over for a moment. He smiled. "Then the Riordan whelp was speaking the truth—at least insofar as there having been other children with him. I am still not certain he knew nothing about the theft of the device. In any case, whether he was aware of it or not, these others must have the G-Seven unit—or at least know where it is."

Gidris nodded. "It would appear so."

Abruptly, Kruge had a thought. He turned to his captain. "My lord?"

Vheled's eyes narrowed. "Speak."

Kruge lifted his chin, proud of himself. "The humans appear to have gone to a great deal of trouble to see that we do not gain access to this device. Perhaps this technology—what do they call it? Terraforming? —is not as benign as it seems."

The first officer's brow writhed with curiosity, but it wasn't in his interest to show anything but disdain. "What does *that* mean, second officer?"

"What it means," the captain interjected, "is that the G-Seven mechanism may be a weapon after all, despite appearances to the contrary." His features hardened. "If so, then we are fortunate it is only in the hands of younglings. Even should they know how to

147

use it, they cannot be equipped to use it *well.*" A pause. "And if we can bring it back to the homeworld . . ." His lip curled. "The possibilities are most intriguing."

Kruge tried to decipher the remark. Did Vheled mean that by laying this technology at the emperor's feet, he would gain even more glory for the Ghevish'rae, and thereby further enhance their political standing?

Or was he talking about keeping the weapon a secret from Kapronek and his Kamorh'dag and using it to achieve power in a different way? He grinned at the prospect.

"You find something about the captain's remarks humorous?" Gidris asked him, not bothering to disguise his hostility.

Kruge straightened, but not out of respect for rank. "No, sir. Certainly not humorous."

"Then why the grin?"

Kruge shrugged. "I was entertained by the *possibilities*—sir."

Eyeing his third-in-command, Vheled held up his hand. "You need pursue this no further, Gidris. I am not offended."

"But Captain—"

"But nothing. There is much to be done, Gidris, and you are the one I've chosen to do it." He watched the Klingon's chest swell at the expression of confidence. "Take a half-dozen men," said the captain, "including Loutek and Aoras out there, and track down the missing children—all of them. When you find them, you will find the device."

Gidris beat his fist against his body armor. "I hear and obey."

This time, Kruge kept his smile inside. Gidris had been prevented from disciplining him, and by the word of the captain himself. It boded well for Kruge's future on the *Kad'nra*.

Perhaps he could not rise in the ranks before this mission was completed. But once it was over, Gidris would do well to watch his back.

Chapter Eleven

To THE CAPTAIN'S EYE, the sacred precincts of the Obirrhat looked as old as civilization itself. The streets were narrow and winding—paths, really, between two- and three-story buildings that leaned together like drunken conspirators. Underfoot, there were cobblestones that the years had worn down and cracked; in a number of places, the stones were missing altogether, leaving nothing but dirt in the gaps.

Statuary, most of it in an advanced state of ruin, appeared at nearly every intersection. The most common subjects were young women and children with their arms full of stony flowers.

The place even smelled ancient, Kirk thought, as they filed through the labyrinthine space between two especially precarious-looking edifices. It had that musty odor one associated with antique books, or the kind of old stone bridges one could still find back in Iowa.

It was the kind of place he might have liked to linger in, to get to know better. That is, if it weren't for the deadly stares and muttered curses that dogged his group's every step.

"Feeling a little unwanted?" McCoy asked.

The captain nodded. "More than a little, Bones. Then again, we should have expected a few funny looks. They must wonder what we're up to."

"That's fer certain," Scotty chimed in. "Especially since we've got a couple of armed Manteil watchin' over us. Nothin' like seein' the enemy paradin' through yer streets t' make ye feel a wee bit insecure."

"Frankly," Farquhar said, "I don't see the point in commenting on it. The first minister made it clear he wouldn't allow us to tour the area without an escort. And now that I've had a chance to see what it's like down here, I'm glad he insisted."

Kirk glanced at the pair of Manteil security guards Traphid had assigned to them. It was true there had been bloodshed in these streets, and there might be more before this conflict was resolved.

But Scotty had a point. Their tour could only look like an attempt to underline the Manteil's authority, and that might make a bad situation worse.

As they emerged from the street and passed a relatively wide, perpendicular thoroughfare, the captain noticed a square full of people a block away. It was the first large, open area they'd seen.

He pointed to it. "What's that?"

The nearer of the two guards said: "The market. It's where the Obirrhat in this area buy their food and clothing."

It looked interesting. Nor did there seem to be much point in merely continuing to walk the streets.

On the other hand, it might irritate the Obirrhat if the offworlders and their guards invaded the marketplace. And they'd done enough invading for one day.

"May we see it?" Farquhar asked.

Inwardly, the captain cursed himself for bringing the subject up in the first place. Fortunately, the guards had their wits about them.

"It is not advisable," one of them told the ambassador. "In such a crowd, it would be nearly impossible to guarantee your safety."

"Good point," Kirk said. "In fact, I think I've seen enough of this place altogether."

The ambassador shook his head. "I disagree."

"What a surprise," McCoy whispered in his captain's ear.

"I think it's important to get all the information we can," Farquhar went on. He smiled, the picture of a reasonable man. "We don't have to go into the crowd. We can stand at the fringe of it."

The guards looked at one another. They frowned.

"I'll take full responsibility with First Minister Traphid," the ambassador assured them. "You have my word on it."

The guards continued to look at one another. Their frowns deepened.

Oh, Lord, Kirk thought. They're going to give in.

But he was wrong. One of the guards turned to Farquhar and shook his head. "I do not believe your taking responsibility would make any difference to the first minister. I am afraid I must—"

He was cut off by a banshee yell. Without thinking, the captain took hold of the ambassador and drove him to the ground behind a wooden pushcart.

A moment later, he was glad his reflexes had been so

sharp. As he peered over his shoulder, he saw a couple of Obirrhat youths spraying gouts of red phaser fire in their direction.

Across the way, Scotty and Bones had managed to find cover behind a piece of statuary. Unfortunately, the captain thought, the council had prohibited the offworlders from carrying arms, or the battle might have ended as soon as it began.

As it was, their Manteil guards held their ground and returned fire. Tactically, Kirk knew, it was a mistake.

One of the Manteil paid the price for it, taking a direct shot. The impact sent him flying back into a wall, where he slumped to the cobblestones, a charred, smoking hole in the center of his chest.

His partner remained steadfast, however. Without flinching, he aimed, fired, and took down one of their assailants.

Before the Obirrhat youth could hit the ground, Kirk saw the blackened ruin that had been his midsection and realized the guards had their weapons set to kill as well.

When the other Obirrhat saw his friend fall, he started to back away, squeezing off a couple of blasts to cover his retreat. They didn't help. Coolly, the surviving Manteil skewered him on a bloodred beam.

The youth fell in a fuming heap at a woman's feet. Stricken with horror, she opened her eyes wide and her fingers climbed into her mouth.

For a second or two, there was silence as the import of what had happened began to sink in. Then the Obirrhat around them started to get ugly.

"We've got to get out of here," the ambassador muttered, recognizing the danger immediately. He was doing his best to maintain his composure, but his eyes were a window on his fear.

"Damned right," Kirk replied. Making sure that Bones and Scotty saw him, he jerked a thumb down the street, in the direction from which they'd come. Then, half lifting Farquhar off the cobblestones, he headed that way. Calmly. Or at least, as calmly as possible under the circumstances.

The ambassador began to accelerate, to break into a run, but the captain held him back. "No," he said. "If you run, it's an admission of guilt. And they'll run after us." He looked about them—saw the eyes, angrier than ever, and the mouths twisted with hatred —and kept his balance despite it all. "Trust me," he told Farquhar. "This is our best shot at getting out of here alive."

A wail went up from the woman at whose feet the youth had fallen—a thin, undulating whine of mourning. Before long, others had joined in. The surviving guard bent and pulled his comrade's body over his shoulder, leaving a bloody stain on the cobblestones. He still had his phaser in his hand, though he had the presence of mind not to make it obvious.

"Captain," Scotty rasped, as his path and McCoy's converged with Kirk's. "Are ye all right, sir?"

The Obirrhat in the intersection had begun to move with them, to track them like a huge, deadly predator with a hundred accusing faces.

The captain nodded, keeping a firm grasp on the ambassador's arm. He still had the feeling that Farquhar might bolt at any moment. And for his plan to work, he needed them all together. If they got separated, there was no telling what might happen.

"We're fine, Mr. Scott. Now let's direct our eyes straight ahead and see if we can keep it that way."

Abruptly, a different kind of cry went up, a more guttural sound, bristling with violence. Kirk ignored it, glancing behind them only once to make sure their guard was with them. Once he saw the Manteil, he trained his gaze on their target—the end of the street—and headed for it.

After that, of course, there would be another street, and maybe another. And then maybe they'd be out of the sacred precinct, and the crowd would be inclined to stop following them. *Maybe.*

The captain wasn't putting all his eggs in that basket, however. Now that his back was to the Obirrhat and they couldn't see his hands, he reached for his communicator and opened it waist-high.

Certainly, he could have done that before. But the Obirrhat might have thought the communicator was another weapon being trained on them, and then the situation might have escalated.

"Kirk to *Enterprise.*"

"This is *Enterprise,*" Sulu responded. "Something wrong, Captain?"

That was the value of serving with a man for a number of years. He could tell you were in trouble even before you had a chance to say so.

"Affirmative, Lieutenant. Have Chief Kyle lock onto my coordinates and beam up five—including two Malurians, one dead and one alive."

He could have asked for security personnel to be beamed down, but that would have been an act of desperation. The potential for a major incident was already there without their throwing more fuel on the fire.

155

Sulu paused on the other end. "Captain, Kyle says there are a great many Malurians within close proximity. It may take some time to isolate the ones who are with you."

"Tell Kyle to move as quickly as he can, Lieutenant. We may not *have* all that much time." Closing his communicator, he put it away.

Nor was he a moment too soon. Obirrhat heads were starting to poke out from warped window openings, demanding to know what was going on. They were answered by the crowd, which seemed to grow larger with each pursuing step.

Kirk turned to the Manteil, who was breathing hard now with the strain of bearing his comrade's corpse. "Put your weapon on stun," he told the man.

The guard looked at him, uncomprehending.

Kirk said it again. "Put your weapon on stun, damn it. Do it *now.*"

"But if they charge us, and they see it won't kill them—"

"Then it'll be to our disadvantage."

The Manteil shook his head. "I don't—"

"What he's saying," McCoy rasped, "is any more killing could make this city a bloodbath, and that's more important than whether the four of us live or die. Now put the blasted thing on stun or *I* will."

Reluctantly, the guard altered the setting.

Out of the corner of his eye, the captain saw something thrown at him. He ducked. As it passed by, he saw what it was: a piece of ancient masonry. Great, he thought. Just great.

Another chunk came whizzing at Scotty. Unable to avoid it entirely, he took a glancing blow off his shoulder.

They were getting closer to the intersection. Hell, they were almost on top of it. A little farther now, a little farther, and the cross street opened up on either side of them.

God help us, the captain mused, if we actually have to get out of here on foot. Before long, it'll be a blasted gauntlet.

As if to give force to his fears, Kirk felt something strike him in the back, hard. He winced but kept going, mindful of the numbers against them. McCoy was hit, too; he uttered a curse, though it was too low for their pursuers to pick up.

After the next intersection, Kirk noticed, the character of the buildings began to change. His earlier assessment was correct—they were within a couple of blocks of the precinct limits.

And still no help from the *Enterprise*. Come on, Kyle, he breathed.

Yet another projectile came slanting down at them, catching the ambassador on the side of the head. When he turned to the captain, fright and indignation fighting for control of him, there was blood trickling down from his temple.

The man was going to run. Kirk could see it in his face.

He tightened his grip on Farquhar's arm. "Don't do it," he told him. "Don't even think about it."

Thrusting his chin out, the ambassador endeavored to do as he was told. But his lower lip was trembling; clearly, he was barely able to contain his outrage.

The stoning continued. At one point, a small child even ran up in front of them and hurled a pebble at Scotty, then jeered before running away again. But they endured it, were even grateful for it, because as long as the Obirrhat only used stones, they had a chance. And all the while, they were buying time for the transporter chief.

Finally, however, someone hurled a piece of rock too big to dismiss. McCoy must have been looking back at their antagonists, because it struck him in the forehead, hard enough to make his knees buckle and oblige Scotty to catch him. For an instant, the doctor appeared to be unconscious. Then, with the engineer's help, he managed to gather his feet beneath him and stagger on, blood streaming down his face on both sides of his left eye.

Still, the captain thought, McCoy was lucky. Thrown with a little more enthusiasm, that rock could have killed him.

Looking skyward, Kirk made another silent appeal to Kyle: *Beam us up, Chief! What's taking so long?*

The stoning got worse—heavier and harder. The captain took a shot in the back of the head that made him bite down on his lip. He tasted blood; before he could spit it out, another missile smashed him in the side of the knee.

They weren't going to last much longer. The Obirrhat were getting more vicious with each barrage. Soon, one or more of them would fall to the ground, and that would be the beginning of the end.

The second intersection loomed in front of them. But before they could reach it, it filled up with rock-wielding Obirrhat who blocked their path.

There was nowhere to go. They were trapped.

Suddenly, without warning, their Manteil guard whipped out his phaser and played it over the crowd in back of them. Not knowing that he'd adjusted it to a nonlethal setting, they fell back immediately, as

some of the Obirrhat in the front rank collapsed to
their knees.

That's when all hell broke loose. The Obirrhat in
the intersection hurled their stones and screamed a
vow of vengeance for their brothers' deaths.

The Manteil turned to fire his weapon at them as
well, but a well-aimed hunk of rock caught him in the
jaw and ruined his aim. Off-balance, burdened by his
comrade's body, he went down.

Nor was there time to go scrambling for the phaser.
There was barely time enough for Kirk to set himself
as the Obirrhat in the intersection rushed them,
bellowing as they came.

He wasn't going to give up, the captain told himself.
He'd faced worse than this a hundred times and
gotten through it somehow. That's what he told
himself. But in his heart, he had to concede that this
might be the exception that proved the rule.

And what a way to go—at the hands of a mob,
probably more scared than he was—fighting over a
bunch of dumb beasts who didn't have a clue they
were being fought over. He could almost have
laughed.

Then he saw the Obirrhat closing with them, and he
decided against it. As the leader of the charge brought
a piece of rock back, preparing to bludgeon him with
it, Kirk shuffled his feet to avoid the blow. The rock
shot forward and missed, but the Obirrhat behind it
wasn't going to be so easy to elude. As the captain
braced for the impact of bone against bone . . .

Nothing happened.

And then he realized why. He was no longer standing in a narrow street in the Obirrhats' sacred precinct, he was on a platform in the *Enterprise*'s

transporter room. What's more, Scotty and Bones were with him, though both of them had seen better days. And so was the Manteil guard, along with his tragic burden.

Dr. M'Benga, Nurse Chapel, and a trauma team had been waiting alongside Kyle for the landing party's arrival. As Kirk and the others came staggering off the platform, each of them found a pair of arms to lend support.

"I'm all right," the captain told the two burly nurses who'd come to his aid. "Really, I'm fine."

"I'll be the judge of that," said M'Benga. He turned to the nurses. "See him to sickbay. And don't let him pull rank on you."

"That's right," McCoy muttered, as another pair of sickbay personnel ushered him off. "Be careful with him; he's a slippery devil." And he winked, bloody face and all.

Kirk was glad to see the doctor still had enough of his wits to poke fun at him. Sighing, he allowed himself to be escorted to sickbay with the others.

Chapter Twelve

THE LOWER HALF OF Traphid's face was twitching as McCoy had never seen it twitch before. "I cannot say how much I regret what happened," he told them. "It was . . ." He searched for the right word, then shook his head in defeat. "I should have anticipated such a turn of events. I should have dispatched more guards to escort you."

Once again, there were eight of them in the hall of government: McCoy, Jim, Scotty, the ambassador, and the four Malurian ministers. The tension in the air was almost palpable.

"You acted as you saw fit," Farquhar replied—diplomatically, of course. He had a dermaplast patch over one eye. "There is no need for self-recrimination, First Minister."

"And with all due respect," the captain added, "even a couple dozen guards wouldn't have been able to keep the Obirrhat in line after what happened to those two young men."

True enough, McCoy thought. Hell, the presence of the guards was what had caused the whole thing. If they'd been unescorted, they might not have roused such a furor.

Traphid frowned. "Yes. Their deaths were unfortunate." His voice hardened. "As was the death of our guardsman. It appears the Obirrhat have gotten their hands on a supply of phaser pistols. We will have to find their source and cut it off."

"In the meantime," the ambassador remarked, "I think we've seen all we need to see. The time has come for us to sit down and talk—to see if we can't work out a solution to all this."

The ministers looked at him. "Of course," Traphid answered. But it seemed to McCoy he had even less confidence in the suggestion than before. "We may begin this afternoon."

Farquhar nodded. "Good. It's best we get started as soon as possible."

"First Minister," Kirk interjected, "I'd like to make a recommendation."

The ambassador smiled sweetly in his direction. "We'll meet with the council this afternoon, Captain. We can present our recommendations then."

"People may be dying as we speak," the captain reminded him. "If we can temporarily defuse the situation, we can prevent that."

Farquhar was about to press his case, McCoy thought, when Traphid raised his hand. "I would like to hear the captain's recommendation," he said.

Yet another rebuke, the doctor noted. When would the ambassador learn?

Kirk turned to Traphid. "I know how closely you embrace your religious beliefs, First Minister. And if

FACES OF FIRE

the situation were not so potentially explosive, I
would not presume to raise this issue. But would it not
serve everyone's interests, including those of the
cubaya themselves, if you were to keep the animals
away from the sacred precinct for a short while?"

Farquhar reddened. "Captain—"

Kirk continued, speaking calmly yet forcefully,
despite the incipient protest. "I know I'm asking a lot,
First Minister. However, this is a unique problem,
and unique problems call for unique solutions."

Traphid and his colleagues listened, their expressions unreadable, at least to McCoy. But the ambassador wasn't nearly so attentive.

"Captain, I believe we are overstepping our bounds.
We didn't come here to remold the cultural values
of—"

"What's more," Kirk plunged on, "there's the safety of the beasts to consider. Imagine if the Obirrhat
had chosen to attack the cubaya that came through in
the first wave, instead of waiting and hoping for a
solution. They could have slaughtered the animals
wholesale." He eyed the first minister. "Perhaps the
next time, they *will.*"

McCoy nodded. Tell 'em, Jim.

"Captain," Farquhar rasped, noticeably perturbed
now, "that will be quite enough." He turned to
Traphid. "First Minister, I must apologize for this
man's affront to your traditions. It is inexcusable, and
it will not happen again, I assure you." With this last
comment, the ambassador turned back to Kirk and
glared. The captain glared back.

Farquhar's finally done it, the doctor thought. He's
even gotten to Jim Kirk—and that's not an easy thing
to do.

Traphid made a gulping sound, drawing everyone's attention. He addressed the captain. "As you say, unique problems call for unique solutions. I will concede as much."

McCoy tried to contain his surprise. Was it possible Kirk had actually pierced the Malurian's dark-ages mentality and let some light in?

"But Captain," the first minister went on, "the ambassador is correct in one respect: you misunderstand our traditions. The cubaya are not simply beasts to us—they carry the living incarnations of our most sacred leaders. There will be no discussion of curbing the rangings of the cubaya. Not for a day; not even for a minute."

The doctor's hopes crumbled as fast as he'd built them up. He should have known better, he told himself.

"As for their safety," said Traphid, "we are concerned. However, we will meet that concern with increased security measures." He paused. "I am the first to admit that this is not an ideal solution, given the volatility of the Obirrhat population in the sacred precinct. But until an ideal solution presents itself, it will have to do."

McCoy cursed inwardly. In other words, he thought, thanks for the help, but next time keep it to yourself.

The captain bit his lip. He seemed on the verge of trying again, maybe using a little different approach. But he must have thought better of it, because all he said was, "I would have been negligent in the performance of my duty if I'd failed to make the suggestion."

The first minister nodded. "I understand." He looked to the ambassador. "This afternoon, then."

"This afternoon," Farquhar confirmed.

When the Klingon entered the rec dome, where half of them were being held, Carol's stomach muscles clenched. She fully expected him to announce that they had caught and killed the human children in the hills, and disposed of them in whatever way Klingons disposed of corpses.

But instead, he asked, "Which one of you is Yves Boudreau?" His words were clipped and guttural but otherwise fairly easy to understand.

The colony administrator raised his head. There was a purplish swelling at the corner of his mouth, where one of the invaders had hit him, and a dark cut over one eye, where he'd been clouted for not responding quickly enough to the one called Mallot.

"Something else? I've told them all I can," he muttered wearily.

That wasn't quite true, of course. Boudreau hadn't given them much more than broad strokes when it came to the G-7 unit.

Nor would he be required to, apparently, until they had recovered the unit. And that was missing, if their captors were to be believed—although they didn't seem to know what had happened to it.

Carol didn't know either, but she had her suspicions. When she'd seen her fellow colonists being rounded up, Mr. Spock wasn't among them. And if *anyone* could take the one-of-a-kind unit and carry it off with him, it would be a Vulcan.

Of course, she couldn't come out and ask their

captors if Spock was missing too, any more than she could ask about David and his friends. Because if the Starfleet officer had eluded the Klingons—and maybe taken G-7 with him—she didn't want to give him away.

Helping Boudreau to his feet, Carol instinctively placed herself between him and the Klingon. After all, the administrator wasn't a young man; the next blow might do irreparable damage.

"Stand away, woman," growled the newcomer.

"What do you want with him?" she asked.

The Klingon's bony brow bunched with anger. "That is none of your concern. Now stand away or you will wish you had."

"It's all right, Carol," said Boudreau. "There's no point in resisting."

He was right; she knew that. But it didn't make it any easier for her to watch him walk by and out the entrance to the dome, followed closely by the Klingon.

The room they occupied was almost as large as the Hall of Government, and with its tall, stained-glass windows, just as impressive, too. A table was set for them on the far end, though their food hadn't arrived yet.

"How could you have *done* such a thing?" the ambassador asked through tightly drawn lips. "How could you have even contemplated it?"

His back to Farquhar, Kirk shrugged. "Seemed like a good idea at the time."

He tried to concentrate on the stained-glass images and not on the ambassador's voice. That way, there was at least a chance he'd get through this tête-à-tête without blowing up.

"A good . . . ?" Farquhar sputtered. "It could hardly have been a *worse* idea." He shook his head. "That's the problem with having ship's personnel participate in diplomatic endeavors."

"Indeed?" Scotty said. McCoy muttered something as well.

The captain could only imagine the kind of looks they were giving the ambassador. He would have liked to do the same. But he wasn't going to take the bait. He wasn't. He was going to memorize every detail of these fine, stained-glass works of art—right down to the number of cubaya in them, which was considerable.

"Indeed," Farquhar replied, without looking at the engineer. His attention was still riveted on Kirk. "We've already forfeited the possibility of meeting with the Obirrhat, thanks to your misguided set of priorities. Would you have us alienate the Manteil as well? Remember our job, Captain—to bring the two sides together. How would you do that? By aligning both of them against *us?*"

Kirk focused on a particularly loathsome-looking pair of the Manteil's holy beasts. He thought they were mating, but he couldn't be sure; the style was far from realistic.

"Are you listening to me?" the ambassador demanded.

The captain took a deep breath, then let it out. "It's my job to listen to you," he said. *But it's not my job to like it,* he added silently.

"Then I suggest you open our afternoon meetings with an apology to Traphid and his fellow ministers for trampling on their beliefs."

Kirk felt a surge of anger. He bit it back. "Apologize?" he echoed.

"That's right. I want them fully cooperative when the talks begin, not harboring a resentment it'll take days to overcome."

The captain looked at McCoy, then Scotty. They looked back sympathetically, no doubt wishing there were something they could do to help him.

But there wasn't. They knew that. And so did Kirk.

"Apologize," he said again. He regarded Farquhar. "You don't think we've apologized enough to them already—for arriving when we did, for wanting to see the beasts and the sacred places at the heart of their dispute, even for taking up their time with suggestions they rejected? You don't think they're a little *tired* of hearing us apologize?"

The ambassador's eyes narrowed. "Captain, some days ago, you expressed a reverence for the wisdom of following orders. Your orders at this moment, I believe, are to assist me in these negotiations." A pause. "Unless, of course, you're refusing to do that—in which case I will be certain to include the fact in my report to the Federation Council."

Kirk didn't give a damn about Farquhar's report to the council. He did, however, give a damn about following orders. Or, at least, enough of a damn not to fly in the face of them because of his personal predilections concerning the ambassador.

"All right," he said reluctantly. "I'll . . . tender an apology." The words left a bad taste in his mouth.

Scotty cursed beneath his breath. McCoy just shook his head.

The ambassador nodded, satisfied. "I thought you'd come to your senses."

The captain flashed back to his conversation with

Carol back on the colony world. She'd asked him if he was happy, if he would trade his captaincy for something else. What might he tell her if she asked that question of him now?

Farquhar cleared his throat, like a rooster crowing over his victory. "If you'll excuse me, I think I'll see what's keeping our lunch. Diplomacy always makes me hungry."

And with that, he strutted out of the chamber, leaving a razor-edged silence in his wake. Scotty was the one who finally broke it.

"Of all the self-important, narrow-minded, stubborn *fops* I've met in my day . . ."

"You can say that again," McCoy told him. "And a lot more, if you like—though you still won't cover the subject adequately." He scowled. "I had him pegged from the moment I laid eyes on him."

Kirk nodded. "So you did, Bones. And I was foolish enough to try to talk you out of it."

"Obviously," Scotty continued, "he's forgotten ye saved his worthless hide not sae long ago."

"Worthless hide indeed," remarked the doctor.

The captain sighed. "It's not the personal humiliation that bothers me so much. It's the fact that the fate of this world is in his hands. I just wish there were something we could do to defuse the situation before the death toll starts to mount." He frowned. "If only there were a way to get in touch with those two Obirrhat ministers—what were their names? Menikki . . ."

"And Omalas," the engineer supplied.

"That's right," said Kirk. "Menikki and Omalas. If we could find them, talk with them, see the matter from their angle, maybe we could get some fresh ideas."

Bones looked at him thoughtfully. "Worthless hide," he repeated. His face seemed to light up. "Hell, maybe there *is* a way."

"What are ye sayin', Doctor?" asked Scotty.

McCoy turned to the engineer. He tilted his head. "Hmm. I wonder . . ."

"Bones?" Kirk probed. "If you've got something on your mind, spit it out."

McCoy's eyes narrowed appraisingly. "You know," he said, "it might not be a bad idea at that."

And before either of his companions could ask again, he let them in on it.

Shading his eyes from the big white disk that loomed directly ahead of him, Loutek stopped to wipe his tearing eyes on his sleeve. How many hours of this could a man take?

Just a little longer, he told himself, *and the damned sun will be out of your eyes. Just a little longer.*

Of course, he'd probably only find another steep, gritty slope beyond it, just like the one he'd been climbing. Cursing, the Klingon resumed his ascent. Loutek hadn't been particularly fond of this assignment at the outset, and his disenchantment was growing by the minute.

First off, he didn't relish the idea of hunting children, particularly human children. There was no honor in it, no challenge.

Second, he hated the place itself. And not just the fact that the sun seemed to be in his face everywhere he went, sending probes of pain into his eyes. Much worse was the air, which, as cold as it was, seemed to suck the moisture out of his very pores.

Coughing for what seemed like the hundredth time, he hawked and spat. And then regretted it, for it only made his throat that much drier and scratchier.

Give me the homeworld any day, he mused. Give me the warmth and the mists and the towering trees for shade. Give me a place where a warrior can *breathe*.

Abruptly, a handful of pebbles came loose underfoot, sending him sliding a meter or so back down the escarpment. Loutek cursed, then trudged up again. It was as if the environment itself were conspiring to prolong this ridiculous search.

Moments later, more careful of his footing now, he came to the top of the slope. The glare of the sun made it difficult to tell at first what was up ahead. Squinting, he finally made it out—not another slope but a deep basin, a valley. Like everything else here, it was reddish brown; not only the inclining walls that defined the place but also the boulders that jutted out of the ground at irregular intervals.

More important, from Loutek's point of view, was that one of the walls was dotted with a series of what looked like openings. Sizable openings. Caves, he mused. Natural hiding places. And shelter from the biting winds—something one would need in order to survive for long up here.

His pulse sped up a bit in anticipation. If the human children were where he thought they were, he would not only put an end to this distasteful task, he would also be commended by the captain. And commendations led to promotions.

Taking out his disruptor, he almost laughed. It was ludicrous to think that he would need it to overwhelm a pack of human brats.

On the other hand, why make things difficult for himself? One glimpse of the disruptor would put to rest any hopes they might have of running away. Better to strike fear into them immediately than to actually have to use the damned thing later on.

Crouching low to minimize his chances of being seen, the Klingon picked out a line of approach. If he descended into the valley on the same side as the caves, the only way they could spot him would be if they had posted a lookout. And though there was no way of knowing if they had done that yet, since the darkness at the cave mouths was impenetrable, Loutek rather doubted it.

Klingon children would have done it, but Klingons knew a lot more about hunting and being hunted. The game of predator and prey was second nature to them.

Loutek made his way into the basin. Ignoring the cold and the blinding white sun, he kept as far to the right as he could, diverging from that plan only when he came across a boulder too big and smooth to climb over.

No sign of movement in the caves. No sounds. So they hadn't spotted him yet.

Of course, the caves could have been empty. There was always that possibility. But he didn't believe it. Being upwind, and probably not close enough to smell anything anyway, he couldn't be certain, yet his every instinct told him that there was someone hiding in those pockets of darkness.

He crept a little closer. Still no indication that he'd been seen. He grunted in disgust. Why didn't humans train their young to protect themselves? Did they expect the galaxy to be that benevolent to them?

Closer still. The Klingon negotiated the largest boulder he'd come to yet, then a smaller one. He had to concentrate on being quiet now, on not dislodging anything that might roll down the hill and give him away.

Step by careful step, he narrowed the gap. The ground cooperated, throwing no surprises in his path. The whole effort was going very smoothly, he thought, very efficiently. And why not? He was Klingon, wasn't he? And not just Klingon but Gevish'rae.

Suddenly, even before he himself knew why, Loutek whirled and pointed his disruptor at a point directly behind him—a place where the big, empty basin met the cavernous blue sky.

There was nothing there. Nothing and no one. He scowled, casting a careful eye over the entire perimeter of the valley. Still nothing. His scowl deepened as he let the barrel of his disruptor drop to his side.

Klingons were taught to trust their instincts, their reflexes. But this time, he thought, his instincts had led him astray.

There was no one around here except for Loutek himself and the human children he was stalking. The other Federation intruders were all under guard back in their colony buildings. And there was no animal life on this world.

Therefore, no threats. Which meant his mind was playing tricks on him.

And small wonder, now that he thought about it. The way his head hurt from that piercing sunlight, it was no surprise his senses were a little muddled.

Turning back toward the cave, he gauged the distance he still had to cover. Less than a dozen meters, he judged. A matter of moments before he found what he was looking for. Working his way around one last boulder, Loutek approached the cave from an angle that would let him drop in front of it from above. There were still no sounds from within, but he didn't let that bother him.

If the cave was empty, which he doubted, he'd have lost nothing by his efforts. And if it was full of children, his discipline would be rewarded.

He just wished it weren't so dry out here. He wished this hunt were over already, so he could return to the *Kad'nra* and breathe again without abrading the inside of his throat.

A few more steps, and a few more beyond that, and Loutek was almost there. He avoided a spot where the dirt looked looser than elsewhere, moving a little farther upslope to find better footing. Then, having circumvented the problem area, he descended again.

Tightening his grip on his disruptor in anticipation, the Klingon crouched and laid his other hand on the ground to steady himself. He didn't want any slipups now, not after he'd made such a flawless approach.

Creeping forward, and forward again, he at last reached his destination, a small ledge directly above the first cave. Gathering himself, he dropped and twisted, training his weapon on the darkness within.

He had expected a cry of some sort, maybe an attempt to scurry past him. Neither of those possibilities materialized. In fact, there was no indication at all that the damned thing was occupied—just a cold breath of air that greedily lapped up the sweat on his feverish brow.

Of course, the humans could have been sleeping in

the cave's recesses. In that case, they wouldn't have noticed him yet. The problem was, he couldn't be sure. After the blinding light of the sun, the interior of the place looked pitch black to him. Impenetrable. It would take a few moments for his eyes to adjust.

Squinting, concentrating, he waited. The seconds passed. Kahless it was cold out here. By comparison, the air in the cave had to feel balmy. Surely it wouldn't hurt to take a couple of steps inside. To get out of this hell of wind and brazen sunlight and into someplace more comfortable, if only for a moment.

Careful to stay alert, Loutek advanced into the darkness. His eyes had acclimated enough for him to make out vague shapes, though none of them were moving. Keeping his disruptor pointed at them, he advanced a little farther.

The shapes still didn't move, not even with the gentle rise and fall of the chest area that usually denoted sleep. Coming closer, he saw why.

They weren't living beings. They were just rocks, situated in such a way as to give the impression of head and torso, arms and legs.

He grunted softly. Funny how much the pile of rocks had resembled humans. He nudged one of the smaller ones with his booted foot, watched it teeter and roll away from its companions.

Funny indeed. Scanning the rest of the cave, Loutek found nothing else of even passing interest. Obviously, the children were in the other caverns, if they were here at all. The only way to know was to check. But he didn't move right away. He lingered, allowing the relative warmth of the cave to leech some of the stiffness from his tired muscles.

The Klingon grinned. It even felt easier to breathe

in here, though there was probably no more moisture in the cave than anywhere else. If he closed his eyes, he could almost imagine being back on the homeworld, in his family's tiny water garden. It occurred to him how pleasant it would be to take off his boots and his heavy, leather body armor and drop into a scented pool for a while.

But duty called. Suppressing a growl, Loutek turned to the cave opening, where the blazing light had become more blinding than ever. His eyes felt as if they'd been stabbed; he had to look away.

He realized then that he would have to make the transition from light to darkness over and over again with each cave search—a tedious process at best, and at worst a painful one.

Unfortunately, the only alternative—to shut his eyes as he went from cave to cave—was impractical. He could just imagine one of the others, or even Gidris himself, coming upon him as he groped his way from one place to the next like a blind man.

Again, he spat—and again he regretted it. What a loathsome assignment this was. A loathsome assignment and a loathsome world.

Crossing back to the cave mouth, Loutek stood and stared out at the terrain. He couldn't discern a thing. It was a curtain of fire, a—

Suddenly a red ball of agony exploded in Loutek's temple. He dropped to one knee.

A moment later, a second ball of pain exploded in the back of his neck. The Klingon flung up his hands to protect himself, angry and confused and at least a little fearful of what was happening to him. Something big and heavy hit his right hand—the one that held the disruptor—but he hung on to the weapon anyway.

He had to see, he told himself. He had to see who was attacking him.

Squinting into the brazen glare, through the blood that was running down his brow and into his eyes, he made out a number of small forms swarming about him like carrion creatures around a carcass. Pointing his disruptor at the nearest of them, he started to depress the trigger.

That's when he felt something on his shoulder—and whirled to look up at a form larger than any of the others. He barely had time to make out the features of a Vulcan before the darkness closed in all around him.

177

Chapter Thirteen

As SPOCK'S FINGERS probed the bundle of nerves at the juncture of neck and shoulder, the Klingon went limp in his grasp. Letting go, he watched the inert body slump the rest of the way to the ground.

There was blood on the Klingon's face, the result of a head wound, which may have been a factor in the ease with which Spock snuck up on him. However, it wasn't until Spock took stock of the children who stood around him—three boys and two girls, their clothing covered with red dirt, each armed with a rather substantial-looking rock—that he put all the pieces together.

"This was a trap," he concluded.

There was a distinct note of surprise in his voice, perhaps even admiration. He immediately regretted the untoward display of emotion.

One of the boys, a child with black hair and narrow features, nodded eagerly. "Yessir," he said, spitting the word out so quickly that Spock could barely understand it. "We spotted the Klingon coming a long way off, so we were ready for him. We got ourselves all dirty and hid in the last cave 'cause we knew he'd try the biggest one first, and when he went in we came out with our rocks and waited for him, and—"

Spock held up a hand. "You need not explain further. I believe I understand the nature of your stratagem."

The boy stopped, though he seemed disappointed. Spock was sorry for that, but there were more important matters to be dealt with right now.

Despite everything, the Klingon hadn't dropped his weapon. Lowering himself into a squat, Spock wrested the disruptor from his adversary's fingers and tucked it into the sample pouch he wore slung over one shoulder. Then, slipping his hands beneath the Klingon's armpits, he drew him up almost to a standing position. Finally, Spock lifted one of the man's arms and draped it over his shoulder.

"What are you doing?" asked the darker of the two girls.

"I am concealing him from view," the Vulcan answered. "In fact, it would be a good idea for us *all* to conceal ourselves from view. At some point, perhaps very soon, this one's presence will be missed and his comrades will initiate a search for him."

A boy with blond hair nodded. He turned to the others. "Come on. Let's pick up our rocks and bring them back inside the cave."

Spock noted the boy's alertness. At least a couple of the stones had blood on them; that clue alone would have been enough to give them away to any Klingon who came to investigate.

What's more, no one hesitated to follow his direction. Obviously, he was their leader, maybe the one who'd come up with the idea to turn the tables on the Klingon.

The Vulcan watched for a moment to see which of the openings the children used as they hid their missiles. As it turned out, it was the cavern just beyond the one the Klingon had entered. Apparently, that was also the egress from which the children had issued as they pelted their victim.

Following them in, Spock headed for the back of the cave, where the slanting ceiling and the dirt floor converged. Kneeling, he deposited his burden there and checked the Klingon's pulse.

Still strong. Despite his wound, he was in no danger.

On the other hand, he wasn't about to wake up for a while. The nerve pinch usually left its victims unconscious for three or four hours.

Spock checked the Klingon's belt for food. Usually, Klingon warriors carried a small amount of it with them out in the field. He wasn't disappointed. A pouch held a number of heavy, brown grain pellets. Not esthetically appealing, but they would have to do.

Extracting the pellets, he joined the children, who had already begun to sit down in a circle nearer the front of the cave. They looked at the alien fare greedily—five hungry faces that seemed much too young to be battling Klingons.

The first officer distributed the grain pellets and watched the children wolf them down. He kept none for himself.

But the blond boy handed half his allotment back. "You have to eat, too," he said.

Spock shook his head. "My needs are different," he explained, which was accurate, if only in the strictest sense.

The child had probably never met a Vulcan before, nor did he have any reason not to believe Spock. Shrugging, he gobbled down the remainder of his pellets.

"You have not had access to food in some time," the Vulcan observed.

"We had some snacks with us," explained the third boy, who had red hair and freckles. "We took 'em whenever we went up into the——" He looked around at the others, then amended his comment. "Whenever we went up to the playground. But the snacks ran out, and it's been pretty hungry here ever since."

The boy with black hair leaned forward. "What's going on back at the colony?" he asked. He swallowed but maintained his composure for the most part. "How are our parents?"

Spock wished he could give him an answer. "I know very little more than you do," he replied. "I left the installation shortly after the Klingons arrived."

One of the girls, a slight youngster with pale skin and delicate features, started to pose her own question. But she must have thought better of it, because she closed her mouth and looked at the ground.

Seated next to her, the other girl asked: "Did you see them kill anybody?" Her gaze was steady, but there was no concealing the trepidation in it.

The Vulcan shook his head. "I did not. Nor do Klingons generally kill unless they must; they are not as bloodthirsty as some would have us believe." He sighed, ever so slightly. This was not a subject he enjoyed discussing with children. Nonetheless, they deserved the truth. "However, I cannot rule out the possibility of fatalities."

The youngsters looked at one another. Some were better at concealing their fears than others. The blond boy seemed to be the best of all. There was something about him that Spock found familiar—something, perhaps, in the way he held himself, or in the way his eyes narrowed as he listened. The Vulcan just couldn't put his finger on it, and the mask of grime on his face didn't make his effort any easier.

The boy spoke up. "Why are the Klingons here, anyway? What are they after?"

"This world is not all that distant from the recognized boundaries of the Klingon empire. It is possible that they are merely asserting their right to it." Spock paused. "However, it is far more likely that they have received intelligence about the nature of the colony's work, and wish to seize whatever new technologies have been developed."

The youngster grunted. "That makes sense."

"What does *not* make sense," Spock told him, "is your assault on the Klingon who was pursuing you."

The children looked at him as if he'd just told them he was a Klingon himself. Perhaps he had been too abrupt in changing topics; that was still an area of human conversation in which he was less than adept, despite the practice his mother had provided during his childhood.

"But we *got* him," the red-haired youth protested. "We had him right where we wanted him."

"Perhaps," the Vulcan replied. "There is no way of knowing what might have transpired if I had not intervened."

"We'll do it again, this time without any help," the dark-haired boy suggested. "And you'll see how easy it is."

Spock shook his head. "I cannot allow a repeat of the maneuver. It is too dangerous. Even the slightest miscalculation could mean your deaths."

They looked at him with hard eyes in hard faces. "Our parents are fighting for their lives," the black girl reminded him. "If it means helping them, why shouldn't we do the same thing?"

"I am certain," the Vulcan said, "that your parents would prefer you to remain safe—to retreat into the hills as far as you possibly can, and to stay there until help arrives."

"And what about you?" asked the blond boy, the leader. "What are *you* going to do?"

It was the one question Spock wasn't prepared to answer. "I do not know yet," he said.

"You're going to try to help the people back in the colony," the dark-haired boy accused, more certain of it than the Vulcan himself was.

"If circumstances allow," Spock agreed, "I will make an attempt to do so."

"And won't your chances be better," the blond one suggested, "if you get some help?"

It was almost logical. The Vulcan gave the youngster credit.

"My chances of helping your parents will be greater, yes. But my chances of losing you will also be greater. It will be a trade-off."

The boy shook his head. "We're not just going to run away and hide." He licked his lips. "We've proven we can help, and we're going to—with you or without you."

Spock cocked an eyebrow. The child had the kind of courage one didn't find too often, even in adults. What's more, he seemed to be an inspiration to the others. The Vulcan sighed. Apparently, he had little choice in the matter. If the children could not be convinced to retreat to a safer place, he would have to protect them. And the only way to do that was to join forces with them.

It was not a situation he found appealing. However, the alternative—letting them brave the danger on their own—was even *less* so.

"All right," he said. "We will work together. However, you must follow my directions. If we are to lay traps for our pursuers, they must be more efficient than the one that caught *him*." He tilted his head to indicate the Klingon who lay unconscious in the back of the cave.

The children looked at one another. The black girl nodded.

The blond boy turned back to Spock. "You've got a deal," he said.

It was settled. "I will need to know your names," the Vulcan told them. "Mine is—"

"Mr. Spock," the blond one said, perhaps a little too quickly. And then, realizing his error, added, "I know."

"And yours?" the Vulcan asked.

For the first time, the youth seemed reticent. Finally, he said, "David."

"I'm Pfeffer," the redhead chimed in.

"Garcia," offered the dark-haired boy.

"Medford." That came from the black girl.

Finally, "Wan."

Spock couldn't help but notice that they all used their last names. All except David. He was the only one who'd given the Vulcan his first name. And reluctantly, at that. Spock filed the fact away for future consideration.

As Kruge eyed the human called Boudreau, the man shook his head. He seemed sincerely puzzled. "I don't understand. I thought I'd explained this already to Mallot."

The Klingon scowled. He laid the blunt tip of his long, thick finger on the colony administrator's chest and pressed against the bone. "You may have explained it to Mallot, human, but you have not explained it to *me.*"

They were standing outside the dome in a cold wind. Though the Klingon was hardly dressed for the weather, he didn't feel any discomfort. He was distracted by his thirst for knowledge.

If G-7 was truly a weapon, he needed to know more about it. And he wanted to hear about it from the man who had developed it—not from Mallot, who, being a Klingon, would almost certainly have his own ambitious agenda.

"Very well," said Boudreau. "What is it you wish to know, exactly?" His expression changed. "Maybe you should tell me what you know already, and I can go on from there."

Kruge couldn't see anything wrong with that approach. "I know," he began, "that a pack of your children are missing. A child named Riordan told us as much."

He looked for another shift in expression and was

rewarded. Obviously, Boudreau had known about the children. And now he knew that the Klingons knew as well.

The second officer went on. "I know that these children have stolen the G-Seven unit, which was at the heart of your installation. And I know that the G-Seven device is a weapon of considerable might, which you do not wish to fall into the hands of your enemies."

A strange thing happened then. It seemed to Kruge that the human almost smiled. Then the Klingon figured it out: the smile was feigned. *To throw me off the track.*

He glared at Boudreau. "Now it's your turn to educate me."

The human looked at him. "What is your name?" he asked.

That took the Klingon by surprise. "Kruge," he snarled. "Why do you ask?"

The prisoner shrugged. "I just wanted to know the name of the man who is going to kill me."

Kruge could feel his black eyes narrowing, bringing his brow down lower. "And why do you think I will kill you?" he asked.

"Because I'm about to tell you that what you believe is a lie—or really, a number of lies. And I don't expect you will like that very much."

The Klingon's lip curled. "Try me," he said.

"All right," Boudreau replied. "To begin with, there are no children in the colony besides Tim Riordan, no matter what he told you. No doubt he lied because he was scared. And frankly, I can't blame him for that."

Kruge looked at him askance. "No children? How can that be? Our sensors picked them up."

The human seemed to hesitate, or was it the Klingon's imagination? Then he said, "They're only echoes. Ghosts. At least, those are some of the things *we* call them when they foul up our ships' sensor readings."

"Ghosts?" the Klingon repeated. "You mean sensor artifacts?"

"That's right—artifacts. Things that appear to be there but aren't. It has something to do with magnetic field anomalies. So you can look high and low for those children you recorded, and you'll never find them."

Kruge pondered that. "Then who took the G-Seven unit?"

"That," said the terraformer, "I don't know. Who's missing?"

The Klingon frowned. "Besides the children—the ones you say aren't there—no one. Everyone is accounted for, except the Riordan whelp." He licked his lips. "Perhaps the boy was lying all along. Perhaps he hid the device himself." He could feel himself growing angry just contemplating the possibility.

"I don't think so," the human said. "You've seen him. Does he seem like the sort of child who would risk his life to keep that unit from you?"

Kruge frowned again. "Admittedly, he does not. Then who?"

"Unfortunately," Boudreau told him, "I can't help you there. But I can tell you this: I wouldn't be too concerned about the G-Seven. It's hardly what I'd call a weapon, or even the basis for one."

Kruge was unconvinced. What kind of fool did the human take him for? Did he think the Klingon would simply accept his word at face value? "Then why has it been stolen—and at great risk?"

The human shrugged a second time. "Again, I don't know for certain. But if I were to venture a guess, I'd say it was to prevent you from developing a countercapability. After all, we will eventually bring along our terraforming technology to the point where we can alter an entire planet. I wouldn't put it past the Klingon Empire to try to undo our alterations, just to keep the Federation from expanding its sphere of influence."

Kruge thrust out his chin. "That is not the Klingon way; at least, it is not the Gevish'rae way." But the Kamorh'dag? He would have to speak to Vheled of this—it almost seemed like something they might try.

Kruge spat on the ground, to show what he thought of the option Boudreau had described. "If we wished to remove the Federation from a world, we would do so. Nor would its environment make it any more or less difficult for us."

"To be honest," Boudreau told him, "that comes as a surprise to me. More to the point, I think it would come as a surprise to the person who took the G-Seven unit." He shrugged. "So you see, it doesn't really matter what you would have done with the G-Seven. What matters is what our thief *thought* you would have done."

Kruge pondered the administrator's words. After a moment or two, he decided they were worthy of further scrutiny. He grunted. "You will return to your dome now."

Boudreau nodded. "As you wish," he said.

Chapter Fourteen

THIS TIME, when they visited the sacred precincts of the Obirrhat, no one even glanced in their direction.

It was more than a little strange, after the hostility they'd encountered only the day before. Almost like being invisible, the captain mused.

He made a mental note to describe the experience to Bones. After all, it was the doctor who had equipped them with facial prosthetics and subdermal dyes and optical overlays designed to make them look like Malurians.

Then it had just been a matter of having ship's stores whip up some garments, the loose-fitting variety favored by the Obirrhat, and voilà! Two denizens of the sacred precinct.

Now the only question was how long the prosthetics would last before the itching forced him to rip them off his face. Why couldn't the Malurians have had features a little easier to wear?

"How's yours feel?" Kirk asked his companion.

Scotty grunted. "Like I've got my face caught in a vise. If I'd known it was goin' to be this uncomfortable—"

The captain darted a look at him. "You'd have done it anyway." His facial muscles started to form a smile, but the prosthetics inhibited it.

The engineer shrugged. "Aye, I suppose ye're right."

Kirk pointed to the open-air market they had glimpsed during their official visit. The crowd wasn't as thick as before; some of the merchants were even starting to pack up their wares. But then, it was almost dusk, and the market evidently didn't stay open at night.

"Looks like as good a place to start as any," he said.

Scotty nodded. "After you, sir."

The Scots accent and the Malurian visage seemed wildly at odds with one another. But then, neither one of them would pass for a native if they had to talk much. They would be wise to restrict any conversation with true Malurians to as few words as possible.

As they approached the market square, the captain scanned the individual stalls. Some offered fresh vegetables. Others displayed long, ornate robes of a vaguely religious-looking nature, and still others showed metal or ceramic cookware. If there was a statue near a booth, and it still had a limb or two, it was used as a display fixture for the merchant's wares.

It smelled different here than in the other parts of the precinct. In a moment, Kirk saw why. One corner of the plaza was piled high with overflowing containers of garbage, and some of it looked ripe enough to have been around when the buildings' foundations were laid.

Personally, the captain mused, I think the cubaya would have liked it around here. Plenty to eat. But then, what do I know? I'm just an ignorant offworlder.

Feeling a tug on his sleeve, he turned to Scotty. The engineer pointed to a spot about midway across the far side of the marketplace.

There was an open doorway there, with a number of Obirrhat standing just inside it. They all appeared to have mugs in their hands. As the humans watched, others came to patronize the place.

"I may nae know much," the engineer said softly, "but I can spot a drinking establishment a mile away."

Kirk grunted. "And information flows fast and loose where there's liquor to loosen the tongue."

Scotty looked at him, screwing up his Malurian brow in concentration. "James Joyce?"

The captain shook his head. "Montgomery Scott. Shore leave on Gamma Theridian Twelve. That little place by the river, with the pretty barmaids and the birds flying around in the rafters."

"Ah," said the Scotsman. "Right you are. I dinnae remember the quote, but I remember the barmaids just fine."

Somehow, Kirk didn't think this place would be quite as frivolous as the one on Gamma Theridian Twelve. But then, they weren't here for a vacation.

"Come on," he told his companion. "Let's see if we can't find a few loose tongues."

Crossing the plaza, they walked up to the open doorway as if they belonged there. Some of the Obirrhat stopped their conversations and glanced curiously at the newcomers as they entered, but no one challenged them.

Inside, they found much what they had expected—meager lighting, shadowy corners full of tables, and a steady, vaguely conspiratorial drone of voices. Much like any other public house the captain had visited.

However, there was one way in which this place was different. There was no bar. And for that matter, now that Kirk had a chance to think about it, no waiters, either.

Yet there were men with mugs in their hands. Obviously, they'd gotten them from somewhere.

"Captain . . ." Scotty murmured.

"I know," Kirk replied, careful to keep his voice down. "Where does a man get a drink around here?"

It was by no means a casual concern. Without mugs in their hands, they stuck out like two very sore thumbs—a condition hardly conducive to the clandestine gathering of information.

Some of those at the corner tables were starting to look at them—warily, the captain judged. Of course, it might have been his imagination, but if they stood there much longer, trying to figure out what to do next, *everyone* would be staring.

Kirk was on the verge of making a quick exit when a youngster seemed to pop up from out of nowhere. He held his hand out palm up and peered at the captain.

The captain peered back. "Yes?" he prompted.

The boy's skin twitched between his cheeks and his jawline. "Don't you want a drink?" he asked.

Damn, Kirk thought. So that's how it works.

"I very definitely want a drink," the captain said. "And one for my friend here as well."

"Of course," the youngster responded. "I'll get one from Phatharas—he never waters them down." But he didn't move yet; he just looked meaningfully at his open palm.

Taking the hint, Kirk reached into the pocket of his tunic and withdrew a couple of pieces of Malurian currency. While much of the planet's economy operated through electronic funds transfer, a primitive system in and of itself, those in the environs of the capital employed an even more ancient method of wealth transfer—metal coins, like those used centuries earlier on Earth.

Fortunately, coins such as that were easy to replicate. The captain handed over the ones he'd been carrying, hoping that they'd be about the right amount. He gathered from the way the boy's eyes lit up that he'd paid more than he had to, but not so much as to arouse suspicion.

"Be quick," he told the youngster, "and the rest is for you." He said it as if a big tip had been his intention all along.

Nodding eagerly, the boy took off. Kirk watched him go out the door, and wondered fleetingly if he'd just been had by a junior-grade con man. After all, he had no guarantee that his emissary would return.

Then again, others had viewed the transaction, and no one had seemed to think it was unusual. Taking Scotty by the arm, the captain indicated an unoccupied table in the darkest of the place's four corners.

The Obirrhat at the neighboring tables scrutinized them as they went by, hardly bothering to conceal their interest. Still, as at the door, no one stopped them or questioned their reason for being here, despite the fact that they were obviously strangers. In a close-knit community like this one, that fact wouldn't go unnoticed for very long.

They sat. And a moment later, much more quickly than Kirk had expected, the boy returned with a tray. There were two mugs on it, which he balanced easily.

Looking around, he spotted his clients in their new location and brought their order over. Lowering his tray onto their table, he removed the mugs from it and set them down before the captain and Scotty. Then, with a glance—perhaps by way of thanks, perhaps to see if they wanted anything more—he departed.

Raising his mug, the captain sampled its contents. The liquid within was milky, spicy, and quite cold—a strange combination, but in this case a pleasant one. And if there was alcohol or any other stimulant in the mixture, he couldn't detect it.

"Not bad," he remarked to Scotty.

The chief engineer shrugged. "It could use a little sprucin' up, if ye know what I mean."

Once again, Kirk was tempted to smile. And once again, his prosthesis prevented it.

For a little while, they sat there, nursing their drinks, while the captain tried to think of the best way for them to start a dialogue with some Obirrhat. Finally, unable to come up with anything particularly clever or original, he opted for the direct approach.

Turning to one of the patrons at the next table, he engaged the man's eyes. The fellow raised his mug a couple of inches in response.

"Good day," Kirk suggested, raising his own mug.

"There've been worse," the Obirrhat agreed. "On the other hand, there've been better."

Among the common people, unlike in the Hall of Government, there were none of those fingers-to-temple gestures Farquhar was so fond of; Kirk knew that from his mission briefing tapes.

"You're new here," the Obirrhat observed.

The captain nodded. "Visiting, actually."

"Hell of a time to visit, what with all the trouble that's going on."

"Actually," Kirk replied, "it's the trouble that's prompted the visit."

That piqued the man's interest. "Oh? Got family here you're worried about?"

The captain paused a moment, as if reflecting. "In a sense," he said at last. "I mean, we're all brothers here, aren't we, when you come right down to it?"

It was plain that the fellow caught his drift. He nodded. "That's the way I feel." He indicated the pair seated across from him. "In fact, that's how we all feel."

Kirk turned to Scotty. "You see? I told you we'd find a good reception in this place."

The engineering chief grunted approvingly. "I never had any doubt of it. After all, this is the sacred precinct. If ye canna find solidarity here in these tryin' times, where can ye find it?"

Their newfound friend sighed aloud. "Times are trying, all right. Just yesterday, the damned Manteil marched a procession of offworlders through the precinct—along with a couple of armed guards. It was a slap in the face, I tell you—a reminder of how little they respect us."

One of his companions chuckled. "True. But we taught them they couldn't do that kind of thing. A couple of our boys came out shooting—even took one of the guards down."

The first Obirrhat made a gesture of dismissal. "That was nothing to be proud of. We lost two to their one, and they weren't much older than the mug-

195

runner who got you your drinks. I count it more of a pity than anything else."

Kirk frowned in sympathy, nor was it entirely an act. He'd hated to see those Obirrhat youths cut down as much as anyone else.

"At least we showed them," the second man piped up. "At least we didn't let it go unnoticed, like we've done in the past."

The first Obirrhat dismissed that idea as well. "So what? Are they going to stop treating us like something less than men? Are they going to cease their abuse of the sacred ground?"

The third man at their table, who had been silent up until now, spoke up. "They'll never stop that. Not unless we *make* them."

"Granted," the first Obirrhat replied. "But there's time enough for that." His eyes momentarily lost their focus. "And no need to lose young lives in the process." As he emerged from his brief reverie, he turned to the captain and Scotty again. "But then, you didn't come here to listen to us argue, did you?"

Kirk shook his head. "With all due respect, no. One can hear the same arguments wherever there are Obirrhat, I think." He looked around, as if leery of spies. "Though there are some in the precinct I'd give much to listen to."

All three of his listeners nodded gravely. "I believe I know who you mean," the first man said.

"Do you know where we might find them?" Mister Scott asked.

The question met with a mixed reaction. It seemed to Kirk the men knew, but were reluctant to give away such important information.

On the other hand, he and Scotty were passing

themselves off as representatives of another region. And communication among the various Obirrhat communities was essential if they were to stand up to the Manteil.

In the end, opportunism won out over caution. "If you like," the third Obirrhat offered, "we can take you to them."

"We would like that very much," the captain told them. "In fact, the sooner the better."

The Obirrhat exchanged glances. "Why not now?" the second one said.

They reached an unspoken consensus. Almost at the same instant, they raised their mugs and drained them. Kirk and Scotty did the same. With all the spice in their drinks, it wasn't easy, but they managed.

"Come," said the first Obirrhat, and made his way toward the door through the growing crowd. The disguised humans followed, and the other two Obirrhat brought up the rear.

Outside, it was full sunset. The sky in the east was a riot of golds and greens, and the dying light was reflected on the ancient walls of the market square. It gave the place an ethereal quality that was almost startling and hard to reconcile with its very earthly appearance during the day.

The third Obirrhat, the taciturn one, must have seen the look in the captain's eye. "Beautiful," he said, "is it not?"

Kirk nodded. "Indeed."

"It's the first time you've seen it?"

"The first time," the captain echoed.

"In that case," the Obirrhat remarked sincerely, "I envy you a great deal."

They crossed the plaza, with its tables and booths

now empty of merchants, retracing some of the steps Kirk and Scotty had taken just minutes earlier. However, instead of heading for the broad thoroughfare, the Obirrhat led them to another exit, the narrowest street they'd seen yet. Truth to tell, it was little more than an alley.

As they entered the cool, deep-shadowed space between the buildings, the captain could see that the passage eventually terminated in a cul-de-sac. So their destination had to be somewhere before that point— one of the various doors that opened on the alley— though none of them looked particularly auspicious.

Of course, that would be the whole point—to look inauspicious. If you're hiding something or someone you don't do it in a place that draws attention to itself.

About halfway to the dead end, the second Obirrhat turned to Scotty. "Where did you say you were from again?" he asked.

"We didn't say," the engineer told him. "But as it happens, we're from Torril."

The man nodded. "Never been there myself," he commented. "Nice place?"

"The nicest," Scotty answered.

Good going, Kirk thought. Very smooth.

Naturally, they'd done some research on the geography of the region and picked a likely town as their point of origin. But not truly being natives, they had to avoid in-depth conversations about the place.

As it happened, the second Obirrhat didn't have a chance to inquire further, because the first one stopped and knocked sharply on a small, wooden door. There was a distinct pattern to the knock, too—two raps close together, followed after a second or two by another, and finally three more in succession.

The door opened. A pair of silvery eyes caught the light, flickering as they glanced from one caller to the next.

"It's all right," the second Obirrhat said. "They're friends from Torril come to have a word with us."

The sentinel grunted, turned to others deeper within, and barked something the captain couldn't quite make out. Then he gestured for them to come inside.

They entered, moving slowly because it was difficult to see—and even more so after the door closed behind the last of them, cutting off the light filtering in from the alley. Reaching out instinctively, Kirk felt a wall and followed it.

They continued that way for what seemed like a long time, considering how small the precinct buildings looked from the outside. The captain used the time to think about what he was going to say to Menikki and Omalas, who might not give them a whole lot of time to communicate once they learned whom they'd invited into their hiding place.

He was still mulling over his choice of words when a small flare of blue light erupted off to his right. A moment later, a second flare erupted on his left. Even before his eyes adjusted to the illumination, the captain could see that whatever corridor they'd been traveling had opened into a large room. It was full of Obirrhat—perhaps a dozen of them, not counting the ones he and Scotty had come in with. In fact, the newcomers were surrounded by them.

The second Obirrhat stepped forward and indicated his companions with a sweep of his arm. "A

Michael Jan Friedman

couple of visitors," he said, "from Torril, come to confer with our leaders."

One of the others in the room eyed them in the glimmering light. "How interesting," he remarked. He looked at Kirk. "I am from Torril. And I've never seen you before in my life."

The captain cursed inwardly. They hadn't taken into account the possibility that delegations from other cities might have begun to arrive already in the precinct—though in retrospect, it seemed a rather large oversight.

A moment later, Scotty paid for their mistake. One of the Obirrhat behind him delivered a crushing blow to the back of his head, driving him to his knees. As the engineer crumpled, Kirk whirled, expecting more of the same.

His expectation was on the money. Moving to his right, he eluded the rock-wielding fist that would have laid him out alongside Scotty. Then, gripping his attacker's wrist with both hands, he pivoted, dropped to one knee, and flung the man over his shoulder.

Screaming at the pain of his broken wrist, the Obirrhat hurtled into two of his onrushing compatriots. Hoping to take advantage of the confusion, the captain went for his unconscious engineer, aiming to scoop him up in his arms and make for the exit.

Unfortunately, it didn't work out that way. Though he managed to reach Scotty without anyone intervening, he'd barely lifted him off the ground before something hit him hard in the side of the head.

His last thought, before he lost consciousness, was that all McCoy's hard work had been for nothing.

Chapter Fifteen

"THEY DID WHAT?" blurted Farquhar, standing at the other end of the doctor's office in sickbay.

McCoy scowled, hating the idea of having to spill the beans—though it didn't seem as if he had much of a choice. "They went back to the precinct."

"Back to the—" The ambassador sputtered. "By themselves?"

McCoy nodded reluctantly.

"Were they out of their minds?" Farquhar raved. "The last time we were in the precinct, we were almost killed." He held out his hands, as if he expected an explanation to drop into them. "What in blazes were they thinking?"

McCoy shrugged. "Probably that they'd be able to end this conflict sooner if they had some input from the Obirrhat side."

"Wait a minute," the ambassador said. "They went to meet with the Obirrhat? Just like that?"

"No, not just like *that*," the doctor told him. "They took some precautions first, of course."

"Precautions? What kind of precautions could keep them safe from a pack of bloodthirsty rebels?"

It sounded like Farquhar's objectivity was starting to slip, Bones noted. But then, getting stoned within an inch of his life will do that to a man.

"Precautions," he repeated. "Like some minor facial surgery to make them look like Malurians."

The ambassador looked at him, amazed. "You performed surgery on them?"

McCoy felt himself getting angry. "Damn it, it was the only way to give them a shot at finding Menikki and Omalas. I figured—"

"So it was *your* idea."

"*Yes*, it was my blasted idea. They needed to get close to the missing ministers. This was a way to do that."

There was silence for a moment. "But now you're worried," said Farquhar.

"You think I'd be telling you all this if I weren't?" McCoy harrumphed. "They were supposed to have been back by now. Something's happened to them. I can feel it in my bones."

"And what would you have me do about it?" the ambassador asked, smiling suddenly. "Tell the council?"

The doctor nodded. "That's exactly right. The council may be the only hope they've got right now."

Farquhar looked at him as if he were crazy. "I meant that as a joke. If the council were to send a squad into the precinct right now, it might destroy what little chance for peace still exists."

"And if they don't," said McCoy, "the captain and Scotty may be goners."

The ambassador shook his head. "No. That's not how it works, Doctor. We can't risk the lives of thousands, maybe millions, to save a couple of foolhardy Starfleet adventurers."

Bones advanced on Farquhar. "Those foolhardy adventurers saved your bacon not so long ago," he rasped. "You can't just write them off like that!"

"*I* wasn't the one who told them to go back to the precinct," the ambassador shot back. "*I* wasn't the one who suggested they risk their lives!"

That stung. For a moment, the doctor thought he was going to slug the other man. Judging by the expression on Farquhar's face, he thought so too.

But in the end, McCoy didn't do any such thing. Because as much as he hated the idea, he knew that the ambassador was right.

"You win," he muttered, turning his back on Farquhar.

"I . . . win?" the ambassador repeated. He sounded incredulous.

"Yes, damn it. You win. We won't go to the council." He grunted helplessly. "We'll just keep our fingers crossed and hope that Jim and Scotty come out of this alive."

For a little while, neither man spoke. Finally, it was Farquhar who broke the silence. "Jim? You call your captain by his first name?"

The doctor looked back at him over his shoulder. "Is there anything wrong with that?" he asked.

The ambassador shrugged. "No, nothing. It's just that . . ." He shrugged again. "I just didn't think it was done. Protocol and all that."

"You know," McCoy said, "there's more to life—and diplomacy—than protocol, Ambassador."

For the first time since they met, McCoy had the feeling that Farquhar was listening to him, *really* listening to him. Then the old stiffness came back into the man's spine and he tugged down on his tunic.

"I'm going to beam down alone," Farquhar told him. "If the ministers ask, I'll say that the captain and his people were required on the ship. To . . . to address some sort of technical problem."

"Fine." The doctor didn't care a whole lot what excuse the ambassador gave the council. He was too preoccupied with thinking of another way to help his friends.

"Dr. McCoy?"

"Mm?"

"I just want you to know that I'm concerned about them as well." He bit his lip. "Captain Kirk and Mr. Scott are brave men. If there's any justice, they'll come back safe and sound."

Bones glanced at him, more than a little surprised. "Thanks," he said.

Farquhar cleared his throat. "You're welcome." Then he turned and exited the doctor's office.

"What kind of trap are you making, Mr. Spock?" It was Garcia who'd asked.

The first officer replied succinctly. "An efficient one."

Under Spock's painstaking guidance, the disruptor's pale blue beam cut a precise and continuous path through the vein of foliated rock—not unlike shale or schist on Earth—that was part of the hillside. Fortunately, this form of mineral accretion was plentiful in this region.

The Vulcan tried to concentrate on his work and not to dwell too much on the number of Klingons he and the children had sighted in the last few hours. Obviously, the net was tightening around them; every moment they spent out here in the open was a flirtation with disaster.

The children, on the other hand, showed no sign of concern. They stood at a safe distance and looked on, their faces dyed a pale blue by the glare of the disruptor beam.

It would not do, he realized, to let them see apprehension either in his expression or in the curtness of his answers. They took their cue from him, and panic was the last thing they needed.

Far better, under the circumstances, to let them in on what he was doing step by step, as if he were a teacher, and they his students. *Yes,* he thought. *That is the approach I must take.*

Unfortunately, while he often held informal seminars on various subjects for new additions to the science section, the first officer had no experience with a group this young. He could only hope that his illustrations were understandable to them.

"On Vulcan," he explained, "there is a predator called a le-matya. It lives in the hills. But in times of drought, when its natural prey becomes sparse, it grows bold and comes down to the plains to forage. Then traps must be set, or the le-matya will steal even household pets."

Pfeffer looked up at him. "You mean like dogs and cats? To eat them?"

Medford made a face. Obviously, the idea didn't appeal to her.

"Not dogs and cats," said Spock. "But their Vulcan equivalents. And yes—to eat them. That is how le-matyas live—by hunting for their food."

As the first officer continued to cut his way through the rock, finding the disruptor only slightly more awkward than a phaser, he recognized the smell of ozone—the same smell he'd encountered on Earth during summer storms. Interesting, he mused, despite all the other matters he had on his mind. The disruption process had some similarities to the application of simple static electricity.

The most important result, however, was that it worked. He would be finished in a matter of moments.

"Of course," he resumed, "on Vulcan, we have access to dead tree branches and leaves. Here we must be somewhat more innovative."

He turned momentarily from his labors to look again at his audience. The children were still watching with great interest.

Finally completing his task, he removed his finger from the weapon's firing pad. Instantly, the disruption barrage stopped.

Now came the difficult part, he thought, the part that required some finesse. He would have to separate the various laminate leaves of which the rock was constructed—originally, disparate materials that had been deposited by whatever forces shaped this planet millennia ago.

Kneeling, he sighted the disruptor along the fault lines of the top layer and the one directly beneath it. Then he depressed the firing pad again.

"When I am done," he announced, "you will be

able to pick up the pieces. That is how light they will be."

The beam lanced out and sliced the leaves apart, starting with the left-hand edge and working its way to the right. A few seconds later, the top laminate was free.

Terminating the beam, Spock stepped back to judge his handiwork. By that time, the children had already begun to approach the rock for a closer look.

Pfeffer looked up at the Vulcan. "Can we touch it? Is it hot?"

"You may indeed touch it," Spock assured him. "You may even lift it up."

The boy's eyes lit up with a mixture of awe and disbelief. Taking the edge of the laminate in his hands, he pulled at it experimentally.

It moved easily. More easily, in fact, than even the Vulcan had expected. Encouraged, Pfeffer pulled it off the rest of the rock.

"Careful," Spock warned. "It is brittle. And we do not want it to break. Not yet, at any rate. Ms. Medford, would you give Mr. Pfeffer some assistance?"

Complying eagerly, Medford picked up the other end of the leaf. Together, she and the red-haired boy carried it down to the strip of level ground at the convergence of this hillside and the next.

"Can I help carry the next one?" Wan asked.

"I see no reason why not," Spock replied. "For now, however, you must stand back again."

Wan, David, and Garcia did as they were told. Once they were safely out of the way, the Vulcan applied his disruptor beam to the separation of the next two leaves.

This time they didn't come apart as easily or as neatly as he'd wanted them to. But there was enough of the top layer left intact to serve their purpose. Wan and Garcia teamed up to carry it.

Only one more laminate was required. With great care, he went to work again, and this cut was the cleanest of all. Allowing the beam to lapse and activating the safety mechanism, he placed the disruptor back in his shoulder pouch.

And none too soon. The sun was dropping quickly in the west; soon it would be too dark to use the weapon without drawing a great deal of attention to themselves.

David looked up at him. Everyone else was at the bottom of the hill.

"Want a hand?" the boy offered, though not quite with the eagerness of the others.

"Please," Spock answered.

Together, they lifted the sheet of rock and brought it down to where the others were waiting for them. As the children watched, still hardly believing one could take apart a rock as if it were a sandwich, they set the laminate down near the others.

The Vulcan scanned the uneven terrain in all directions, to make sure there were no Klingons approaching. Then he turned his attention to the pit. It was a man's height in diameter and twice as deep, excavated only minutes earlier by the force of the borrowed disruptor. Using his eye to judge the proper measurement, Spock took the Klingon weapon out again and cut a slot in the hole.

"What's that for?" asked Garcia.

"The idea," the first officer told him, "is to take one of these leaves we've carried here and place the bottom edge of it in the slot, then lean the other edge up against the side of the pit. The second leaf will rest on the first at a more or less perpendicular angle, and the third will rest on the second in much the same way."

"Like a house of cards," observed Medford.

Spock was familiar with the analogy. "Yes. We will subsequently cover the topmost sheet with loose dirt and pack it. With a little care, it will look like part of the path and nothing more."

"I get it," said Wan. "When someone steps on it, he falls in."

The Vulcan nodded. "If all goes according to plan, the brittle top sheet of rock will give way, followed by the one below it and the one below that, until our passerby finds himself at the bottom of the hole."

"Just like the animal you were talking about," said Pfeffer. "The . . . le-matya?"

"Correct. Just like a le-matya that comes hunting too close to a Vulcan family estate."

"Mr. Spock?" asked Wan.

"Yes, Ms. Wan?"

"Why couldn't you just shoot the Klingons with your disruptor? I mean, you're so good at sneaking up on them and everything . . ."

Spock shook his head. "I may be able to do that to one Klingon, or two," he said. "But such tactics have limited utility. Eventually, I would be detected in the act, surrounded, and destroyed. This way, we may accomplish the same purpose with a much more limited exposure to danger."

"I knew that," claimed Pfeffer. "What a stupid question."

The Vulcan regarded him. "There is no such thing as a stupid question, Mister Pfeffer. Particularly when one is as young as Ms. Wan—or yourself."

Pfeffer looked cowed. "Sorry," he muttered.

"No apology is necessary, at least not to me." He turned back to the girl. "In any case, Ms. Wan, we may change our tactics if we can obtain additional disruptors. But for the time being, we must resort to more circumspect methods."

Wan nodded. "I understand," she told him.

It was gratifying to know that, especially in view of what he had in mind for her when the sun came up again. "Now," said Spock, taking in the rest of the children at a glance, "I would appreciate some help from all of you. We must cover this hole while we still have the light."

For a long time, there was darkness, peaceful and unbroken. Then a harsh whisper: "Captain, wake up."

Even before he threw off the last heavy tatters of his dreamless stupor, he recognized the voice. It was Scotty's. Good old Scotty. Always reliable, always there when you needed him.

As Kirk opened his eyes and turned to follow the voice to its source, he had already begun to put together the features that went with it: the round, light-complected face, the dark brows, the warm, brown eyes full of intelligence and good cheer. He wasn't prepared for the deep-set, silver orbs that peered at him out of a leathery visage as black as any void he'd ever seen.

In fact, he would have jumped to his feet if he'd been able to. Unfortunately, that wasn't an option because of the thick, coarse ropes binding his hands and feet.

"Damn," he breathed out loud, trying desperately to figure out how a Malurian had managed to steal his friend's voice. Then he remembered.

He knew where he was, and how Scotty's words could be coming from a Malurian mouth, and why they were tied up. And though it calmed him to think he hadn't lost his mind, it was hardly pleasant to realize they were in the hands of a rebel faction that had already demonstrated a penchant for violence.

Scotty's pale, almost luminous eyes narrowed in their prosthetic sockets. "Sir, are ye all right? For a minute, I thought they'd brained ye altogether."

The captain managed a smile. "No. I've still got my wits. Or most of them, anyway."

"They've taken our communicators," Scotty said.

Kirk nodded. Their captors had been thorough.

He turned from Scotty to survey their surroundings. They were in a small chamber with a single window, which let in a gray shaft of light not far from where they were sitting. The door was set into the far wall. Kirk was reasonably certain it was locked and probably well guarded into the bargain. In fact, he thought he heard voices on the other side of it.

He tested his bonds. They'd been tied by an expert. And there was nothing in the room sharp enough to cut them with.

Not that these were obstacles he couldn't get past. There was always a way out, if one thought about it.

In this case, for instance, the window offered two advantages. If they smashed it, they'd have all the sharp edges they needed to sever their bonds. And the opening looked big enough for them to wriggle through.

Of course, with their ankles bound the way they were, they'd have no choice but to hop over there. An awkward process, to be sure, but one they could have put up with. That is, if escape had been their top priority, which it wasn't. They hadn't come all this way to go home empty-handed. Their purpose was to establish a dialogue with the Obirrhat. And the best way to do that was to stay put.

"With all that paraphernalia on yer face, it's hard fer me t' tell what ye're thinkin'," Scotty observed.

"What I'm thinking," the captain told him, "is that, contrary to appearances, we may be in a pretty good position. If we can convince our—"

He was interrupted by the creaking of the door as it pushed open. A moment later, a trio of Obirrhat entered the room.

None of them looked particularly well disposed toward their prisoners. And two of the three carried phasers in a way that suggested they had no qualms about using them.

"I see you're awake," noted the unarmed Obirrhat. And then, to his companions: "Get them on their feet."

The phaser bearers did as they were told. Each of them took an arm and hauled a prisoner up off the floor.

It was rough treatment, but Kirk offered no resistance. This was one of those times when his mouth would help him more than his muscles.

"Damned Manteil spies," the unarmed Obirrhat spat. "Did you really think you would fool us with your story about coming from Torril?" He took a step forward. "Now, I want to know two things. Who sent you? And for what purpose?"

The captain grunted. "Before we get into all that, I should tell you we're not what we seem to be."

Their captor's eyes narrowed. "What is that supposed to mean?"

"We're aliens," Scotty explained. "Members of the Federation diplomatic team assigned to help end your conflict with the Manteil."

"Aliens?" the Obirrhat echoed. "How can that be?"

"I know," Kirk said. "It's hard to believe. But it's the truth." He raised his hands to his face and touched his cheek. "This is all the product of prosthetics and subdermal dyes. Underneath it all, we're human."

"I see," the Obirrhat remarked, though he sounded skeptical, to say the least. "And I suppose there's a way to prove what you say?"

The captain nodded. "You could open my shirt. The disguise only covers our faces and hands."

Still looking suspicious, the man gestured to one of his companions. "Do as he says, Zaabit."

The one called Zaabit tucked his phaser into his belt—behind him, so that the prisoner couldn't grab it while they were at close quarters—and began unfastening the front of Kirk's tunic. After a moment, he gasped.

"What is it?" asked the Obirrhat in charge.

"He wasn't lying," Zaabit replied, turning to face his comrade. In his surprise, he'd presented his back to the captain, giving him a golden opportunity to grab the phaser. But under the circumstances, Kirk refrained.

The leader seemed to look at the prisoners in a new light. "So you really *are* the offworlders," he said.

213

"We really are," the captain confirmed. "And we didn't come to the sacred precinct to spy on you. We came to find your leaders, Menikki and Omalas. The former ministers. We wanted to talk with them."

Their captor's face twitched. "What about?"

"We need to hear their side of the story," Kirk explained. "If there's a way out of this conflict, we're not going to find it dealing with the Manteil alone."

The Obirrhat digested the information. "I am sorry to disappoint you," he said at last, "but Menikki and Omalas are not here. And even if they were, they would not waste their time speaking with you."

"Waste their time!" Scotty blurted, his indignation rising to the surface. Even with a Malurian cast to them, his eyes seemed to blaze.

"That is correct," the Obirrhat told him, cutting him off. "For that is what it would be—a complete and utter waste of time. There is no possibility of reconciliation with the Manteil. They are obsessed with those damned cubaya."

"Perhaps," the captain suggested, "we should let Menikki and Omalas make that decision for themselves. After all, we represent an objective third party in the—"

"Enough," their captor announced. "I do not need an offworlder to tell me what is best for my people."

There was something about the way he said the last phrase—"my people"—that gave Kirk pause.

"You're one of the ministers," he said.

The Obirrhat nodded. "I am Menikki. So you see, I am an expert on the Manteil, particularly those on the council. And when I say I do not believe your intervention will accomplish anything, I know whereof I speak."

"With all due respect," Scotty said, "ye've nae even tried it. If ye'd only come back to the negotiation table—"

"Why?" the minister asked him. "So I can be told yet again that our sacred places are meaningless, that they are somehow less important than a herd of dirty beasts? So I can be humiliated by men who can't see beyond their own absurd beliefs?"

"All right then," the captain interjected. "Stay here and do what you have to. But give us a better idea of what your needs are so we can try to formulate a solution on our own."

Menikki snorted. "You mean provide an education for you? And then send you back to the Manteil?"

Kirk nodded. "Something like that. We just need more to go on. All the information we've heard so far has been supplied by the council. And as you know, that's a pretty one-sided situation these days."

The minister shook his head. He looked incredulous. "Is it possible you really believe we will let you go?"

The captain frowned. This was definitely *not* a positive development.

"What do you mean?" he asked.

Menikki's face twitched—a sign of regret? "I mean we cannot let you live. Not after you have seen our hiding place."

Kirk's mouth went dry. Out of the corner of his eye, he saw Scotty turn to look at him.

"That wouldn't be very intelligent," the captain argued. "You may have taken our communicators, but my people know we're in the precinct. If we're gone too long, they'll tell Traphid."

"We do not fear Traphid," the minister told him.

"That's foolish," Kirk said. "The Manteil could come in here and crush you anytime they want to. You know that. And our deaths will only make them want to do so that much sooner."

Menikki shrugged. He turned to the armed Obirrhat standing on either side of the captain and Scotty.

"Dispose of them," the minister instructed.

His comrades raised their phasers. And Kirk had no doubt about the level of destruction the weapons were set for.

So much for my mouth, he thought. It's time to try the alternative.

Before the Obirrhat beside him could press the trigger, the captain lashed out with his bound-together hands and knocked the weapon aside. Then, allowing the surprised Obirrhat no time to recover, he reversed directions and belted him across the mouth.

The Obirrhat staggered backward, his weapon clattering to the floor. Kirk lunged for it, but bound as he was, he didn't quite make it. As he hit the deck, bruising his ribs in the process, he found the device just inches beyond his outstretched hands.

By then, however, the Obirrhat had taken in the situation and was reaching for the weapon as well. Desperately, the captain gathered his knees underneath him and propelled himself forward again.

This time, he made it. His fingers closed on the device just in time for him to whirl and point it at his antagonist.

Finding himself on the wrong end of the weapon, the Obirrhat withdrew his hands and backed off.

Only then did Kirk dare to glance in Scotty's direction. As it turned out, the engineer hadn't fared quite as well as his captain. He'd trapped his captor's head in a vicious-looking leglock and, though the Obirrhat didn't have possession of his weapon, neither did Scotty. It was lying on the floor, just beyond their awkward attempts to reach it.

As Kirk watched, Menikki started for the unclaimed device. The captain fired a bright red warning shot, which scarred the floor between the minister and his objective. Menikki looked up at him, eyes wide.

"If I were you," the captain said, "I'd back off." He turned again to his own adversary, before the man could get any ideas. "I mean all of you."

With a sigh of relief, Scotty relaxed his legs and let his opponent's head slip out. "Damn," he said, "I'm glad I didnae have t' keep that up much longer."

As the Obirrhat retreated, giving the remaining weapon a wide berth, Scotty wriggled over and took charge of it. Then he pushed himself up to a kneeling position and glanced back at Kirk.

"I can cover them, sir, while ye make yerself a wee bit more comfortable."

Indeed, the Obirrhat looked stunned. Obviously, they hadn't had much experience at this sort of thing.

The captain nodded. "Thank you," he told Scotty. Creeping over to the wall, he sat up and rested his back against it. Then, digging in with his heels, he shimmied up the vertical surface into a standing position.

"All right," he said, training his weapon on their captors. "Your turn, Mr. Scott."

A few moments later, the engineer had pushed himself to his feet as well. He turned to Kirk, probably trying to smile beneath his prosthesis. "Nice work, sir."

"Likewise." Turning to the Obirrhat, he said: "And now, I'd like to try a somewhat different approach."

"So would I," said a voice from beyond the open doorway. And barely an instant later, a hunched and elderly figure came through.

Menikki cursed, then interposed himself between the newcomer and the humans. "Do not hurt him," he pleaded. "He presents no danger to you."

"We're not going to hurt anybody," Kirk assured them. "Not if we can help it."

"It is all right, Menikki," said his fellow minister. "I believe him."

Menikki frowned. "You are too trusting, Omalas."

The older Obirrhat shrugged. "Perhaps. Or maybe you are not trusting enough."

Taking advantage of the distraction, Scotty aimed his phaser at the ropes that bound his ankles. It took the dark red beam only a moment to slice through.

Not a bad idea, Kirk mused, and did the same for his own bonds.

"That was unnecessary," Omalas said. "We could have untied your ropes."

The captain grunted. "It didn't seem the matter was entirely up to you."

The Obirrhat looked amused; the corners of his eyes crinkled as he regarded his fellow minister. "Menikki is hotheaded sometimes," he replied. "But he usually follows my lead."

The younger man shook his head. "Not this time, Omalas. There is too much at stake here—not only our lives and those of our people but the success of the whole revolt. Without you and me, who will lead it?"

Omalas pointed to the Starfleet officers. "This man has offered us a way to settle our dispute without further bloodshed. Is that not worth taking a few chances for?"

Menikki harrumphed. "It is a false hope they offer us, even if they themselves believe otherwise. The Manteil are as stubborn as bedrock. You know that as well as I do."

"It may be," Omalas countered, "that the Manteil say the same thing about us." He looked at Kirk for confirmation. "True?"

The captain tried to smile, but the prosthetics wouldn't allow him. "I'm afraid so," he said, nodding.

The older Obirrhat eyed him. "And even with two such intransigent combatants, you believe you can forge a lasting peace?"

Kirk nodded. "We've done it before."

Omalas seemed satisfied. "Very well, then. I will not come out of hiding to meet with Traphid and the others; we may not meet with the kind of welcome you anticipate. But I will see to it that you have whatever information you need to do your job."

Menikki made a hissing sound. Apparently, he still had some reservations about letting the offworlders live.

"Thank you," the captain told Omalas, ignoring the younger minister's reaction.

"In the meantime, though, you must return our phasers. I fear that the rest of our comrades, who await me just down the hall, would misunderstand if they saw you with a weapon in your hands."

Kirk hesitated. Could the Obirrhat be trusted?

Then again, did they have a choice in the matter?

"Come, my friend," said Omalas. "You've asked me to rely on your word. You must rely on mine."

Reluctantly, the captain placed the phaser in the

Obirrhat's hand. Muttering a curse beneath his breath, Scotty followed suit.

"Excellent," said the Obirrhat, restoring the phasers to their proper owners. "Now come with me," he told the humans, "and I'll have someone remove the rest of your ropes. Then we can talk all you like."

Chapter Sixteen

KIRK WASN'T VERY HUNGRY, but Omalas insisted that they eat. "No one ever learned wisdom on an empty stomach," he told them.

Leading them into a small room with a chest of drawers, a wooden table, and some chairs, he asked them to sit. Then he had a fellow Obirrhat bring bread, a pitcher of cold scented water, and a couple of mugs.

As it turned out, the Obirrhat bread—round and hard on the outside, sweet and soft on the inside— tasted as good as any meal Kirk could remember. Scotty seemed to be enjoying it as well. Tearing off another sizable chunk, he shoved it into his mouth and chewed vigorously.

"Careful, Mr. Scott," Kirk jibed. "You'll split a prosthesis."

The engineer grunted as he lifted a mugful of water. "Seein' as how we've already blown our cover, sir, ye'll excuse me if it's nae my first concern."

Omalas himself sat at the table with them but declined to eat anything, a fact that at first gave the captain pause. But then, he told himself, if the Obirrhat had wanted to do away with them, there were easier methods than poisoning.

"Not that I don't appreciate the hospitality," Kirk said, "but why is it so important that we eat?"

The minister smiled. "Because you will not have another opportunity until you have finished becoming wise. It is our law."

That seemed to get Scotty's attention. "Ye know," he commented, "such an enterprise might take a fair amount o' time."

Omalas shook his head judiciously. "Not more than a single night."

Scott looked at the captain. Kirk shrugged.

When they were finished with the fare the Obhirrat had set before them, Omalas himself cleared the table of crumbs with his bare hand. Then he went over to the chest of drawers that stood against the wall.

"You say you wish to understand the Obirrhat?"

The captain smiled. "That's why we're here, at no small risk to life and limb."

"Good," said Omalas. Opening a drawer, he extracted three ancient-looking, leather-bound books. With unmistakable reverence, he placed them on the table.

"All you need to know of us," he told them, "you will find in these."

Kirk reached out and touched the nearest of the tomes. As he'd guessed, the leather was oily to the touch. Obviously well cared for.

He looked up and saw Omalas scrutinizing him. "You have such books where you come from?"

The captain withdrew his hand. "Yes. We do."

Sitting down, the minister drew one of the tomes to him and opened it to the first delicate, yellowed page. Tilting his head, he indicated that the humans follow suit.

Carefully, they did just that.

Aoras sighed.

They'd been searching for the human children for a day and a night, a remarkable—and remarkably *frustrating*—amount of time, considering who their prey was. But Gidris had refused to ask for help from either the captain or the *Kad'nra*.

And now the search had led the two of them to this flat, narrow notch between two slopes. Down here, out of the wind, it wasn't quite as cold as elsewhere. But the sun was still a damned knife in each eye.

And the sun wasn't the only problem.

"Kruge is a fool," said Gidris, between clenched teeth.

Aoras didn't answer. He knew better.

After all, Kruge may have come after Gidris in the chain of command, but he came before Aoras. And it wasn't wise for one to criticize one's superior, even in the company of a greater superior.

Besides, Aoras told himself, Gidris wasn't really speaking to him. Nettled by his inability to find the human children, the man was indiscriminately venting his spleen at anyone who'd ever crossed him, and Aoras just happened to be there.

"First, he grins like an imbecile at the captain's remarks. Then, when I take him to task for it, he tells me he's *intrigued by the possibilities.*" Gidris snarled. "I'll give him more intrigue than he bargained for."

Aoras didn't want to hear that sort of talk, even if he didn't understand very much of it. It was too dangerous.

Someday, no doubt, Kruge would challenge Gidris for his position on the *Kad'nra*. And if Kruge became first officer, Aoras certainly didn't want to be known as the man in whom Gidris had confided his personal likes and dislikes, particularly when Gidris's greatest dislike was Kruge.

Despite Aoras's silent wishes to the contrary, Gidris railed on. *"You need pursue this no further,* he tells me. But wouldn't I have *loved* to pursue it! Wouldn't I have relished the opportunity to sweep Kruge's maggot-infested head from his palsied shoulders!"

Please, thought Aoras. Save it for another time and another set of ears. I'm too young to wake up with a dagger in my throat.

Eyes bulging, dark with anger, Gidris reeled off a string of curses, and then remained silent for a while, as if finally answering Aoras's plea. Aoras had no doubt, however, that the second-in-command was continuing his tirade in the privacy of his own brain.

Now there was only the sun to contend with. Couldn't the damned Federation colonists have chosen a place that wasn't so—

Suddenly, something on the path ahead caught his eye. Stopping dead in his tracks, he realized what it was.

A child. A human child.

And her back was to them—she hadn't seen them yet. With luck, she might lead them to the rest of the pack.

Aoras put his hand in front of Gidris to alert him. But the first officer had seen her too, and he brushed his companion's hand away with more than a little disdain.

Then they waited, all but holding their breath, still as statues, not daring to move lest they alert the girl and give her a chance to sound the alarm. The human children had been devils to find; neither Gidris nor Aoras wanted to waste what seemed to be a stroke of great fortune.

Fortunately for them, the child seemed oblivious to her surroundings. She was doing something with her long, black hair—twisting it into a braid, Aoras thought—and the effort seemed to occupy her completely.

Or at least that's how it appeared. But just before she would have disappeared around a bend in the slope to their left, some sixth sense gripped her. The girl turned and saw them. Wide-eyed, she fled.

The chase was on. Aoras plunged ahead, legs churning, striving to make up the distance between them. Normally, he'd have taken his time, believing no mere human child could elude them for long. But these children had managed to keep them guessing for hours now; they had earned the right to be taken seriously.

Gidris was right beside him, matching him stride for stride. He'd already whipped out his disruptor, prepared to use it if it meant fulfilling his mission—and cementing his position in the captain's good graces. Not wishing to appear uncommitted to their success, Aoras pulled out his weapon as well.

Then something happened, Aoras wasn't sure what. The next thing he knew, the ground had slid out from under him, there was the sound of something snapping, and dirt was hissing all around him.

He was tumbling down into darkness, though that only lasted for the briefest of moments. Then he felt himself hit bottom, hard, and a weight that could only have been Gidris slammed down on top of him, knocking the wind out of his lungs.

As he lay there gasping in the dust-clotted air, he realized that Gidris was unconscious, or worse. Nor did he have the strength to move the man off him; his whole being was involved in desperately trying to pull air down his throat. But even through the mist of still falling debris, he could make out a light above, a light twisted and torn by some sort of fragments he couldn't quite identify. That's when it came home to him: the hole they'd fallen into was deep, *very* deep. Too deep, certainly, to have been made by nature.

An instant later, there were flashes in the light, flashes that reminded Aoras of disruptor fire. He tried to shout, to tell whoever was firing to stop, that there was someone down here. But it was no use. He couldn't get out anything more than a painful wheeze.

What in hell's name was going on? The tastes of fear and anger mixed in his open mouth. Who'd dug this hole? Why were they being fired on?

And then it came to him. *Kruge.* He'd decided to take advantage of the situation to become second-in-command, and—

But why do it this way? Why not just pick them off at a distance? Did he want to show his men how clever he was? Wait, that didn't make sense. The girl—she'd been part of it, hadn't she? How could Kruge have enlisted her? No matter. It *had* to be Kruge—who else could it be?

Meanwhile, the disruptor fire continued, flaring in the darkness. Little by little, the debris above Aoras was removed, improving his view. And he was able to drag enough air into his lungs to groan in protest—to let the disruptor wielder know there was someone down here, just in case it wasn't Kruge.

As he'd expected, however, it didn't stop the barrage. If only he knew where his own disruptor had gone. But it was lost when they fell into the hole: by now, it could have been eaten up in one of the blasts.

Helplessly, Aoras watched as a figure came into view at the lip of the pit, gaining definition as the fragments above him were blasted out of existence.

Strange. It didn't look like Kruge. For that matter, it didn't look like a Klingon at all. Finally, the disruptor had cleared away enough of the debris to show him his captor's identity. Aoras's eyes opened wide with loathing.

A Vulcan! And in a Starfleet uniform, no less!

Even with only half his breath back, he managed to spit out a curse. He understood now how the G-7 unit had disappeared and how the children had managed to elude them so well. They were led by a Starfleet officer!

"Go ahead," he rasped. "Kill us! We will not go unavenged!"

The Vulcan peered down at him. "I have no intention of killing you," he said. "I only wished to make certain you were unarmed and had nothing to climb over in your attempts to get out. If I were you, I would conserve my strength. You are likely to be down there for some time."

And then he vanished, amid what sounded like a chorus of childish laughter. Confused, feeling as if he'd just dodged a dagger, Aoras just stared at the circle of blue sky above him until Gidris began to stir.

Aoras grunted. The second-in-command would never believe this. *Never.*

"Sir?"

It was Scotty, sitting across the table from him. The engineer was peering at Kirk with bloodshot eyes.

"Sorry," said the captain, shaking his head. "I guess I must've dozed off for a moment."

"It's all right," Scotty told him. "After stayin' up all night readin' these scriptures, I'm feelin' a wee bit woozy m'self."

Kirk looked around. "Where did Omalas go?"

"He didnae say," the engineer reported. "Only that he'd be right back."

Now the captain remembered. "That's right," he muttered. "How long ago was that?"

"Just a couple o' minutes, sir." A pause. "After all that, have ye got any ideas? Fer solvin' the cubaya problem, I mean?"

Kirk smiled unenthusiastically. The Obirrhat's holy book had covered every subject from dietary laws to funeral rites, from farming tips to marriage vows. The rules governing the sacred precinct had been only a small portion of the information contained in the scriptures. "Can't say I do, Scotty. You?"

"Not a one. Not yet, anyway."

Abruptly, the door opened, and Omalas stood on the threshold. He had a tray of fresh bread and a cold pitcher on it, the same as the night before.

"To celebrate the acquisition of wisdom," he explained.

There was something else on the tray as well—two somethings, in fact. Their communicators.

"After we celebrate," Omalas told them, "we will blindfold you and bring you back to the place where you were—" He smiled. "Where you lost consciousness. Then you may call up to your ship or return to the Hall of Government, whichever you prefer. But I would not recommend lingering in the precinct. Menikki is not happy about the way I have accommodated you. He will not hesitate to use force if he finds you skulking about again."

"I understand," said the captain. "But you need not worry. We got what we came for."

The question now, he mused, is whether we can *do* something with it.

Vheled seethed with anger. "Say that again," he told Kruge.

The second officer met his gaze. "The first officer seems to have vanished. Also, Loutek, Aoras, Iglat, and Shrof." If he was pleased about the apparent breakdown of Gidris's efforts, he didn't let on. "Only Dirat and Rogh are left, and they have been unable to complete their assignment."

The captain cursed and spat. "How difficult can it be to find a pack of human brats?"

Kruge shrugged. "Not very difficult, one would think. If you wish, I will take a second squad and investigate."

Vheled scowled. "No," he said. "Stay here. Until I return, you are in charge of the mission."

The second officer's eyes narrowed. "Until you return?"

The captain nodded. "Yes. I am going out there myself to see what this is about, and to finish the job

Gidris started." He grunted. "You may find yourself first officer of the *Kad'nra* sooner than any of us expected, Kruge."

The second officer responded with a subtle grin. "I would be pleased to serve you in whatever capacity you deem appropriate," he said.

Vheled growled. "I'll bet you would. Now, round up some men for me, and good ones—Chorrl, Engath, Norgh, Zoragh. And the Nik'nash, Grael. We have already wasted more than a day on this foolishness; I want to finish it as quickly as possible."

Chapter Seventeen

McCOY WAS IN SICKBAY, muttering to himself, trying to figure out why the new biomonitors still wouldn't work right, when he heard the sound of approaching footsteps. Whirling, he saw two Malurians standing in the middle of sickbay.

His first impulse was to call for security. What in blazes were Malurians doing on the *Enterprise*, much less *here*?

Then he realized that they weren't Malurians at all. "Jim!" he cried. "Scotty!"

"In the flesh, if not exactly our own," Kirk joked.

"For a moment," the engineer said, "I didnae think ye recognized us."

For a moment, the doctor mused, *I didn't. Damn, but I do good work!*

But what he said was, "Balderdash." And then, "It's good to see you two. I was starting to wonder what happened to you." He paused, and he could feel his cheeks turning hot. "At one point, in fact, I even wondered out loud—to the ambassador."

The captain looked at him and frowned. At least, McCoy thought it was a frown. It was hard to tell with Kirk's prosthesis getting in the way.

"Sorry, Jim," he added. "I was worried. I thought we might have to send the Manteil in after you." He cleared his throat. "Fortunately, it didn't come to that."

The captain nodded. "It's all right, Bones. I understand. Now, if you're not too busy with those monitors, could you get this thing off my face? It feels like a Tetracite mudpack."

Tetracite mud was famous for the nearly microscopic parasites that inhabited it. Nor was the analogy lost on the doctor, who once spent an itchy week recovering from those parasites' bites.

"Actually," said McCoy, "if I recall correctly, it was Mr. Scott who had his prosthesis applied first. In all fairness, I think his should be the first to come off."

The engineer held up his hands to signal his indifference. "I dinnae mind—"

But Kirk cut him off. "The doctor's right, Scotty. You go first."

"Sir, I—"

"And don't argue to be polite," the captain continued. "You know you hate that prosthesis as much as I do."

His protest subsiding, Scotty went over to the nearest biobed. "All right," he told McCoy, "work yer magic, Doctor."

Crossing the breadth of sickbay, Bones opened a drawer and got out a freshly charged laser-scalpel.

"Just be sure the prosthesis is all ye remove," Scotty admonished.

The doctor smiled. "No promises, Commander. Now shut up and lie down. This won't take but a minute."

While he was waiting, Kirk opened his communicator. McCoy could hear the device click in the background.

"How's it going up there, Mr. Sulu?"

The helmsman had been sitting in for the captain up on the bridge, of course. His response was quick and efficient.

"Couldn't be better, sir. Welcome back."

"Thank you, Lieutenant. Carry on." And then, as an afterthought, "You're taking care of my fire-blossom, aren't you?"

This time, McCoy heard Sulu chuckle before he answered. "It's one of my top priorities, Captain. Why? Can't you smell it from sickbay?"

Kirk chuckled too. "Carry on." There was another click, as the captain closed the device.

By then, the doctor had excised the bulk of the prosthesis from Scotty's face. The engineer's skin was still black, naturally, and his eyes were still silver, but at least his features had been restored.

"Och, but it feels good t' get that off," said Scotty.

"Hold still," McCoy warned him, "or you might lose something I'm not supposed to take off." Then, without losing his focus on the laser surgery, he asked, "So, Jim? Did you get what you went down there for?"

Behind him, the captain grunted audibly. "Hard to say, Doctor. We managed to speak with Omalas and Menikki, all right. We even got a chance to read the

233

Michael Jan Friedman

Obirrhats' holy scriptures, with Omalas's help. But we're still not within sniffing distance of—"

Suddenly Kirk snapped his fingers. "Damn it, Bones! That's it!"

Deactivating his scalpel, McCoy turned to look over his shoulder. "I'll have you know I'm trying to conduct surgery here! Now, what the devil are you shouting about?"

The captain was fairly beaming. "I've got the solution, Doctor, the answer to the Malurians' problem. And wait'll you hear what it is."

"Go ahead," McCoy told him. "I'm all ears."

"Just sae long as it's you an' not me," Scotty quipped.

Before Kirk had gotten a dozen words out, they knew he was on to something.

I could get used to being in charge, Kruge told himself. Surveying the inside of the dome the captain had claimed as his headquarters, he placed his feet up on the desk in front of him and nodded. *I could get used to it very easily.*

And he vowed that someday he would get used to it. After all, once Gidris was eliminated, which might have taken place already, if the state of affairs up in the hills was as bad as it had sounded, he would have to set himself a new goal. And what more appropriate target could he set his sights on than a captaincy? If not of the *Kad'nra,* then of some other vessel.

With all this internecine warfare between the Kamorh'dag and the Gevish'rae, there were bound to be some positions opening up. All he had to do was move the right pieces and—

234

The door opened abruptly, and one of his guards, a powerful man named Oghir, took a single step into the dome. "Second officer, I have news from the *Kad'nra.*" He paused, hesitating. "From Haastra."

Haastra? The security chief? Removing his feet from the desk, Kruge planted them on the floor and leaned forward. "What news?" he barked.

Oghir was obviously not happy about what he had to impart. "There has been an accident, second officer. An act of—" He paused a second time.

Leaping to his feet, Kruge growled: "Enough! I will hear it from Haastra himself!" And so saying, he snapped his communicator off his belt and activated it. It took a moment before the security officer responded.

"Kruge?" he asked. "I must speak with the captain!"

"The captain is busy," the second officer told him. "I am in command here."

He heard a muffled curse but no objection. Normally, Haastra answered only to the captain himself. But if Vheled had left Kruge in charge, the security chief couldn't bypass him.

"We've had an explosion in one of the cargo holds," said Haastra. "Next to the warp engines."

Kruge felt his lips drawing back over his teeth. "Sabotage?"

"Without question."

"Any idea who did it?"

"None—yet."

"Damage?"

"Extensive. Until we can repair the warp drive, we've been hobbled—limited to impulse power."

Michael Jan Friedman

Kruge spat. He didn't look forward to telling Vheled about this; no wonder the man before him had been so reluctant to speak.

"Get repairs under way, then," he snarled. "I want the engines ready again in a matter of hours."

"Of course," Haastra replied. But there was a note of irony in his voice, as if he doubted the chief engineer could meet such a demand.

"And Haastra," the second officer continued, "see to it that the culprit is identified and taken into custody. The captain will not want to return to hear that there is an unknown saboteur in our ranks."

He could imagine the security chief bristling at that last remark. "I don't need *you* to remind me of that," Haastra retorted.

And then the conversation was over. Kruge put away his communicator and glared at Oghir.

"Well?" he snapped. "What are you waiting for? Get back to whatever it was you were doing!"

The man didn't need to be told twice. The doors had barely slid open before he was gone.

Alone with his thoughts, Kruge pounded his fist on the desk in front of him. It jumped, its legs creaking as they scraped against the floor.

A saboteur! It was an outrage! And if Haastra didn't find him soon, the security chief might not be the only one whose head might be forfeit.

Suddenly the second officer didn't feel quite so comfortable being in charge.

There was an air of tension in the Hall of Government, a feeling of hostility that had not been there before. Kirk couldn't help but notice it as he, McCoy, and Scotty followed Farquhar into the chamber.

Traphid and the other Manteil ministers stood grim-faced around their conference table, beneath their spired metal ring. A monitor stood before one of the windows—dark for now but soon to be illuminated with the narrow-cast images of Omalas and Menikki. There was a security guard on either side of the monitor.

Stopping before Traphid, Farquhar put his fingers to his temples. "We are grateful for your indulgence, First Minister."

The Manteil returned the gesture, but only in a perfunctory sort of way. If Traphid had seemed impatient before, he now appeared downright anxious.

Nor was his behavior difficult to understand, what with all that had transpired in the last few days. In the first minister's place, Kirk would have been anxious, too.

"If you can stop the bloodshed," Traphid told the ambassador, "it is *we* who will be grateful." His face twitched. "Though I must remind you, our dedication to the cubaya has not diminished. Nor will we give ground on the subject of their rights and well-being."

Farquhar nodded. "We understand, First Minister. And I assure you, we have in no way underestimated your dedication to the sacred beasts. Nor, for that matter, have we taken lightly the concerns of the Obirrhat."

Traphid looked approving. "Good. Then let us proceed."

As the humans moved to their places before the monitor, however, the ambassador snuck a look at Kirk, as if to say: *Don't make a liar of me, Captain.*

Kirk frowned. It wasn't Farquhar's disapproval he was worried about.

At a sign from Traphid, the security guards on either side of the monitor moved to activate the device. A moment later, the screen came alive.

It showed Omalas and Menikki in a bare, windowless room that gave no indication of where they might be. After all, there was no guarantee that the Federation's plan would be acceptable to both sides, and if it was not, the Obirrhat didn't want to give away the whereabouts of their leaders.

Of course, the Manteil could have traced the signal if they'd wanted to, but Traphid had given his word that that wouldn't happen. And to set the minds of the Obirrhat even more at ease, the council had provided them with a half-dozen switching-and-transmission units, which could be used to relay the original signal and disguise its source.

Omalas looked at Traphid. "Good day, First Minister."

Traphid returned the scrutiny with apparent equanimity. "And to you, my colleague. Perhaps, if fortune smiles, it will be a good day for all of us."

One didn't have to listen hard to hear the strain in their voices and the sorrow for those who had already been lost. But their words, at least, were civil. Even hopeful, the captain thought.

He cleared his throat. Farquhar took notice.

"The idea we are about to present is Captain Kirk's," the ambassador announced. "I ask that you turn your attention to him."

All eyes fell on Kirk. Taking a deep breath, he launched into the speech he'd prepared the night before.

"As you all know, Lieutenant Commander Scott and I had an opportunity to visit with the Obirrhat in their sacred precinct. Minister Omalas was kind enough to show us his people's holy book."

That was McCoy's cue to hand the captain the electronic slate he'd carried into the room with him. "Good luck," the doctor muttered under his breath.

"Thank you," Kirk replied. He looked down at the slate, addressing both those present in person and those pictured on the monitor.

"Correct me if I'm wrong, Minister Omalas, but your protest concerning the free movements of the cubaya is based on the following passage: *No beast of forest or field shall set itself down on the sacred soil.*"

The quote was exact. Kirk had gotten it from Omalas himself earlier this morning through a direct comm link with the *Enterprise.* So when the captain looked up, it was no surprise that the Obirrhat minister was nodding.

"That is indeed the basis for our protest," he agreed. "It is why we cannot tolerate the animals' presence in our ancient precinct."

"All right, then," the human said. "Now, some time ago, we suggested to the council that a predator—a gettrex, for instance—might be domesticated and left in the vicinity of your sacred ground."

"That would be an *outrage,*" blurted Menikki. "The gettrexin are even less welcome than the cubaya!"

"So we were informed," Kirk assured him. "We then amended our suggestion—replacing an actual predator with the scent of one. That, too, was deemed inappropriate. As was a chemical compound that simulates such a scent. We even offered to supply a compound that copies the scent of a beast never seen on this planet, and that was rejected as well."

"As it should have been," Omalas confirmed. "All

of those possibilities would come into direct conflict with our scriptures, as we interpret them."

The captain looked at the Obirrhat on the monitor. "Fine. No beast-smells. But what about *other* scents?" He paused for effect. "How about the scent of a flower?"

Again, he consulted the slate. *"You shall adorn the sacred stones with all manner of flowers and growing things, for they freshen memory and quicken the heart.* Isn't that how your scripture is worded, Minister Omalas?"

The Obirrhat grunted—again, no surprise. "So it is. Nor have we ever objected to flowers in the sacred precinct." His face twitched—with curiosity, Kirk thought. "But I do not think a plant will accomplish your purpose, Captain. I have never heard of one that would keep a cubaya away with its scent. In fact, the beasts are notoriously attracted to most strong-smelling flowers."

"That's correct," Kirk told him. "As long as you limit the discussion to Malurian flowers." He turned to Scotty.

Whipping out his communicator, the engineer opened it and said: "Mister Kyle, you can send down the specimen now."

It took only a second or two for a small, black object to materialize at Scotty's feet. When the process was completed, everyone could see that it was a shiny, black globe.

The engineer knelt to pick it up, then turned it over to the captain. Accepting it with a nod, Kirk pressed a small stud on the side of the globe.

Immediately, the top half split into two sections and each one retracted, revealing the object's contents: a flowering plant with long, dark-blue petals and a large, prickly-looking, gray stamen. The captain held it out to the monitor and the Obirrhat ministers, as if it were a gift of surpassing beauty.

Which it was, Kirk mused, if you were of the opinion that peace was beautiful.

"What is it?" Menikki asked.

"A Klingon fireblossom," the human told him. "Not the kind of specimen you'd want to plant just anywhere, unless you wanted to kill all the growing things around it. This one was kept in our ship's botanical gardens, separate from all our other plants. But more important," Kirk said, "the fireblossom emits a scent that the cubaya are sure to find unpleasant."

Traphid sniffed. "I don't smell a thing," he remarked.

"Of course not," McCoy interjected. "You're not a cubaya. And that's the beauty of it. No Malurian will be bothered by the scent, but it'll keep the beasts at a considerable distance."

Omalas regarded the doctor. "You know this for a fact?"

Bones nodded. "I've had an opportunity to gather plenty of sensor data on the cubaya, so I know how their olfactory systems work. Seems they bear more than a passing resemblance to a Klingon beast called a puris, and puris avoid fireblossoms like the plague. You can bet the farm on it: the cubaya will be no more enamored of these flowers than they are of the worst-smelling gettrexin on the planet."

Menikki's eyes narrowed. "Do you think we will call off our revolt on your word alone?" He made a derisive sound in his throat.

"There's a way to prove I know what I'm talking about," McCoy replied. "I've already begun synthesizing compounds that copy the scent of the fireblossom. We can place them in the path of the cubaya, and if they turn away, we know we've got something."

"And if not?" asked Menikki.

"Believe me," McCoy told him, "there won't *be* any if not."

"For us to believe, we must be present," Omalas noted.

"Of course," the doctor agreed.

Menikki turned to his fellow Obirrhat. "You mean come out of hiding? That is impossible."

Omalas snorted. "There is another saying in the scriptures, my friend: *For the overly cautious, everything is impossible.*"

Chapter Eighteen

IT WAS A RELATIVELY simple matter for Transporter Chief Kyle to locate the main herd of cubaya. Anything that big was difficult to miss.

Nor was it any more difficult to transport the inhabitants of the Hall of Government—including the Manteil ministers, their guards, Farquhar, and the three Starfleet officers—out to a place just ahead of the herd. Or to beam down a couple of crewmen with some beakers full of synthetic fireblossom scent.

The hard part was locating Omalas and Menikki and *their* guards, with only street directions to go on. But somehow, Kyle had managed that too.

Now they all stood together on a gentle incline overlooking the mother city, watching the wind send ripples through the high, blue-green ground cover. Fortunately, it was blowing in the right direction— out toward the cubaya, who were getting closer by the minute.

Closer not only to them, but to the opened beakers left on the ground at intervals of roughly thirty meters. For all intents and purposes, they'd created a wall of fireblossom fragrance, which would cause the beasts to veer off, if all went according to plan.

Kirk, who happened to be standing next to McCoy, put his hand on the doctor's shoulder. "Tell me, Bones, just how confident *are* you that this artificial stuff will work?"

Bones scowled. "There's no reason it shouldn't," he replied.

"You're not answering my question," the captain said.

"Damn it, Jim, I'm a doctor, not a veterinarian. It takes time to perfect these things."

Kirk nodded. "I was afraid you'd say something like that."

The ground beneath their feet shook under the weight of the oncoming herd. And so far, the animals showed no intention of turning away from them.

Not that they were in any real danger. The cubaya weren't going fast enough to trample them, and the beasts typically went around obstacles rather than through them. But if the cubaya got past the scent barrier, the city wasn't all that much farther down the slope—a journey of only a day or so at the rate the beasts were making headway. Before long, they'd be flooding the sacred precinct.

That's why this had to work. Because if they didn't stop the cubaya, the Obirrhat would stop them, and the conflict would attain a whole new level of violence.

The beasts were less than a hundred meters away

now, breasting the grasslike ground cover as if it were the river the captain had first seen them in. They still gave no sign that the contents of the beakers were having any effect on them.

Kirk noticed the Malurians exchanging glances: Omalas with Menikki, Traphid with his fellow Manteil. Though he was still no expert on native facial expressions, he didn't think they looked particularly confident.

And they were losing what confidence they did have with every thundering step the cubaya took. Nor could the captain blame them.

Eighty meters. Seventy. Sixty.

Kirk sighed. He'd really thought he had this thing licked.

Fifty. Forty. Thirty.

"Come on," McCoy said out loud, addressing the nearest of the beakers. "Do your stuff, damn it! Do it *now!*"

Suddenly, as if the doctor's exhortations had cast a charm over the cubaya, the beasts in the first rank slowed down and frantically began to change direction. The next rank did the same. And then the rank after that.

Pretty soon, the whole herd was splitting down the middle, turning to the right or left, and running parallel to the line of beakers. The group of Malurians and humans watched, apprehension turning to disbelief and disbelief to outright jubilation.

"All *right!*" McCoy cried. "I knew it'd work!"

The captain didn't have the heart to remind him of his earlier remarks. The important thing was that it had worked.

"Captain Kirk."

He turned to see Omalas standing by his side. "Yes, Minister?"

"You have my gratitude. In fact, you have the gratitude of this entire world."

Out of the corner of his eye, Kirk saw Farquhar watching. Watching and listening. The captain shrugged.

"The Federation sent down a team, Minister. If there's credit to be given, it should be given to all of us equally."

Omalas nodded. Judging by the look in his eyes, he seemed to understand. "Then that is what I will do—give credit to you all." He leaned closer. "But most of all to you, my friend in wisdom."

And then he went over to Farquhar to fulfill his promise.

As Vheled materialized in the space between the red-dirt hillsides, he looked to Grael. In accordance with the captain's previous instructions, the man opened his communicator and spoke into it.

"How far?" asked Grael.

"Perhaps thirty meters," came the slightly static-troubled response from Terrik, who had pinpointed the location of every Klingon that had gone out with Gidris—again, on Vheled's orders. "Just around the next bend."

"Excellent," said Grael. He closed his communicator and put it away.

Enough was enough, the captain told himself. Normally, he wouldn't have thought it necessary to employ technology in the hunt for mere children. But these children had somehow proved more resourceful than they'd expected—unless, of course, Gidris had simply bungled the job.

Either way, Vheled was taking no chances. He wanted to end this, to find the G-7 unit, and find it quickly, before their glorious victory in the name of the Gevish'rae became tainted with rumors of ineptitude.

The captain gestured in the direction Terrik had indicated. "Engath, Chorrl, take the advance position. Norgh, bring up the rear. Move!"

They moved, and swiftly. As the group advanced, wary and alert, Vheled nodded with satisfaction. He wanted no room for error. No possibility of running into the same problems Gidris had encountered.

They'd barely begun their march before Engath and Chorrl signaled back to them. Apparently, Terrik's reading had been an accurate one. And there was no danger, or their gestures would have conveyed as much.

In fact, there was something of a smile on Engath's face. And as Vheled approached their position, he noticed that Chorrl had one too, though he hid it better.

A moment later, he saw the reason for their amusement. The only thing up ahead was a large hole in the ground.

But Terrik had gotten a reading of two Klingons here. And if they were nowhere else to be seen . . .

They had to be in the *hole*.

If this mission had been someone else's responsibility—if someone else's career had been on the line and not his—Vheled might have thought it humorous himself. As it was, his fury climbed the inside of his throat like a small, vicious predator.

Stiff-necked, he advanced on the pit. Stopped at the edge. And peered down into the darkness within. His eyes were used to the bright sunshine that plagued this place, but he could make out vague forms. Two of them, he decided. And neither seemed to be aware of his presence.

Disgusted, he kicked some dirt into the hole. It made the figures stir, even elicited a curse. They stood up, giving him a better view of their faces.

One was Gidris. And the other Aoras.

"Captain!" cried the first officer, caught off-balance. He seemed to be bleeding from a head wound. "I—I am glad to see you. We were tricked—"

"By whom?" Vheled thundered. "A pack of human *children?*"

"No," said Aoras, "not children alone. They have a Vulcan with them. It was he who arranged this trap, who—"

The captain's answer was to kick again at the brink of the pit. Dirt rained down on the pair trapped below, silencing Aoras's protest.

"Sons of puris! What is a single Vulcan? What did he do, wrap you in his legendary mind-magic and convince you to leap into this hole?"

"Captain Vheled," cried Gidris, trying to explain, "he wasn't one of the colonists. He wore the uniform of Starfleet!"

Starfleet?

Starfleet!

The thought was like salt rubbed into a wound. If Starfleet was involved, their entire mission was in jeopardy. And it had taken him this long to find that out!

Before he even knew he had drawn it out, Vheled

fired his disruptor into the pit. There was a flash of deadly blue light. When the darkness closed down again, the hole was empty. Gidris and his companion were gone.

The captain bit his lip. He couldn't allow his emotions to rule him that way. This wasn't a brawl in some pleasure palace. This was a mission, and he was the one on whom success or failure hinged.

If he wanted to be in command of the situation, he first had to gain command of himself. Taking a deep breath, he put the disruptor away.

Not bothering to use Grael as a go-between, he took out his own communicator and contacted Terrik. The response was prompt.

"Yes, my lord?"

"Forget my initial instructions," Vheled told him. "I'm no longer interested in finding our men. Let them rot. Right now, all I care about is finding the children. And one other—an adult. A Vulcan."

There was a pause on the other end, naturally. Terrik must have been as surprised as the captain himself was. "Immediately," he replied.

Unfortunately, Klingon sensors were not as sophisticated as the Federation kind. It would take Terrik some time to scan for the Vulcan, even knowing his approximate coordinates.

Vheled could wait, however, if that was what it took to do this *right*.

There was nothing on the forward viewscreen but a pallet of streaming stars—always a pleasant sight but doubly so this time. The Malurian conflict had been one of the thorniest problems Kirk had ever faced; he was glad to have it behind him.

"Estimated time of arrival at Beta Canzandia Three?" he asked Chekov.

"Four days, sixteen hours, and tventy-nine minutes, sair."

The captain smiled to himself, noting how his navigator had rounded off the figure. Spock would have given it to him down to the hundredth of a second, not that it was even vaguely necessary.

It would be good to see Spock again and to hear his comments on what had transpired back at the colony. Knowing the Vulcan, he'd not only tracked down that suspected trouble with the G-7 unit and corrected it but also turned the problem into an advantage. By now the device was probably growing plants that *exceeded* the performance expected of them.

"Sir?"

Kirk, in his command chair, turned at the sound of Uhura's voice. "Yes, Lieutenant?"

His communications officer looked vaguely troubled. "It's Starbase Twelve," she told him. "They say that there may be something wrong with the Beta Canzandia colony."

The captain could feel the muscles in his jaw tightening, but he stayed outwardly calm. "Details, Lieutenant."

Uhura frowned, relaying the information as she received it. "It seems the colony missed its scheduled check-in transmission. And when the starbase attempted subspace contact"—she bit her lip—"there was no answer."

Kirk swallowed. *Carol.* And *Spock.*

And Beta Canzandia wasn't far from Klingon territory—though it didn't have to be the Klingons. It could have been any number of things.

"Thank you, Lieutenant. You can inform Starbase Twelve that we're on our way."

Before Uhura could begin to comply, the captain had swiveled around again. "Mr. Sulu, take us up to warp nine."

But even at that speed, it would take them nearly a day to reach the colony. Kirk hoped that whatever the problem was, it could wait.

David was sitting in a shallow defile, munching on the last of the Klingon rations with all the other kids, when they heard the scuffle of footfalls above them. Immediately Spock drew his disruptor pistol and motioned for everyone to get as low as possible.

There were rasping, guttural noises that David had come to recognize as Klingons talking to one another. And then a sharp smack that sounded for all the world like a fist hitting a naked cheek.

Down in the half-light of the defile, David held his breath and looked around. The other children looked scared but also alert. When his eyes met the Vulcan's, he saw an incredible calm there. Calm, even in the face of terrible danger.

Spock put a finger to his lips. He didn't want anybody to say anything, not even a whisper, in case the Klingons didn't know yet what they'd come upon.

Was it possible their luck had finally run out? Or would the invaders find nothing amiss and keep on going? Then one of the cliffs that made up the defile exploded in a flash of sudden, blue force. As Spock and the children ducked, the fragments of dirt and rock pelted them, covering them with a fine, red silt.

"Come out, Federation scum! Come out, or I will destroy your hole—and *you* along with it!"

David felt his pulse racing. He could see the expressions on his friends' faces, and they were no longer just a little scared. They were a *lot* scared.

For their sake, David tried to set an example. He tried to be as cool and unemotional as Spock was, no matter how agitated he was deep down inside.

He wondered how many of the invaders were up there. If it was only two or three, there was a chance the Vulcan might be able to surprise them with his disruptor.

No—they had to know he had a weapon. Otherwise they wouldn't have bothered to fire from a distance. They just would have leaned in and trained their disruptors on them. And how would they know about the disruptor unless they'd come across one of the traps and freed the Klingons within? David bit his lip. Maybe they'd found more than one of the traps. Maybe they'd found—

Without warning, the cliff wall erupted again in a gout of blue chaos. This time there was more rock and less dirt, and it hurt where it hit them.

"You think you can play a game with me?" roared their tormentor. "You think you can outwit me as you outwitted the fools who pursued you earlier?"

There was raucous laughter—not from just two or three but from what sounded like a large group. It was cut short.

Down in the defile, David's heart was pounding against his ribs. They were outnumbered, and probably all of their enemies had weapons like the one that was eating away at their hiding place.

But as frightened as he was, as hopeless as the situation seemed to be, he refused to give in to the

Klingons. He knew that after all he and his friends had done to the marauders, they wouldn't be allowed to live even if they surrendered.

If he stayed where he was, though, if he didn't move or cry out, he didn't think the others would give themselves up either. And that might give Spock a chance to somehow get them out of this.

He'd no sooner thought that than the Vulcan began firing his disruptor—but not at the Klingons. He trained it at the wall of the defile.

At first David couldn't figure out what Spock was doing. Then, as the weapon bored its way into the earth, he began to see the Vulcan's plan. He was making a tunnel. An escape tunnel. And maybe he had more in mind than just escape, David realized. If Spock could come up *behind* the Klingons and surprise them . . .

A moment later, the Vulcan's head and shoulders followed his disruptor beam into the narrow passage he'd created. Another moment, and he was gone altogether.

No sooner had he disappeared than the Klingon above them resumed his barrage. Blue light blazed, gouging a huge hole in their protecting wall.

"Last warning!" called the marauder. "Your last chance to save your worthless lives!"

Though David could no longer see him, Spock was digging furiously. But he needed time to get to a position from which he could help them.

Again, the wall of the defile was savaged by the Klingon's disruptor beam. And again. Half-buried in dirt and debris, stinging from the force with which it was propelled at him, David gritted his teeth.

The other kids were like red-dirt creatures that had burrowed to the surface. With Spock gone, they looked at him for guidance.

And he wasn't about to back down. The Vulcan had to have all the time they could buy him.

Come on, Spock! Come on!

But as David braced himself for the next blast, the sky suddenly rained Klingons. Before he could scramble away, or even try, he was grabbed by a pair of large, powerful hands and thrown roughly over the brink of the defile.

Then another Klingon grabbed him by the front of his jacket and picked him up off the ground. David found himself staring into the eyes that looked like two chips of obsidian. Beneath them, a mouth full of sharpened teeth grinned crookedly.

"Finally," the invader snarled, in a voice like two rocks being ground together. "The little puris who've been leading us on such a merry chase."

Consumed with a hatred that matched his fear, David struggled. He kicked at the Klingon, punched at him, but his thick, leathery body armor seemed to keep him from harm. The grin widened.

And then another of the brutes bellowed, as if in pain. "The Vulcan! Terrik confirmed that there was a Vulcan!"

Abruptly, the grin on the face of David's captor vanished. Hugging the boy to him with crushing force, he trained his weapon on the defile.

"Find him!" cried the one who'd first noticed Spock's absence—obviously their leader. "Find him or I promise you, you will not live to see the homeworld!"

The Klingons still in the defile clawed furiously through the red earth and shattered rock, but to no avail. One even used his disruptor, despite the risk to his fellow invaders.

"He's not here!" one of them cried finally.

"Fools! He *must* be there! Can he have disappeared into thin air?"

It was then that David saw it—a tiny upheaval of red earth, shot through with scattered, pinprick beams of blue light not ten meters from the place where they'd been hiding. He looked around quickly. No one else seemed to have noticed—not the Klingons, not even the other children.

He turned the other way and resumed his struggles, desperately trying to distract their captors. "Let me go!" he yelled. "Take your hands off me!"

David's efforts only made the Klingon hold him that much tighter. But they served their purpose, he saw, as he stole a glance at the upheaval. The blue light was gone, but he could make out Spock's hands now, overturning slabs of dirt to clear a path to the surface.

What's more, the Vulcan was working quickly. In another couple of seconds, he might raise himself to the point where he could fire on the Klingons.

"Let me go!" David cried, with renewed intensity. And finally landed a solid blow to his captor's mouth.

The Klingon spat out a curse and thrust the boy away from him. Seeing his chance, David pulled the brute's hand to him and bit it. The next thing he knew, he was lying face up on the ground, stunned but free. The Klingon was holding his hand in pain and glaring down at him.

As he lunged for the boy, David spun away, narrowly avoiding his antagonist's grasp. Then he scampered in the opposite direction from the site of Spock's emergence, sliding and stumbling on the uneven terrain, blood thumping in his ears.

"After him," someone roared. "And quickly, or your hide will be forfeit!"

The words had barely left the Klingon's mouth before David felt a weight descend on his ankles, pinning them together. Though he put out his hands to break his fall, he hit the ground with breathtaking impact.

Rumbling a curse, his captor snatched him up and struck him. "Insolent slug! Try that again and I'll hobble you for good!"

David's face stung from the blow. His ankles hurt, too. But he didn't care. Because past the assembled Klingons and their captives, he could see Spock pulling himself out of the ground. As he watched, the Vulcan freed himself up to his armpits, then his waist.

But just when he thought Spock was going to pull it off, to get the drop on their antagonists, he heard a child's voice cry out: "Mr. Spock!"

The Klingons whirled, albeit in different directions. But at least a few of them whirled in the *right* direction—and trained their disruptors on the dirt-encrusted Vulcan. One of them held Garcia in front of him.

"Go ahead," he told Spock. "Try it and the whelp will die first."

The Vulcan frowned. He had no choice. He'd lost the element of surprise.

Slowly, reluctantly, he laid his disruptor down on the ground in front of him. A moment later, one of the Klingons came by to pick it up, and as he straightened, he backhanded Spock across the face.

"That," said the invader, leering, "is for wasting my time." Turning, he signaled to a couple of the other Klingons. "Drag him out of there. There are questions that still need answering."

Chapter Nineteen

SPOCK DIDN'T RESIST as he was torn rudely from the tunnel and sent sprawling into the children's midst. Two more Klingons pulled him to his feet and made him face the leather-bound giant in command.

"You have stolen the device called G-Seven," the Klingon spat. His eyes were inches from the Vulcan's. "I want it."

Spock met the invader's scrutiny and returned it. He could have lied and said he knew nothing about the unit. But he was a Vulcan; lying did not come easily to him.

Besides, it was patently obvious that either he or one of the children had taken the G-7 mechanism. And he was far better suited to enduring the Klingon's brand of questioning than the children were.

"Well?" pressed his inquisitor.

The Starfleet officer remained silent, though he knew it would not endear him to the Klingon.

The invader's eyes flashed black fire. Taking

Spock's face in his gauntleted hand, he squeezed. The contact was unpleasant, even humiliating, but the Vulcan endured it.

Then, suddenly, the Klingon whipped his head to one side, releasing it. "You will never tell," he decided. "Torture would be wasted on you—though I may engage in it anyway, purely for my entertainment, when time is not a consideration."

He turned, seeking something. Finally, his eyes alighted on David.

"A human, on the other hand, may not be quite so reticent," the Klingon rumbled. "Especially such a small human." He gestured, and the blond boy was brought to him.

Even at close quarters, David didn't flinch. He did his best to look the Klingon in the eye.

The invader had chosen poorly, Spock reflected. Of all the children he had at his disposal, the blond boy would be the least likely to tell him anything.

Or perhaps I am misjudging the Klingon's intent, he thought. Perhaps this was all a show based on the belief that Spock would break down rather than see David tortured.

Nor would the Vulcan have hesitated to give away the whereabouts of the G-7 unit if he thought it would ensure David's safety. However, Klingons were not known for their merciful natures . . . nor for their short memories. Having been thwarted this long, they would have their revenge, even if their demands for the device were met.

"Where is the terraforming unit?" the Klingon asked.

David would not have said even if he knew. His attitude was positively Vulcan.

Spock regretted that the children were involved in this. He had tried to send them deeper into the hills. He had tried to put their safety before his own. But they had made the choice to stay with him and to help. They were faced now with the fruits of their decision.

"Where is the mechanism?" the Klingon snarled.

David glanced at Spock and remained silent.

But the boy's link to the Starfleet officer did not go unnoticed. The Klingon's ebony eyes glittered beneath the ridge of his brow.

"It seems," he observed, "this child draws his courage from the Vulcan. Well, that resource can be stripped from him easily enough."

He turned to a couple of Klingons whose hands were not full with the other human children. With a jerk of his shaggy head, he indicated a nearby outcropping of red rock.

"Take him around to the other side," he commanded. "Then we will see how much of his foolishness is his own."

Spock watched, prevented from intervening by the half-dozen disruptors aimed at him, as the Klingons grabbed the boy and brought him around to the far side of the outcropping.

The wind was cold as it swept through the hills, making even the sun seem to shiver. Vheled looked at the boy.

And David looked back with defiance in his eyes. An almost Klingon sort of defiance, despite the fact that he was in the grip of two brawny warriors. Despite even the disruptor in the Klingon captain's hand. Vheled smiled inwardly.

Apparently, the boy's courage was his own, not the Vulcan's. This one was different from the Riordan child, the one who had succumbed to tears back at the installation. But he was still a child. More than likely, he would break. And if he did not, it was of no great import. He would die and another child would take his place. Eventually, Vheled would find the weak link in the chain. It was only a matter of time.

"You know what I want," the captain said. He raised his disruptor until it was even with the boy's eyes, until he could look right down its barrel. "Give it to me—or perish. It is that simple."

The human blinked a couple of times. But he didn't weep. And more to the point, he didn't give Vheled the information he sought.

This was getting infuriating. It was time to shed some blood, the captain decided, to show the humans he meant business.

"Stand back," he told his men, so they wouldn't be caught in the disruption effect. As they obeyed, he pressed the end of the barrel against the spot between the child's eyes. In a way, Vheled hated to reward valor with death. But in this case, he had no choice.

Suddenly, there was a flare of blue radiance. But not from the weapon he held against the human, from somewhere else.

As he looked up, he saw that one of his men had fired on the other. And Chorrl, the one who'd been fired upon, was disintegrating before his eyes.

The captain of the *Kad'nra* didn't know what was happening, but he knew that it wasn't good. It wasn't until the Klingon's disruptor swung in his direction that he began to understand the extent of the problem.

"Grael," he said. "What are you—?"

There was no time to finish his question. Grael's finger was depressing the trigger.

Hurling himself out of the way, Vheled narrowly missed being disrupted. The blue beam lanced past him and shattered part of the outcropping.

As the captain landed on the ground, he rolled and came up firing. Unfortunately, his aim was shaky, and he missed his target by a good half a meter.

Even more unfortunately, Grael's second shot was perfect. Vheled could feel himself being ripped apart; the pain was like nothing he had ever imagined. He doubled over, his weapon slipping from his hand.

But even as he perished in the atom-tearing wake of the disruption radiation, the captain of the *Kad'nra* managed to raise his head long enough to glare at Grael and hurl one hissing curse at him:

"Traitor!"

For a moment, Grael stood over the remains of his former comrade and his former captain, trying to accept the reality of what he had done. Somehow, he'd believed that treachery would be an easier thing to swallow the second time around.

He was wrong. It was worse—much worse. But there was no turning back now. He had only begun to fulfill his unholy pledge to Kiruc, first by sabotaging the *Kad'nra*, and then by killing Vheled to keep him from bringing back the colonists' terraforming technology.

There were still a half-dozen other Klingons on the other side of the outcropping to deal with. And then Kruge and his group, back at the installation.

First things first, he decided. He would have to find

a way to wipe out his remaining crewmates—preferably without being killed himself. After all, the whole point of this was to ensure his continued survival.

So wrapped up was Grael in his thoughts, he almost forgot about the human child—who now stared at him with strange, blue eyes. Returning the stare, the Klingon suddenly got an idea.

It was a risk, Grael told himself. But it also might be his only chance. Going over to what was left of Vheled, he picked up the captain's disruptor and held it out to the boy.

The human looked reticent, suspicious. He didn't move.

"Take it," the Klingon rasped, so no one else could hear. "You want to help your friends, don't you?"

The child nodded. "Yes," he said softly.

"Then this is your chance. Take it."

The boy weighed his decision for another second or two. Then he came forward and held out his hand. Grael laid the disruptor in it.

"You know how to use it?" he asked.

The human nodded again. He pantomimed pressing the trigger.

"Good," said Grael. He directed the boy to one edge of the outcropping. "You stand there." Indicating the other end of the rocky mass, he said, "I'll stand here. When I give you a sign, take out as many as you can."

The child's eyes narrowed. There was a question in them: *Why?*

Grael didn't answer. It was none of his concern.

Silently, they moved to either end of the outcropping. As the traitor craned his neck around it, the scene beyond gradually came into view. The Klingons had herded the children and the Vulcan together so they could surround them and watch them more easily. Apparently, no one had heard the brief disruptor battle. Nor had enough time passed for them to suspect anything was amiss.

Grael turned and gave the signal. Then, unbeknownst to the boy, he waited for him to fire first. That would ensure that the Klingons' fire would initially be directed at the human, not at the traitor.

After all, why incur more danger than he had to? Let the child run interference for him. The only aspect of his plan that might have worked better was the human's aim. His first burst went well wide of the Klingon nearest to him.

Everything else worked like a charm, however. No sooner had the Klingons realized they were being fired upon than they returned the favor, blasting away at the source of the blue beam.

Grael couldn't tell if the boy was hit or not—nor did he much care. The important thing was that he had provided a distraction.

With unerring accuracy, the traitor cut down two of his comrades in quick succession. A third saw him and got off a shot but not a good one. And a fraction of a second later, he too was writhing in agony.

Then a couple of beams sizzled past too close for comfort, and Grael had to retreat behind the outcropping. Two more blasts struck the edge of the formation, pulverizing it; fragments rained down all over.

Taking a deep breath, the traitor stuck his head out past the rock again and fired. Again he was successful, and a comrade fell.

Four down, two to go. But before Grael could score another victim, the Vulcan made it unnecessary. Coming up behind one of the Klingons, he grabbed him at the juncture of neck and shoulder and the warrior collapsed.

As the sole remaining invader turned to fire at the Starfleet officer, a couple of the human children tried to tackle him from behind. And when the Klingon tried to cast them aside, it left him open for the Vulcan's attack.

A single blow was all it took. The Klingon crumpled as if his bones had turned to frail swamp reeds.

Only then did Grael check to see the status of his young accomplice. The boy, it seemed, was unhurt. And he still held the disruptor.

"Your job is done," the traitor told him. "Give me back the weapon."

As before, David hesitated. Grael eyed him. Would he actually have the courage to test a Klingon's trigger finger? At point-blank range?

Suddenly inspired, Grael pointed his disruptor in the direction of the human's comrades. "Don't test me," he said. "I'm on your side—if you allow me to be."

Maybe it was the threat to his friends; maybe it was something in the Klingon's voice that smacked of the truth. In any case, the child lowered his weapon and tossed it to Grael.

The Klingon caught it and grunted. "A wise choice." Then he came out of concealment, only to see the Vulcan kneeling to recover a weapon from one of the fallen.

"I wouldn't touch that if I were you," he said.

Like the boy, the Vulcan seemed to weigh the

various elements of the situation. In the end, he withdrew his hand.

That gave the Klingon the chance to complete his work here. He destroyed his two unconscious comrades, then their weapons.

While he was doing this, the Vulcan remained impassive, only the merest shadow crossing his face. But the children's faces openly displayed their emotions: horror and revulsion.

"They were your enemies," said Grael, when he was finished. "Why not be glad they are gone?"

"What you did was unnecessary," replied the Starfleet officer. "They would have remained unconscious for hours."

"Unnecessary?" the Klingon echoed. He leered. "Maybe for your purposes, but definitely not for mine."

The Vulcan regarded him. "I must confess," he said, "I do not understand your motives—or for that matter, your objectives."

"My motives," Grael told him, "are my own. And my objectives, at least insofar as you need know about them, are to confound this mission and take us back to the homeworld. In fact, I will be encouraging our departure sometime later today." He pointed with his disruptor in the direction of the colony. "That should give you time to return to your installation and free your human friends while you still have the chance."

The Vulcan maintained his scrutiny. "An act of mercy?" he asked.

The Klingon shook his head. "You know better."

Accepting that as the truth, the Starfleet officer looked to his young charges. "Come," he said. "Let us do as he suggests."

Only the boy with the yellow hair and the strange blue eyes gave Grael a last look. The rest just followed the Vulcan past the outcropping and into the distance.

When he was sure they were gone, the Klingon holstered his disruptor, sat down where he could rest his back against the outcropping, and contemplated his deeds.

Kruge was pacing the commandeered dome when the door opened again. As before, it framed the powerful form of Oghir.

"Second Officer? It is Grael."

Oghir's expression was no more sanguine than before. Kruge cursed and opened his communicator. "Grael? This is the second officer. Report! What is happening?"

Grael's tone was hollow, flat, as if his emotions could not begin to keep up with the disasters that had been taking place out there. "They're all dead," he reported.

The second officer shook his head. "What nonsense is this?"

"They're all dead," the man repeated. "Captain Vheled, First Officer Gidris, everyone. I'm the only one left."

It took a moment for the words to sink in, and then another before Kruge could get himself to believe them. "Who killed them?" he asked. "Not the human brats?"

"No, not children. There are no *children* out here, Second Officer. Only adults—Starfleet officers." A pause. "It's a trap of some kind, I think. As if they *wanted* us to come here, to try to steal their technology . . ."

Kruge resisted an impulse to hurl his communicator at the dome's curved wall. He should have known mere children couldn't outwit an experienced warrior like Gidris. He should have *known*.

And so should Vheled have known. He should have taken more men, maybe even directed long-range disruptor fire from the *Kad'nra*.

But now it was too late. According to Grael, the captain was dead. And so were their hopes for obtaining the full measure of this colony's scientific advances.

Abruptly, Kruge realized he'd gotten what he'd wished for. He was in charge—not just for a little while, but indefinitely.

The knowledge sobered him. "Stand by," he told Grael.

"Aye-aye, sir," came the response.

Curbing his fury, Kruge considered his options. He didn't have many.

He could take the few troops that were left to him and confront the Starfleet force in the hills, but that seemed like a losing proposition. If this was a trap, as Grael had suggested, who knew what else lay in store for them out there?

The second option was to cut and run. To beam up with whatever data Mallot had been able to coax from Boudreau and his computers and content themselves with that.

Naturally, the second option grated on Kruge's nerves. For one thing, they would look like puris, slogging home with their tails between their legs and their mission only partly accomplished, and that would not help the Gevish'rae cause in the least. For another, Boudreau had lied right to his face. He must have known what awaited them in the hills; he must have been in on it. And Kruge hated it when people lied to him.

On the other hand, what else was there for them to gain here? There was still a chance that the G-7 device was a formidable weapon; in his heart, he still believed that. But there was also a chance that the damned thing had never existed in the first place.

Maybe the whole installation was just bait for the Federation's trap. Maybe when they got back to the homeworld and analyzed all Mallot's data, they'd find out that it was gibberish—more bait.

Still, they couldn't go back with nothing of value. They couldn't—

With the suddenness of a summer storm in the Fesh'rin hills, Kruge's course of action became clear to him. He spoke into his communicator again.

"Grael?"

"Yes, Second Officer?"

"I am now the *captain*," Kruge reminded him tautly.

"Yes, Captain?" the man amended.

"Contact the ship and have yourself beamed up. And alert the transporter tech. There will be more to follow."

"As you wish—*Captain* Kruge."

Still standing just inside the door, Oghir looked at him. "We are leaving?" he asked tentatively.

Kruge nodded. "Yes. We are leaving. But not alone."

The man looked puzzled. "Not alone?" he echoed.

"Of course not," said the new captain of the *Kad'nra,* as he brushed past Oghir on his way out the door. "The colonists will be coming with us."

And with Oghir trailing him, he headed for the domes where Boudreau and the other lying humans were being kept.

A small, nondescript gray ball appeared in the distance on the main viewscreen. The captain knew what it was: there was no point in calling for magnification.

"Approaching Beta Canzandia Ten," Sulu reported, from his customary position at the helm. His voice was stretched tight, but no tighter than Kirk's nerves. The trip had seemed to take an eternity. "Estimated time to Beta Canzandia Three is twenty-three minutes, thirty seconds."

"Still no response from the colony," Uhura contributed.

The captain leaned forward, lodging a knuckle in the space between his chin and his lower lip. Probably they'd beam down and find the problem was nothing more than a communications unit on the blink. Or some damned interference pattern in the atmosphere.

And Spock would look at him as if he'd been crazy to tear across space at warp nine. *As you can see, sir,* he would say, eyebrow raised in incredulity, *we are quite unharmed.*

At the navigation board, Chekov was hunched over his controls as if to get a better look at one of his monitors. Suddenly the ensign whirled around in his seat.

"Sair, I've got a Klingon wessel on my screen—and it's in orbit around the colony planet!"

The captain absorbed the information in an instant and formulated a course of action.

"Maintain speed, Mr. Sulu!" He touched a pad on the armrest of his command chair. "Mr. Scott?"

"Aye, sir."

"We've got trouble up ahead—Klingon trouble. I want phasers and photon torpedoes primed and ready!"

"Ye've got 'em," Scotty assured him.

Kirk's mind raced. What were the Klingons up to, anyway? Just asserting what they claimed were their borders—or something more than that?

Could it be they were after the terraforming technology? He certainly wouldn't put it past them. The Klingons had seen benign Federation technologies as threats in the past; why not now?

Damn. The colonists had no defenses, no way of fighting back. They'd be helpless against the likes of a Klingon raiding party.

If they'd hurt Carol . . . or Spock . . .

Abruptly he realized his hands had become fists. With an effort he relaxed them, then tapped his armrest again. "Mr. Leslie."

"Sir?" came the almost instantaneous reply.

"Prepare a security team. It looks as if we're going to have to take a colony back from the Klingons."

Leslie caught on quickly. "We'll be ready in five minutes, sir."

"Five minutes will be satisfactory," the captain told him.

It would be about twice that before they reached Beta Canzandia Three. Kirk knew they'd be ten of the longest minutes in his life.

Chapter Twenty

FROM THE VANTAGE POINT of the playground, Spock and the children lay on their bellies and surveyed the situation below. It was deceptively peaceful down among the colony buildings.

"How will we know which domes they're being held in?" asked Garcia.

"They are the ones that will be guarded," the Vulcan answered. "In any case, that will be my problem—no one else's. I will go down there alone."

The children all looked at him, defiant, longing to accompany him even after the scare that their captors had put into them.

Then David spoke up. "Mister Spock's right," he said. "This is something he can best do alone."

The first officer regarded the boy approvingly. In some ways, the Vulcan mused, he was no longer a boy at all. And in that instant, as he considered his strange, young ally, Spock suddenly realized what he found so familiar about him.

No, he told himself upon reflection. It was not possible; surely, the captain would have mentioned such a thing. Unless . . . he didn't know himself. And then the rest of the truth became apparent to him, unfolding like a scroll. Except, of course, for the identity of the child's mother.

"As David says," Spock went on, unflustered, "I have a better chance of succeeding if I try it on my own."

None of them looked happy about it, but they gave in. With a quick glance over his shoulder at the faces he would never forget, the Vulcan started down toward the domes of the installation.

The descent from the hills to the colony proper took Spock almost precisely seventeen minutes, as he'd expected. However, it took him almost that long again to find the guards posted around the outpost's buildings. Fortunately, he spotted them before they spotted him.

The Klingons were talking, which made it a bad time to approach them. He could hardly sneak up on one while the other was watching. After a minute or two, however, an opportunity presented itself. One of the guards walked away—either to report to a superior or to take care of his physical needs.

He was gone no more than half a minute before Spock crept around the edge of the dome, came up behind the remaining Klingon, and grabbed him at the base of his neck. Despite the guard's brawny physique, he was out instantly.

Catching his victim as he fell, the Vulcan took him under the armpits and dragged him into the dome. As he hoped, the doors slid aside at his approach.

"My God," someone gasped.

Looking over his shoulder, Spock saw the clot of frightened colonists. One of them pointed to him. He recognized the face.

"It's Spock," said Boudreau disbelievingly. He saw the unconscious Klingon and laughed. "How in blazes did you do *that?*"

"No time to explain," the Vulcan replied. Dropping the guard just to one side of the entrance, he slipped the Klingon's disruptor out of his belt. Then he straightened. "However, I would appreciate your help in attracting the other guard's attention. The more noise, the better."

Finding Carol Marcus among the uninjured, he tossed her the disruptor. She caught it, then looked at him.

"In case my methods prove unsuccessful," he told her. "Though I advise you to keep it out of sight for the time being."

"Mister Spock," Dr. Marcus said. She still looked as if she was in shock. "The children—"

"They are all fine," he said brusquely. "Now Doctor—the noise, if you please."

Marcus nodded. Then she and her fellow prisoners made a clamor that the remaining guard could not have helped but hear. A couple of seconds later, the doors slid away again and the Klingon took a step inside. His disruptor was in his hand, trained on the colonists ahead of him. Having already noticed his partner's absence, he was grim and alert.

He glimpsed Spock out of the corner of his eye in time to whirl and avoid the intended nerve pinch. However, he was too slow to press the trigger on his weapon before the Vulcan laid him low with a whip of a right hook.

I must remember to thank the captain for that maneuver, Spock mused.

This time, he handed the disruptor to Boudreau. Taking it, the scientist grunted. "Never thought I'd see the day I'd be carrying one of *these.*"

"As I indicated earlier," Spock told him, "it is merely a precaution. Do you know where the rest of your colleagues are?"

Boudreau nodded. "One of the other domes. But I'm afraid I don't know which one."

"No need to worry," the Vulcan assured him. "I found this one. I will find the other."

"Don't you want some help?" asked Dr. Marcus.

Spock shook his head. "I would prefer to see you escape while you can. Even without the disruptors, you should not have a problem in that regard."

The blond woman seemed to be on the verge of arguing with him, but in the end, she refrained. "Come on," she told the others. "Let's get out of here and let Mr. Spock do his job."

Something in the way she said that made the Vulcan think. And in the next instant, the last piece of the puzzle fell into place. David . . . *Marcus?* Yes. David Marcus.

Spock waited until the last of the humans had filed out of the opening. Then he took off in the opposite direction, searching for the other prison dome and the remainder of the scientists.

Down below, the installation was just as quiet as before. Just as still, in fact, as if there were nobody there at all.

"It's taking too long," judged Pfeffer.

"It is *not,*" said Medford. "He's only been down there a couple of minutes."

"At least there hasn't been any shooting," Garcia contributed. "I haven't seen any flashes, anyway."

That recalled for all of them their initial horror at observing the colony's takeover. For a moment, no one spoke. And Wan shivered—actually *shivered*.

Then David broke the silence. "He's doing fine. I know he is."

Mr. Spock just inspired confidence in him. Even when they were looking down the muzzle of a Klingon disruptor, David was certain that the Vulcan would get them out of it.

It made him want to be more like Mr. Spock despite his mother's warnings to steer clear of him. It made him want to be the kind of person that could maybe one day help the Vulcan out of trouble the way Spock had helped David and his friends out of theirs.

Not that he'd ever get the chance, of course. But that was the kind of feeling that the Vulcan aroused in him.

He still had no father. But if he needed someone to use as a standard, as a yardstick against which to measure himself—well, to David's way of thinking, he could do a lot worse than Mr. Spock.

"Wait a minute," said Garcia. "What's that?"

There was movement among the domes. A line of people—not Klingons but colonists. They were slinking toward the edge of the installation nearest the children.

"It's our parents," Wan breathed. "And the others. They're escaping!"

David nodded. He knew he could trust Spock. He *knew* it.

Pfeffer started to get up, intending to go down and

meet them. But Medford grabbed his arm, as she'd once grabbed Garcia's.

"What, are you crazy?" she asked. "What if they get caught? Then we'll be caught too."

She was right. Even now they had to be careful. Even now, when it seemed as if everything was on the verge of being all right, they had to hold themselves back—just in case.

With agonizing slowness, the colonists threaded their way out of the installation and up the hill. Spock was with them. David could see the blue of the Vulcan's shirt as he shepherded everyone else along, gesturing for them to move quickly. After a while, they were close enough for the children to make out their faces.

David saw Wan's parents up in front, and Pfeffer's, and Garcia's. But where was his mother? Scanning the incline, he swallowed.

Then, miraculously, he *saw* her. She was walking beside Dr. Boudreau in the back of the group. And of all things, she had a phaser in her hand!

One of the colonists caught sight of them and pointed them out to someone else, and suddenly a bunch of them came running up the hill, their arms outstretched, their eyes alight, and their mouths open, making sounds of joy.

There was no longer any reason to stay hidden. There was only a burst of warm feeling that made David's throat start to close up, and before he knew it he was running down the hill toward his mother, as crazy as the rest of them.

When she saw him, she ran too, until they came together and hugged. They hadn't hugged that way in years, since he was a little kid, but they hugged that way now. And try as he might, David couldn't keep back the tears, not completely.

"Are you all right?" his mother asked, wiping tears from her own eyes with the back of the hand that held the phaser. She leaned back and looked at him, at his face. "My God, you look so skinny. What have you been eating?"

He shrugged. "Not much, I guess."

And then he became aware of all the other reunions that were taking place around him. He couldn't hear much more than snatches of conversation, but they sounded good. They sounded right.

"—and we hid in the caves, and it was cold but we huddled together—"

"—so we knocked him over the head, and then Mr. Spock—"

"—*trapped* the *Klingons?* What do you *mean* you—"

Everyone was crowding together and excited. And there were more of the colonists moving up the slope to join them all the time. Dr. Riordan was among them, with his wife and son not far behind.

For a second or two, David's eyes met Timothy's and held them. David was reminded of the story his mom used to tell him, of the Pied Piper and the little boy who was left behind when all the other children followed the piper into the mountain.

That's the kind of look Riordan had on his face. As if he'd been left behind and deprived of something valuable. Except in the story, it hadn't been the little boy's fault he'd been left out; he was lame, and he couldn't help it. As Riordan flushed and turned away from him, it occurred to David that not every handicap was something you could see from the outside.

Then he forgot about Riordan and looked at the others trudging up the hill to the playground. Though he couldn't actually be sure unless he counted, it looked to him as if they'd all made it.

All of them.

As Kruge approached the nearer of the two lab domes in which the colonists were imprisoned, he was quickly changing his mind. He would still take hostages, of course. But someone would have to *pay* for this humiliating state of affairs and pay dearly.

He had a couple of individuals in mind. One was Boudreau. The other was Timothy Riordan.

After all, the homeworld scientists wouldn't need *all* the humans to piece together the terraforming technology. One or two, even someone of Boudreau's stature, would hardly be missed, and before he actually pressed the trigger, maybe he would see them all grovel. Yes. He would enjoy that.

He was so intent on his revenge, he didn't even notice that the doors to the dome were unguarded. Oghir, on the other hand, was more alert.

"Captain," he rasped. "The sentinels. Where are they?"

Kruge slowed down and looked around warily. Indeed, where were they?

Then he spied the pair of boots that protruded just beyond the curve of the dome and, advancing on them, found the guards stretched out on the red dirt, unconscious.

With a roar of rage and frustration, he lunged for the doors. Just before he would have banged into them, they slid aside, revealing to the *Kad'nra*'s new captain the incredibly *empty* interior of the dome.

279

Lurching outside again, he headed for the other dome. Anger was building inside him like a disruptor charge as he anticipated the worst . . . and found it. The second dome was just like the first—empty as a tomb.

The prisoners were gone. Where? He removed his communicator from his belt, opened it in order to contact what few men he had left at the installation, and was surprised to receive a communication from the *Kad'nra.*

It was Haastra. "We have a problem, Second Officer. There's—"

"Captain, Haastra. I am now *captain.* Both Vheled and Gidris are dead."

There was silence for a moment on the other end, as the security chief absorbed the information. Nor was Kruge surprised. Vheled's death represented a personal failure on Haastra's part, though there was nothing he could have done to prevent it. Security chiefs were always held responsible for their captains' welfare. Nor did new captains generally retain old security officers, and Kruge had no intention of being an exception in that regard.

Finally, Haastra said with obvious distaste and disappointment, *"Captain,* then. As I was saying, we have a problem."

"Then we have a *number* of them," Kruge retorted. "What is wrong now?"

The security chief was calm—as calm as any man could be who'd just learned his fate was sealed. In fact, he almost seemed to gloat as he replied, "There is a Federation vessel bearing down on us. It will be here in a matter of minutes."

Kruge felt himself shaking, not with fear but with

fury. How could everything be going wrong all at once?

"Beam us up," he spat into the communicator. "Every Klingon who still lives is to be brought back to the ship immediately. And be prepared to break orbit as soon as we're aboard."

"As you wish," said Haastra.

He stared at the central dome, the one with all the computers in it, and bit his lip. If only he'd still had the prisoners. Then his return to the homeworld might not have seemed like such a defeat.

As an idea came to him, he grunted. The humans had beaten them—beaten *him*. But before he left, he would show them that Klingons do not take such losses lightly.

"Captain," said Oghir, "what—?"

Kruge cut him short with a quick, chopping gesture. Pulling out his disruptor, he pointed it at the central dome and opened fire.

Blue-white light snaked out at his massive target, spraying over its surface, enveloping it, consuming it. After a moment, Kruge could see inside through a burning, gaping hole, to the computer work stations within. After another moment, the computers themselves began to spark and smoke, and finally to explode into individual balls of flame.

Grinning at the carnage, the Klingon continued to fire. With the explosions continuing, the flames began to blend into a single conflagration. Above the string of blazing work stations, the latticework of white, plastic tubing started to melt and come apart.

And then, in one unexpected paroxysm of destruction, the entire dome erupted like an awakened volcano. The heat seared Kruge's face, but he didn't back off. It felt *good*.

Better yet, it was spreading to other domes in the area. They too were beginning to go up in flames.

It was just an inkling of what the Federation could expect from Kruge, Captain of the *Kad'nra*. Just a taste of the revenge he would work on them some day.

As he savored the prospect, he realized he was beginning to dematerialize. His last sight was of the raging inferno that would slowly but surely claim the entire installation. In the greater scheme of things, it was pitifully small consolation; but for the time being, it would have to suffice.

David had never seen the kind of celebration that took place on the hill below the playground. Adults and children were hugging and kissing and laughing all at once. Only Spock didn't participate. He kept a wary eye on the installation at the base of the slope, where the Klingons were still a threat.

Pulling his mom behind him, David went over to the Vulcan. Spock noticed and cocked an eyebrow, glancing first at the boy and then at his mother.

"You need any help?" David asked.

The Vulcan shook his head. "No. Not at the moment." And then, to David's mother, he said: "Your son is a very brave young man." The observation came without any obvious signs of emotion.

She nodded. "Yes. I know."

Something passed between them, an exchange that David didn't quite understand. Nor did he get much of a chance, because in the next instant, there was the boom of some sort of explosion. And another. And then a whole series of them, one right after the other.

Open-mouthed, David looked down at the installation and saw flames—big red tongues of it, rising from the lab dome.

"My God," someone said. "They're burning the place down!"

Dr. Boudreau stepped forward. He too had a disruptor in his hand, and he looked as if he would have liked to use it.

As David looked on, the flames spread to the other domes. To the rec dome, where they had their parties and their holiday celebrations. To the supply dome, where he'd met Dr. McCoy . . . To the dome where he and his mother had lived—where he'd eaten and done his homework and dreamed his dreams of a lusty, green Earth.

He felt as if his whole life was going up in smoke. And then he looked at his mother, and he realized that her garden was burning, too, and the plants into which she'd put so much loving care.

All of it was burning. And there was nothing they could do except watch and feel helpless.

"The Klingons are breaking orbit, sair!" called Chekov.

The image on the viewscreen bore him out. With the magnification all the way up now, Kirk could easily make out the Klingon vessel as it veered off from the angry, red sweep of Beta Canzandia Three.

The captain was surprised. It wasn't like the Klingons to cut and run, particularly when the odds were more or less even.

"Scan them, Mr. Sulu. Tell me why they're so eager to retreat."

The helmsman's answer seemed to take a long time,

283

though it was probably only a matter of seconds. "They're partially disabled, sir. Energy readings correspond with impulse power only."

Kirk leaned forward. Impulse power, eh? Interesting.

"Any humans aboard her?" he asked Sulu.

Again a wait—one the captain didn't have patience for. If the Klingons *had* taken hostages, he would have to move quickly.

Finally, the answer: "No, sir. No humans aboard."

Kirk leaned back in his chair, momentarily relieved, and watched the Klingon ship continue to put distance between them.

Chekov turned in his seat. "Shell I plot a pursuit?" he asked.

The captain was tempted, but he shook his head. "No, ensign. Plot an orbit." No matter what kinds of atrocities the invaders might have been guilty of, his first priority had to be the colonists. They might be hurt, dying . . .

He clenched his teeth at the thought and swore that if the Klingons had hurt his friends, they would yet have an opportunity to regret it.

Rising from his seat, Kirk turned and headed for the turbolift. "Take the conn," he told Scotty, who was sitting at his bridge station. "I'm beaming down with the landing party."

"Aye, sir," the engineer responded.

Before Scotty could move to the captain's chair, however, the lift doors closed and Kirk was on his way to the transporter room, a prayer on his lips.

Chapter Twenty-one

KIRK, LESLIE, AND THEIR security team beamed down into an inferno. Everywhere they looked, there was a colony dome ablaze.

Carol, he thought.

The captain turned to Leslie, shielding his eyes from the terrible heat. "Where are they?"

If the colonists were still down here, in one of these domes, he had to get them out. He wasn't sure how, but he had to try.

Leslie took out his tricorder and scanned the area in a full circle from where they were standing. Sweating profusely, he wiped his forehead on his sleeve.

"They're not here," he reported. "Not anywhere in the installation."

Kirk knew full well that that could be good news . . . or bad. The tricorder only responded to *living* beings. If the scientists were dead already . . .

Whipping out his communicator, he barked, "Mr.

Sulu. I want a sensor scan of this place—a radius of two kilometers from my position." He frowned. "With particular attention to human and Vulcan life-forms."

"Coming right up, sir." There was a pause, during which the captain could hear the helmsman relaying his command. Then Sulu came back to him. "There's a group of humans just west of the installation, and one Vulcan. Do you need more detailed data?"

Breathing deeply, Kirk shook his head, even though he knew Sulu couldn't see it. "No. No, thank you, Lieutenant. Kirk out."

Leslie smiled. "They got out."

"Apparently," the captain replied. He looked around at the fiery domes. "Come on. Let's see if there's anything around here we can still salvage."

David was sitting at the edge of the playground, looking down at the still-smoking domes and trying to imagine what had happened, trying to reconstruct the events that had led up to the destruction of the colony, when Spock gave the all-clear.

Apparently, it was safe for them to return to the installation. The Klingons were gone now, Spock's ship had called him to tell him so. The fires had been put out, ironically, by strategic phaser fire.

A couple of the domes on the far side of the colony had even been salvaged. The terraformers would have places to live until new structures could be erected to replace the old.

As the group, children as well as adults, began to move down the hillside, they had the look of a people that was going home. There was hope in their eyes, David thought, not bitterness. Relief, not anger.

Even Dr. Boudreau, who had been livid at the sight of the domes going up in flames, had calmed down considerably when Spock ordered the G-7 unit beamed over from its hiding place in the hills. The colony administrator had been cradling the device in his arms ever since, carrying it like a big, shiny baby.

But as he took his mother's hand and descended the slope, David felt strangely detached from the spirit of relief and hopefulness. He felt as if the colony's destruction was a nightmare that could have been avoided.

Sure, the *Enterprise* had sent the Klingons packing, but from what the Klingon in the hills had said, the invaders were probably going to leave the planet anyway. If they'd just been left alone—if they hadn't been confronted and provoked by the presence of the Starfleet ship—would they have trained their disruptors on the domes?

If the *Enterprise* hadn't butted in, the boy thought, would his home still be standing? And the lab dome? And all the rest of them? David shook his head. They hadn't needed any help from Starfleet. They'd done fine without them. But the *Enterprise* had interfered anyway. And *this* was the result.

His sense of horror grew worse with each step. By the time they reached the bottom of the hill and entered the installation, he felt even more detached than before. Distant, in fact—distant and numb. It was as if he were walking with someone else's legs, surveying the charred wrecks of the domes through someone else's eyes.

Though the smoke was lifting up into the air, driven by a stiff wind, the pathways between the blackened, skeletal domes seemed flooded with something thicker and harder than air. It was like walking underwater, David imagined. Or through a dream.

His mother was expressionless. Her features may as well have been carved from rock. But her hand, the one that held David's, gave her away. It was trembling ever so slightly in his grasp.

Unburned tatters of dome material reared and flapped at them as they passed by. They reminded the boy of huge beasts, writhing in agony. Writhing and dying.

The smell of smoke made his eyes start to water. But he wouldn't cry; he wouldn't give even the *appearance* of crying. Setting his teeth, David pressed on.

Why had it been necessary for the military to show up, with its phasers and its photon torpedoes and its bluster, and make the Klingons angry? *Why?*

Abruptly, his horror turned to anger. It lodged in his throat, slick, hot, and throbbing. It spread to his belly, where it smoldered like white-hot coals.

The group began to split up. Here, the Pfeffers stopped at the ruin of what used to be their home and peered into the wreckage. There, the Wans walked toward a clump of spiderlike remains.

Why? David asked again—silently, so no one heard his pain. *Why?*

Then he and his mother came in sight of the place where her garden used to stand. There was movement there—not colonists but Starfleet people, in their red or gold uniforms. Directly ahead of them, one of the men from the *Enterprise* knelt in the scorched tangle that was once a patch of living things. David recognized him, too.

It was the captain, the one called Kirk. The one who had confronted the Klingons.

The man looked up at the boy and his mother. He was holding something. It was so desiccated, so black and twisted, that it took David a moment to figure out what it was. Finally, he recognized it.

It was one of the Klingon plants. One of the fireblossoms.

Where did that captain get off touching his mother's plants? *He* was the one who'd destroyed her garden in the first place, just as clearly as if he'd pressed the trigger on the disruptor himself.

What right did he have to look sad? To look as if he *cared*—now, when it was too late?

Suddenly, David's anger surged and spilled over, and the world melted, caught in the heat of his righteous fury.

It didn't seem to Kirk it had been that long since he'd authorized Spock to give the all-clear. So when he looked up and saw Carol, he was surprised.

But he was even more surprised to see her holding the hand of the blond boy. Not that he hadn't seen the boy around the colony; most likely he had, but until he'd had this chance to see the youngster next to Carol, he'd had no idea that they were related.

Now, as he compared their faces, the conclusion was inescapable. It was Carol's son—no doubt about it. But why hadn't she told him? Why had she—

And then he took another look at the boy, and he had his answer.

My God, he whispered inwardly, suddenly finding it hard to swallow. He felt a smile taking over.

I've got . . . a son? he thought. And then, liking the sound of it: *I've got a son!*

That's when Carol and the boy turned their heads

and saw him standing there, looking at them. *Gaping* at them is more like it, he mused.

The captain started toward them, not sure of what he would say when he got there, not sure of anything except the inexorable pull of his own flesh and blood. The youngster's expression slowly began to change. . . . But not to one of joy. Instead, his mouth twisted and hardened as if he'd just eaten something he didn't like. And even then, Kirk didn't quite catch on, until the boy barked something at him—something about Klingons and destruction—and the captain realized what had contorted those young features.

It was hatred—pure, seething hatred. And it was all directed at him.

Horrified, he asked himself: Why? What had he done?

"David!" Carol took him by the shoulder and whirled him around to face her. She shook her head as if she couldn't believe what she'd heard.

"David," she said, this time in a more measured tone, "what are you saying?"

The boy scowled and took a step back. But when he spoke, his voice was level, almost calm.

"He did this, Mom. It's his fault."

"His . . . fault?" she repeated. "What do you mean?"

For a moment, the youngster seemed on the verge of telling her. Then, biting his lip, he just turned and walked away.

Carol looked at Kirk, hoping he would have an explanation. Of course, he didn't. He just shook his head in helpless bewilderment.

She started after the boy, but the captain held her with a cry: "Carol!"

Carol stopped and turned, looking miserable. "Yes," she said. "He is who you think he is. Now I have to go find him. I have to—" She frowned. "We'll talk later."

Numb, he nodded. "Later." He watched Carol disappear around the curve of a ruined dome.

But in the space of a couple of moments, Kirk had fallen from the pinnacle of jubilation to the depths of dark confusion. And in the wind that whistled through the installation, he could still hear the boy's bizarre and discomfiting accusation: *His fault . . . his fault . . .*

Chapter Twenty-two

CAROL BREATHED IN DEEPLY. The air in the Bois de Boulogne was clean and fragrant. Unless one peeked through the branches, it was impossible to tell that there had been a disastrous fire somewhere nearby.

And neither she nor Jim was peeking in that direction. They had too much on their minds now to be thinking about the colony or anything else.

Fortunately, she'd been able to leave David with the Medfords. He seemed to like them, and she wouldn't have felt right about abandoning him to his own devices at a time like this.

Resourceful as he'd proven himself, her son was no Klingon hunter. He was a ten-year-old boy, and all his fear and horror had had to come out some way. It was just too bad that Jim had been forced to bear the brunt of it. He didn't in any way deserve what happened. He was just in the wrong place at the wrong time.

"What did you tell him?" he asked, frozen vapor trailing out of his mouth. "About his father, I mean."

She folded her arms across her chest. Once again, the classic defensive posture, she knew. But she didn't care. "The truth—to an extent. That I met his father a long time ago; and that his father went away before he was born."

Jim shook his head. "McCoy knew, didn't he?"

She nodded. "I made him swear not to tell—on the basis of patient privilege."

He grunted. "Well, that explains why he was avoiding me for a while there." He looked at her. "It must have been hard, raising him by yourself all these years."

Carol shrugged. "Not as hard as you might think. He's a good boy."

"Spock told me what happened out there in the hills. He's more than just a good boy. He's something . . . I don't know. Something *special.*" The captain sighed. "I wish I could take some credit for that. I wish I . . . had had some part in him, Carol."

She met his gaze, but she didn't say anything. What *could* she say?

Finally, he had to ask it. "Why, Carol? Why let me go on all this time, not knowing?"

"Why?" she echoed. She smiled wistfully. "Because it was better for everyone concerned. If you'd known, what could you have given him? A couple of days here and there? You'd only have felt guilty for not spending more time with him. And David wouldn't have understood having to play second fiddle to your career."

Jim looked at her. "Was it better to have no father at all? Or anyway, none he could point to?"

"I won't tell you that was easy," she conceded. "Not for him or for me. But at least it was a clean break. He didn't have to wonder where he stood from day to day.

He didn't have to figure out why he wasn't a priority for his father, the way he was for his mother."

"That's not fair," he said softly. "You didn't give up your career any more than I would have given up mine."

Carol took his hands in hers and squeezed. "I didn't *have* to," she told him. "In my kind of work, there's a place for a family. For a child. I'm not saying you're a terrible person for wanting to be a starship captain. But you've got to admit, David couldn't exactly have toddled around your bridge while you were out there fighting Klingons."

He sighed. "No. I don't suppose he could have." He withdrew his hands and gazed at the treetops, where the sun was caught like some kind of splendid bird. "And now he hates me."

"That'll pass," she assured him. "I'll make sure it passes. I'll explain that you weren't to blame for any of this—that for all we know, you saved our lives as much as Spock did."

Jim eyed her. "I appreciate that. But I'd appreciate it more if you took it a step further."

She felt herself stiffen at the suggestion. "You mean tell him who you are."

He nodded. "I mean tell him he has a father. Someone who cares about him, even if he's not around." He licked his lips, searching for the right words. "Carol, I'm not telling you how to raise him. Obviously, you don't need any advice from me on that count. But it's wrong to keep my identity a secret. If I were a boy—especially a boy David's age— something like that would be important to me. Hell, it would make all the difference in the world."

She recalled David's questions about his need for a father. Maybe Jim was right. Maybe.

And then again, maybe it would be like opening Pandora's box. Knowing his father was a starship captain, David might someday want to be like him. And she desperately didn't want David to go flitting around the galaxy, giving up all promise of a home and a family for the exotic lure of faraway places, and probably breaking some poor girl's heart in the process. No, she didn't want that for her son at all.

"Promise you'll tell him about me," Jim urged. "Not now. But when he's over what happened today. When you feel the time is right."

She shook her head. "I can't. Not right off the bat. I'd have to think about it—a lot."

He didn't look happy. "You mean *really* think about it? Or just tell me you're going to so you can get me off your back?"

Carol smiled. He knew her too well. She'd made a pledge to McCoy that she'd never truly intended to keep. And here she was, trying to make the same kind of pledge to Jim.

But Jim Kirk wasn't a stranger. He was the man she'd once loved—a man, she admitted, if only to herself, that she loved still.

It wasn't right to lie to him. It wasn't right to wear a mask of deception. If she agreed to think about telling David the truth, she would have to really search her heart.

"All right," she said finally. "I'll *really* think about it. You've got my word. As long as you promise me something in return."

"Anything," he told her.

Carol looked into his eyes, hoping he would understand. "Don't suddenly turn up on this planet, or on the next one we're working on. Don't try to insinuate yourself into his life."

Jim's mouth became a tight line. "Would I do that?" he asked ironically.

"Absolutely," she replied. Seeing his pain, she put her hand against the side of his face. "Let him find his own way, Jim. Let him grow up making his own decisions. Then, if he wants to seek you out, I won't have any objections. Deal?"

After a moment, he nodded. "Deal."

Carol heaved a sigh. "Good. Now that that's settled, you can tell me how it went at Alpha Maluria Six."

It was not difficult to find the children. Of the two domes still standing, only one was being used by Dr. McCoy to treat the injuries suffered by the colonists.

As Spock entered, he scanned the interior of the structure. They were all here, all those he wished to address. However, they were scattered throughout the crowd. It would be necessary to speak with each one individually, he decided.

But before he could even begin to carry out his intention, it was rendered unnecessary. All at once, it seemed to him, the children turned and saw him standing there, and as if responding to an unspoken command, they each got up and came over to him.

First Pfeffer and Wan, whose parents had been sitting together—no doubt sharing their experiences of captivity. Then Garcia. And finally Medford and

David, who had been at the far end of the dome watching Nurse Chapel attend to Medford's father.

Dr. McCoy looked up from his own patient to see the youngsters threading their way among the adults. Far from mocking the first officer as he often did, he smiled. Approvingly, Spock thought.

When the children had all assembled around him, the Vulcan eyed each one in turn. Then he held up his right hand and splayed it to form a V between his middle and ring fingers.

"On my planet," he told them, "this is how we say good-bye: *Live long and prosper.*"

Wan looked at him. "Are you leaving now?"

He nodded. "Yes. I am leaving."

With a concentrated effort, she imitated the position of his fingers. It pleased him.

"Live long and prosper," she said.

Then Pfeffer, who didn't do quite as good a job with the gesture. "Live long and prosper."

Garcia and Medford needed their other hands to keep their fingers in the right configuration. But the words came easily enough.

And finally, there was David. Like a Vulcan born, he held up his hand, fingers spread. "Live long and prosper, Mr. Spock."

The first officer nodded. "Well said." And then, as he had planned, he addressed David in particular: "Hatred is illogical."

He had been concerned that the boy might not understand. However, he understood perfectly. It was evident in his eyes and in the set of his jaw. It might not change his mind about the captain, of course. But then again, the Vulcan mused, it might.

Spock widened his purview to include the rest of

them. "Prosper and live long," he told them. "All of you."

And then he left the dome.

Kirk was in the ship's botanical garden, taking a few moments to admire his fireblossom, when the doors to the cabin opened and someone walked in. He looked to see who it was, and was surprised to note the presence of Ambassador Farquhar. The man had kept pretty much to himself, it seemed, from the moment they left Alpha Maluria.

Farquhar nodded. "Captain."

Kirk smiled politely. "What brings you here, Ambassador? I didn't know you were a rare-plant aficionado."

Farquhar grunted. "I'm not. But then, I'm not a lot of things, I suppose."

The captain regarded him. "Such as?"

The ambassador frowned. "On second thought, never mind what I'm not. Let's talk about what I *am*—and that's grateful."

Kirk was taken aback, to say the least. "Grateful?" he echoed. "For what?"

Farquhar's temples worked savagely. "I very nearly made a mess of things down on Alpha Maluria Six. And on more than one occasion, I'm afraid. But somehow, you managed to pull my rear end out of the fire. And the Malurians' along with it."

The captain shrugged. "I stumbled through it and got lucky, that's all. In the final analysis, I guess that's all any of us can do." He paused. "Besides, I made my share of mistakes this time around. If I'd listened to you in the beginning—if I'd trusted you a little more

298

instead of playing it by the book—we might've prevented the bloodshed before it ever got started."

"You mean," said the ambassador, "if I'd given you *reason* to trust me, instead of badgering you from the get-go." He shook his head. "You see, that's what worked for me at Gamma Philuvia. And before that, on Parness's Planet. As long as I kept everyone on the ship off-balance, I pretty much got what I wanted. Then I turned on the charm when I got planetside, and everything just seemed to fall into place."

Kirk nodded. "When something works, there's a tendency to stick with it. Hell, I've been tempted that way myself."

"But it's not going to work every time," Farquhar added. "I see that now." He considered the fireblossom, reached out and touched one of its petals. "The solution you came up with was a stroke of brilliance. I could be an ambassador for a hundred years and never match it."

The captain looked at him. "Does that mean you're not going to try?"

The ambassador turned to face him. "Of course not." He attempted a smile, and nearly got there. "It means I'm going to try *twice* as hard." This time, his smile went all the way. "And I pity the captain who expects me to get in his way."

Amen to that, Kirk thought. However, what he said was: "I'd stay and chat a little more, but I'm due up on the bridge."

"Don't let me keep you," the ambassador told him.

The captain chuckled. "I won't." And a moment later, he was on his way out into the corridor.

Amazing, he mused. Every now and then, it

Michael Jan Friedman

seemed, a leopard *could* change its spots. Kirk was still thinking about Farquhar when he reached the bridge. As he stepped out of the turbolift, he took stock of the personnel on duty. Everyone was present and accounted for.

Sitting in his command chair, noting the red sphere of Beta Canzandia Three on the main viewscreen, Kirk gave the order: "Take us out of orbit, Mr. Sulu. Half-impulse."

"Aye-aye, sir," the helmsman replied.

The captain watched as the planet slowly began to fall back into the recesses of space. Even on impulse power, the *Enterprise* would lose sight of it in a matter of minutes.

This was a new experience for him. He had departed from hundreds of worlds, some at this leisurely pace and some a great deal more quickly. But he had never left quite so much behind.

If things had worked out differently, he might have been one of the terraformers who had remained with the colony. A husband. A father. A family man. But he had made his choice long ago—made his bed, as the expression went. Now he had to lie in it.

Spock and McCoy stood on either side of him. Both were silent, giving Kirk a chance to be alone with his thoughts. But not *too* alone.

"It shouldn't take too long for them to rebuild," McCoy said finally.

"Not long at all," Spock agreed. "Their new domes should arrive in a matter of weeks."

Kirk nodded. "And with Dr. Boudreau's G-Seven unit intact, they'll be back in business inside a month. Of course, Starfleet's going to have to pay a little

300

more attention to this sector in the future. The Klingons didn't get what they were after. They may be back."

The Vulcan shook his head. "I do not believe they will return, Captain, at least not in the near future. Given the actions of the Klingon who rescued us, I would speculate that Beta Canzandia Three was more of a political pawn than an actual strategic objective."

"I see," said McCoy. "And since when have you become an expert on Klingon nature?"

Spock raised an eyebrow. "All scientific theory is based on observation and extrapolation, Doctor. I am merely applying the same procedures to social theory."

Bones rolled his eyes. "People aren't energy emissions, Spock. They're not quanta. They're unpredictable."

The first officer nodded. "Yes. Predictably so."

McCoy glared at him. "What kind of rhetorical double-talk is that?"

"It is not double-talk at all, Doctor. It is—"

"Enough," Kirk barked.

Immediately, his companions fell silent. Swiveling in his seat, he regarded them.

"You know," he said, "I've heard the two of you go head to head more than once. But I don't think I've ever heard quite as specious an argument as this one." He paused. "If I didn't know better, I'd think you were trying to distract me from something."

Bones and Spock exchanged glances. "I haven't the slightest idea of what he's talking about," McCoy commented. "Do you?"

The Vulcan shook his head. "I too am at a loss."

Kirk frowned. "Right. Uh-huh. Whatever you say."
Turning back to face the viewscreen, he allowed himself a smile that neither of them could see. And also, a reflection. He was leaving much behind. But he was also taking much with him. After all, there were families—and there were *families*.

Epilogue

To KIRUC'S EYE, the observation post didn't seem nearly as ominous as on the occasion of his last visit. Of course, this time he knew for certain whom he was meeting, and why.

Zibrat and Torgis must have felt much the same way. When he told them he had to approach the benighted complex alone, they didn't argue quite so much as they had before.

The orange light was in the window again; Kiruc felt good as he approached it. And why shouldn't he? He'd accomplished all he set out to do, down to the last loose end.

Even Karradh's wish had been satisfied. The first officer of the Fragh'ka was dead, killed in a hunting "accident," and the way was open for Karradh's son to replace him.

Yes. I have done well, even if I must say so myself.

As he got closer to the complex, he was able to discern silhouettes in the orange glow. Was it necessary to show them that he was unarmed? He chided himself instantly for even wondering. Of course it was. This was the *emperor*.

No sooner had he raised his hands than Kapronek's bodyguards came out and encircled him. They were like carrion birds on a puris carcass, it seemed to Kiruc. A strange image under the circumstances, but it seemed to fit.

Disruptors in their hands, they escorted him the rest of the way to the main building. Again, the emperor was waiting for him. At the door, Kiruc observed, security was not as tight as before. There were only a couple of warriors stationed there. But then, the council was not the cauldron it had been a few weeks ago. Kapronek must not have been expecting any serious assassination attempts.

Once the visitor was inside, the guards withdrew without being asked. Another sign of the improvement in the political climate, Kiruc mused.

"You look well," the emperor noted.

Kiruc wished he could say the same of Kapronek. Somehow, the man looked less massive than at their last meeting. Less . . . imperial, somehow.

"I thrive on serving my emperor," Kiruc replied. It was a correct thing to say.

"Do you?" Kapronek harrumphed. "One thing is certain. Your emperor has thrived by your serving him. And your people as well." He frowned. "At least for the time being."

Kiruc looked at him. "The time being, my lord? I thought the Gevish'rae threat had been defused by the abject failure of the *Kad'nra* and the resulting fall of Dumeric from the council."

The emperor nodded. "Defused, yes. It will be some

time before the Gevish'rae can successfully challenge me at court again." He paused. "But not forever. The Thirsting Knives will always be at our throats—always. They will never give up. That is the way of the predator. Indeed, it is the path of courage."

Kiruc shook his head. "You make them sound almost . . . admirable."

"I *do* admire them," said Kapronek. "I admire their hunger. Their perseverance. And I envy them their future—for someday we will not be so vigilant, and they will overwhelm us. We Kamorh'dag will fall to them as surely as grain falls to a scythe. That is a certainty."

Kiruc found he had a bitter taste in his mouth. To contemplate eventual defeat, when victory was so fresh . . .

But then, he was no emperor. Their minds worked differently than those of other men.

"There is one detail that needs clearing up," he remarked. "The matter of Grael, the Gevish'rae who aided us at Pheranna. Should he be allowed to live?"

Kapronek thought for a moment, then shrugged. "I should say so. He may be of use to us again sometime." His sea green eyes narrowed. "Yes, Grael will live."

The intonation pattern suggested that someone *else* would die. Kiruc waited to hear who, but the emperor said nothing. He only continued to stare at him. And slowly, gradually, Kiruc's blood turned to ice.

"No," he muttered, struck by the injustice of it. "I served you well. You told me so yourself."

"I have no complaint concerning the service you did me," Kapronek told him. "My complaint is with the service you did Karradh. You see, the first officer

305

of the *Fragh'ka* was kin to me—though you could not have known that."

"Kin?" Kiruc repeated numbly. "Kernod?"

"Yes. A grandson, by a line that runs through one of my concubines. As I said, you could not have known." His striking, pale eyes seemed to blaze for an instant with emerald fire. "Still, he was my grandson. And I cannot allow him to go unavenged."

Kiruc swallowed. "Did Karradh know?"

The emperor smiled grimly. "He may have."

Then I was duped, Kiruc thought. Tricked into doing something for Karradh that he would never have dared do himself. And all so his damned son could become a man.

He glanced out the window; all was darkness. But Torgis and Zibrat were out there somewhere. Now he knew why they hadn't put up much of a fight this time, when he'd ordered them to stay behind. Now he knew—nor did he blame them, really.

Without thinking about it, he quoted Kahless out loud: "When one's emperor commands, all other loyalties become secondary. When one's emperor commands, no sacrifice is too terrible, no price too great."

Kapronek looked approving. "Very good. Also from the *Ramen'aa,* isn't it?"

Kiruc nodded. "It is." He licked his lips. "May I have the option of dying with honor?"

"You may," the emperor told him. "In your own home, if you wish. After all, you have earned it."

Kiruc grunted. "I am grateful." He pounded his fist against his chest. "Good-bye, Kapronek."

The emperor fixed him on the spit of his gaze. "Good-bye, Kiruc, son of Kalastra."

As Kiruc turned and left the room, he cursed himself for his stupidity. How could he call himself a student of Kahless and not have remembered the most famous saying of all?

Watch your back. Friends may become enemies in less time than it takes to draw a dagger.

Grimacing at his own carelessness, he went out into the darkness.

STAR TREK ®
THE NEXT GENERATION ™

REUNION

Michael Jan Friedman

Captain Picard's
past and present
collide on board the
USS *Enterprise*™

POCKET
B O O K S

444-02